A faint sound from a dark side passage made Kasimir turn his head. The warning had come just in time; he found himself confronted by a wild-faced man, who struck at Kasimir with a desperate blow. Turning with a simultaneous thrusting motion of his torch, Kasimir did his desperate best to parry. The assailant flinched away from the torch at the last moment.

Kasimir swirled his cloak and continued with thrusts and feints of the torch. The man, who had a long knife in his hand, fell back. The two men stalked each other.

As soon as Kasimir called out for help, the other man lunged at him again. Kasimir parried with the torch as best he could, stood his ground and swung his club, hitting his assailant on the shoulder. The long knife went clattering to the floor.

A moment later, two Firozpur troopers had materialized in response to the physician's yell, destroying the local darkness with their torches and taking charge of the howling prisoner.

Also by Fred Saberhagen
published by Tor Books

THE THIRD BOOK OF LOST SWORDS
STONECUTTER'S STORY

FRED SABERHAGEN

A TOM DOHERTY ASSOCIATES BOOK
NEW YORK

THE THIRD BOOK OF LOST SWORDS: STONECUTTER'S STORY

Copyright © 1988 by Fred Saberhagen

A TOR Book
Published by Tom Doherty Associates, Inc.
49 West 24 Street
New York, NY 10010

Cover art by Maren

ISBN: 0-812-55288-1   Can. ISBN: 0-812-55289-X

Library of Congress Catalog Card Number: 87-51397

First edition: May 1988
First mass market edition: March 1989

Printed in the United States of America

0 9 8 7 6 5 4 3 2 1

CHAPTER 1

TWO hours before dawn the dreams of Kasimir were disturbed by a soft noise at the tent wall no more than a sword's length from his head. The noise was the distinctive purring, gently snarling sound made by a sharp blade slitting the tough fabric.

Once this sound had been identified somewhere inside the unsleeping portion of Kasimir's brain, the remnants of his dream—a strange adventure involving the gods of the desert, and enormous distances of space and time—went flying off in tatters. Still, complete wakefulness did not come at once. With his eyes open to the partial darkness inside the tent, he saw by the filtering moonlight a figure moving silently. This figure had come in through the tent wall and gone out again by the same route before he who observed it was fully awake. But Kasimir had no doubt that he had seen it, a man's form, looking as slender and dangerous as a scorpion, clad in dark, tight-fitting clothes, face wrapped for concealment. Nor had he any doubt, when this apparition went gliding smoothly out through the wall of the tent again, that it was carrying a long bundle wrapped in rough cloth, held tightly under its right arm.

Kasimir sat up straight. He was alone in the tent now. No one else was sleeping in it tonight. Though it was quite

1

large, much of the space inside was taken up by the more valuable portions of the caravan's cargo.

The intruder certainly hadn't been Prince al-Farabi, leader of the caravan. Nor was Kasimir able to identify that mysterious form as any of the Prince's followers who had been traveling with him across the desert. Then who—?

Almost fully awake at last, Kasimir leaped to his feet. Just at that moment an outcry of alarm was sounded at no great distance outside the tent. He dashed for the door but it was tied loosely shut, as was usual at night, and undoing the knots delayed him briefly.

Hardly had he got out into the open air before he collided with a figure running toward the tent.

"Thieves!" the other man shouted, right in Kasimir's face. "Robbers! Awake! Arouse and arm yourselves!"

Judging by the growing uproar, the other thirty or forty occupants of the camp were already doing just that. Other voices were shouting alarm from the perimeter. Men poured out of the half-dozen sleeping tents, and weapons flashed in the light of rising flames. Smoldering cookfires and watchfires were being quickly rekindled. Lieutenant Komi, second-in-command to the Prince during this journey, trotted past Kasimir, barking orders to his men. And now, in the middle of all this half-controlled turmoil, strode the Prince himself with his robes flying behind him. Al-Farabi was tall and dark and at the moment a menacing figure with scimitar in hand. He was demanding to know where the alarm had started.

Kasimir confronted him. "Prince, an intruder was in the cargo tent, where I was sleeping! He came through the wall. I—I wasn't in time to stop him—"

"What?" In a moment Prince al-Farabi had sprung to the side of the tent where the cloth had been slit. This was on the side opposite from the normal entrance, whose flap was now hanging open after Kasimir's exit. In the fabric of the

2

tent's rear wall, Kasimir saw now, were two vertical slits, one right beside the other, only a couple of handspans apart. Of course, it must have been their cutting that had awakened him.

The Prince stepped into the tent through the largest of these rents, which was a full meter long.

Peering in through the same aperture, Kasimir saw, by the torchlight that glowed in through the walls, the tall man bending over the heap of baggage that occupied the center of the tent's interior. For a few moments the Prince tossed things about, obviously in search of something. Then al-Farabi straightened up to his full height, giving a great wordless cry as of bereavement.

Kasimir followed the Prince into the tent through its new entrance. "Sir, what's wrong?"

"It is gone." The face al-Farabi turned to the younger man was ghastly in the muted glow of firelight entering the tent from outside. The Prince appeared to be swaying on his fcct. Almost shouting, he repeated: "It is gone!"

"I saw a man inside the tent with me when I woke up," Kasimir stammered, repeating the little information he could give. "He went out carrying a long bundle under one arm. I started to give the alarm but by then he was already gone."

Groaning unintelligibly, the Prince stumbled past Kasimir and out of the tent through its normal doorway. Again Kasimir followed.

Shouts coming from guards at the perimeter of the camp now reassured everyone that the animals were well and none of them had been stolen. But a moment later a new alarm was sounded. One of the guards, who had been posted nearest to the tent where Kasimir slept, had just been discovered lying motionless in the sand.

"Bring him here beside the fire!" Kasimir ordered sharply. "And one of you fetch my kit from the tent." It was the automatic reaction of a trained physician to a medical emergency. In a moment three men came carrying the fallen one, and laid him down on clean sand in the firelight.

The physician went to work. He found that the victim was certainly alive, and a preliminary examination disclosed no sign of serious injury. Kasimir hardly had a chance to begin a more detailed investigation when the man began to stir and grimace, moaning and rubbing the back of his head.

"Someone must have struck me down from behind," the young tribesman murmured weakly, trying to sit up.

"Sit still." Kasimir's exploring fingers found no blood, or even any noticeable lump. "All right, I suppose you'll live. Doubtless the hood of your robe saved you from worse damage."

Aware that the Prince had approached again and was standing beside him, Kasimir turned to repeat this favorable report. But then the young physician let the words die on his lips. The tall figure of al-Farabi, wild-eyed, stood gesturing with both arms in the burgeoning firelight. "The Sword is gone!" the Prince shouted in a despairing voice. It was as if the full enormity of his loss was still growing on him. "The treasure has disappeared!"

While others gathered around, Kasimir stood up from beside the fallen guard and moved still closer to the desert chieftain. In a voice that tried to be soothing he asked: "You mentioned a sword, sir. But how valuable was it? I had no idea that we were carrying any—"

"Of course you had no idea! Of course!" The tall man cast back his hood and pulled his hair. "The presence of Stonecutter was intended to be a secret."

"The presence of—"

"Of a Sword, the Sword of Siege itself! A priceless weapon! It was loaned to me by my trusting friend Prince Mark. And now it is gone. Argh! May all the gods and demons of the desert descend upon me and snuff out my worthless life!"

"The Sword of Siege," breathed Kasimir. "It is one of the Twelve, then." And suddenly the extreme dismay of the Prince was understandable.

Practically everyone in the world knew of the Twelve Swords, though comparatively few people had ever seen one of them. They were legendary weapons, for all that they were very real. They had been forged by the god Vulcan himself more than thirty years ago, in the days before the gods—or most of them at least—had disappeared.

Kasimir wanted to ask how the Sword of Siege had come to be traveling with them, in this rather ordinary little caravan—but that was not properly any of his business. Instead he asked: "Is it possible to overtake the thief?"

"Already I have sent some of my swiftest riders in pursuit," said al-Farabi, who was now standing with his face buried in his hands, while his own people gathered round him in dumb awe. "But to find and follow a trail at night . . . we will of course do all that we can, but I fear that the Sword is gone. Oh, woe is me!"

While Kasimir and others watched him helplessly, the desolation of the Prince became more intense and at the same time more theatrical. He tore at his hair and his garments, saying: "How will I ever be able to face Prince Mark again? What can I tell him? Even the worth of all my flocks and all my lands would scarcely afford him adequate compensation."

"Prince Mark?" Kasimir could think of nothing more intelligent to say at the moment; still, he felt that it was up to him to reply. All of the Prince's own people who were watching looked slightly embarrassed, and he had the impression that al-Farabi's outburst of grief was increasingly directed toward him.

The Prince had paused and was regaining a minimum of

composure. In a milder voice he said: "Know then, my young friend, that my great friend Prince Mark of Tasavalta, despite many misgivings on his part, was generous enough to loan me secretly the Sword called Stonecutter. Why, you ask? I will tell you. In one far corner of my domain, hundreds of kilometers from here, there is a nest of robbers that has proven all but impossible to eradicate, because of the nature of the rocky fastness in which they hide. With the Sword of Siege in hand, to undermine a crag or two would be no great problem—but now the Sword is gone from out of my hands, and I am the most miserable of men!"

Kasimir felt moved to compassion. Ever since they had first encountered each other, a month ago, al-Farabi had been a most kindly and generous host, willing to provide an insignificant stranger with free passage across the desert.

"Is there anything that I can do to help you, Prince?" the physician asked. Though he had never visited Tasavalta, he knew it was a land far to the northeast, bordering on the Eastern Sea, and he had heard that its rulers were respected everywhere.

"I fear that there is nothing anyone can do to help me now. I fear that I will never see the Sword again." Al-Farabi turned away, seemingly inconsolable.

Gradually the excitement in the camp quieted. With a double guard now posted, the fires were allowed to die down once more. An hour before dawn the riders who had been sent in pursuit of the thieves came back, reporting in Kasimir's hearing that they had had no success. When daylight came they would of course try again.

Kasimir, lying awake in his blankets in the cargo tent, hearing the extra guards—now that it was too late—milling around outside, thought that few members of the caravan were likely to get any more sleep during the last hour of the night. But at last, after vexing his drowsy mind with the apparently minor, pointless, and insoluble problem of why the tent wall had been slit twice—one gash was only a minor one, not really big enough for anyone to crawl through—he dozed off himself.

His renewed sleep was naturally of short duration, for at first light the camp began to stir around him once again. As soon as full dawn came, al-Farabi sent out a different pair of trackers. Then he ordered camp broken, and, with the remainder of his men, his passenger Kasimir, and the laden baggage animals, pushed on along the caravan's intended route toward the Abohar Oasis and, a day or two beyond that, the city of Eylau.

Choosing to ride side by side with the young physician, the Prince explained that his men as well as their animals needed to rest and replenish their supply of water at the oasis before undertaking what promised to be a lengthy pursuit into the wilderness. And al-Farabi himself appeared even more fatalistically certain than before that the Sword was permanently gone.

The conversation between the two men faded, and most of the day was spent in grim and silent journeying. The pace was steady and there were few pauses. In late afternoon tall palms came into view ahead, surrounded by a sprawling burst of lesser greenery. They had arrived at Abohar Oasis.

Several other groups of travelers, Kasimir observed, were here ahead of them; indeed he thought that there would probably be someone resting here almost continuously. He had already learned it was an unwritten rule that peace obtained in the oases, and that the rule was usually observed even when bitter enemies encountered one another. Water was shared, fighting rescheduled for some other time and place.

On this occasion, there was certainly shade and water in

plenty for all, and no question of fighting. The Prince gave no sign that he observed any enemies of his Firozpur tribe among the people who were already resting at the oasis— and as for Kasimir, he was not aware of having an enemy anywhere in the world.

As soon as the caravan had halted the Prince directed his people, working for once in shade, as they busied themselves seeing to the animals, and laying out their campsite for tonight. Meanwhile Kasimir, wanting to enjoy a walk in the grateful shade himself, left them temporarily and went exploring.

He moved along cool, well-worn footpaths bordered by grass and shrubs, between inviting pools. Eventually, having chosen the largest and deepest pool of the oasis to quench his thirst, he noticed as he approached it that on the far side of the pool, upon a little knoll of grass, there stood a richly furnished tent. Though it was no bigger than a small room, such a pavilion obviously belonged to someone of considerable social stature if not of great wealth.

Kasimir threw himself down upon a little ledge of rock at the near edge of the pool to drink. As he finished and arose, wiping his lips, there arrived near him at poolside a woman from some tribe whose dress Kasimir was unable to identify. As she was filling her water jar, he questioned her as to whether any single traveler, or pair of them perhaps, had arrived at the oasis since last night.

She answered in a melodious voice. "No, I am sure, sir, that your party is the first to arrive today."

"How do you know?"

"My family has been keeping watch on every side, for some kinfolk who are to meet us here."

"I see. By the way, whose tent is that across the pond? Have you any idea?"

"Certainly." The woman seemed surprised at Kasimir's ignorance. "That is the tent of the Magistrate Wen Chang. He has been here for several days."

Kasimir blinked at her. "*The* Wen Chang?"

The young woman laughed again. "There is only one Wen Chang that I know of. Only one that anyone knows of. From what remote land have you come that you do not know him?"

"I know of him, certainly." Now the conviction was growing in Kasimir's mind that it was, or ought to be, somewhat below the dignity of a physician to stand here debating with a girl who had been sent to fetch water. He turned and started round the pool, ignoring a smothered giggle behind him.

The tent ahead of him was silent as he approached it, the entrance flap of silken fabric left half open. If this pavilion were really occupied by the legendary Wen Chang, then it appeared that the gods might be favoring Prince al-Farabi and his friends with a matchless opportunity.

The Magistrate Wen Chang was a renowned judge, whose fame had spread far from his homeland, which lay well to the south of the desert. In the more fanciful (as Kasimir supposed) stories, Wen Chang was credited with the ability to see into the secret hearts of men and women. It was said that he knew, as soon as he laid eyes on any group of people, which of them were innocent and which were guilty. It was even alleged—Kasimir had heard this variation once—that the Magistrate could tell, just by staring at the thief, where stolen treasure had been hidden. But Kasimir had never heard that the famed Wen Chang was wont to travel as far as this from his usual base of operations.

When Kasimir was still a score of strides from the tent's doorway, the flap opened fully and a tall, imposing man emerged from the dim interior. He was dressed for desert traveling in a gray robe, almost plain enough to be that of a pilgrim.

If this was indeed Wen Chang, he was a younger-looking man than Kasimir had expected, with black hair and a proud narrow mustache still quite innocent of gray; but there was that in his bearing that convinced Kasimir he was indeed confronting the famed Magistrate. From his elevation upon the little knoll the tall man squinted through narrowed eyes in Kasimir's direction; then he ignored the approaching youth and went unhurriedly to the edge of the pool, where he knelt down and with a silver cup scooped up a drink.

Meanwhile Kasimir had come to a stop about ten strides away, where he stood waiting in an attitude of respect.

Presently the tall man rinsed his cup, hurling water from it in a little silver spray, and rose unhurriedly to his full height. His eyes, turned again on Kasimir, were remarkably black. It seemed to the young man that those eyes glittered whenever they were not squinted almost shut.

Kasimir cleared his throat. "Have I the honor of addressing the Magistrate Wen Chang?"

"It is my name. And that was formerly my office." The voice was precise, and spoke the common tongue with a slight accent of a kind Kasimir had seldom heard before. "Whether you are honored by the mere fact of talking to me is something you must decide for yourself."

"Honored sir, I am honored. And I really think that the kindly fates have sent you here. Or they have sent me here to meet you. There is a matter in which your help is greatly needed."

"So?" The tall man eyed the youth intently for a moment. Then he said: "I believe this grassy bank provides a finer seat than any of the pillows in my pavilion. And out here the view is finer too. Let us make ourselves comfortable and I will hear your story. Mind you, I promise nothing more than a hearing."

"Of course, sir, of course." Kasimir let the older man choose a spot to sit down first, then cast himself down on the grass nearby. "Let me think—where to begin? Of course, forgive me, my name is Kasimir."

"And you are on your way to Eylau, to seek employment through the White Temple there."

"Yes, I—" Kasimir forgot his hope of making a good impression so far as to let his jaw drop open. "How could you possibly know that?"

The other made a gesture of dismissal. "My dear young man, I did not know it, but the probabilities were with me. The size and arrangement of the pouches you wear at your belt—the cloth container for drugs, the lizard-skin for items thought to have some potency in magic—these identify you as a physician, or at least as one who has some pretensions of skill in the healing arts. Certain other details of your appearance indicate that you have already been more than a few days in the desert—therefore you are now traveling toward the city, which is only two days' march from here, and not away from it. And once an itinerant physician has arrived in Eylau, where would he most likely go, but to the White Temple of Ardneh, a clearinghouse for jobs in his profession?"

"Ah. Well, of course, sir, when you put it that way, your deduction seems only reasonable."

"'Only,' did you say?" The Magistrate sighed. "But never mind. What is this most disturbing problem?"

Listening to the hastily outlined story of the theft, Wen Chang allowed his epicanthic eyes to close almost as if in sleep. Only slight changes of expression, tensions playing about the thin-lipped mouth, indicated to Kasimir that his auditor was still awake and indeed listening intently.

Kasimir in his relation of the events of the previous night had just reached the point where he had begun his examination of the stunned guard when the Magistrate's eyes opened, fixing themselves alertly at a point over Kasimir's left shoulder.

The young man turned to look behind him. Prince al-Farabi, walking alone, his eyes looking haunted and wary, was advancing toward them along the shaded path beside the pool.

Kasimir jumped to his feet and hastened to perform introductions. The two eminent men greeted each other with every indication of mutual interest and respect.

Then Kasimir announced: "I have taken it upon myself, Prince, to appeal to the Magistrate here for his help in recovering the missing Sword."

Once more al-Farabi demonstrated grief. "Alas! I fear the treasure has gone beyond even the power of Wen Chang to bring it back—but of course I would welcome any chance of help."

"Having just undertaken a long journey which came to naught," said Wen Chang, "and being in no particular hurry to return to my former place of service—there have been political changes there, which I find unwelcome—I have been waiting for two days at this oasis, in hopes of receiving some sign from the Fates to direct me. It appears to me that your problem may well be the sign I have been looking for. I have long been an admirer of Prince Mark of Tasavalta, though I have never met him; for that reason alone I would like to see that his property is recovered. Also, from what I have heard of this problem so far, there are certain aspects of it that are intrinsically interesting."

"Thank you, sir!" Kasimir cried.

"Almost," said al-Farabi, "you allow me to begin to hope again!" He wiped his forehead with the edge of his robe.

A few minutes later, the three men were seated more formally if no more comfortably inside the larger pavilion of the Prince, which by now had been erected in cool shade at the other side of the oasis from the pavilion of Wen Chang.

Here inside the Prince's tent, with a small cup of spiced wine in hand, Wen Chang began to ask questions, probing into one detail after another of the disappearance of the Sword.

"In what sort of container was the Sword carried? And why was it stored in that particular tent when the caravan stopped?"

"It was wrapped in blue silk, and that in turn in coarse gray woolen cloth, that it might seem an ordinary bundle and attract no special attention. And when we stopped for the night the Sword was always placed, in a pile with certain other pieces of baggage, in the same tent as my valued passenger here, who has been passing through my domain under my protection. I had no reason to believe that tent less safe than any other. Rather the contrary, as it was near the center of our small encampment."

"Nothing else was stolen last night? From that tent or any other?"

"Nothing."

"And was the pile of baggage in the tent disturbed?"

"It was very little disarranged, or perhaps not at all; until I began to search through it in hopes that the Sword might still be there. Alas!"

Wen Chang sat back in his nest of pillows. "Then it would appear that the thief, or thieves, knew just what they wanted, and where to lay hands upon it."

"So it would appear, yes." And al-Farabi once more raised his hands to hide his face.

Kasimir tried to reassure him. "They might have been—I suppose it is likely that they were—helped by powerful magic. Perhaps even the magic of one of the other Twelve Swords. Wayfinder, say, or Coinspinner. I have never seen those Swords but either of them, as I understand the tales, may be an infallible guide to locating some desired object."

"Then would that we had them both in hand today!" the Prince cried out.

Wen Chang was nodding thoughtfully. "That the thieves

had either of those Swords is a possibility, I suppose. Or some lesser magic might well have been strong enough to let the robbers find what they wanted. Was any wizard traveling with you?"

"None, Magistrate." Al-Farabi shook his head. "I am a simple man of the desert, who lives more by the sword than the spell. With such trivial magical powers as I myself possess, I have of course already tried to get Stonecutter back. But as I say, I am no wizard. I suppose you will be able to bring to bear much stronger spells and incantations?"

"Probably not."

The Prince blinked at him. "Sir?"

"I prefer to rely upon a stronger tool even than magic."

"And what might that be, Magistrate?"

"Intelligence, my friend. Intelligence." The Magistrate drank spiced wine, and sighed, pleasurably. He moved a trifle on his pillows, like a man settling himself to play a round of some congenial game. "Now tell me. Who, before your caravan set out, knew that you were carrying Stonecutter with you?"

"Among my own people, only myself and Lieutenant Komi, the commander of the escort—and I would trust Komi as I trust myself. Our fathers were blood brothers, and I have known him all his life."

"*I* certainly had no inkling of the Sword's presence with the caravan," Kasimir put in.

Wen Chang nodded slightly at him, prolonged the look appraisingly for a moment, then returned his narrow-eyed gaze to the Prince. "And who, not among your people, would have known that you were carrying Stonecutter with you?"

Al-Farabi took time to give the question serious thought. "Well—the only people I can think of would be the Tasavaltans who delivered the Sword to me at the other edge of my domain. They were three, including Prince Mark himself, and one of his chief wizards, and the strong man called Ben of Purkinje. It was plain to see that the Prince trusted his companions as thoroughly as I trust Komi. And why would a man connive to steal his own Sword?"

The Magistrate was frowning. "There might be several answers to that question. If there is a good answer in this case, it is not immediately obvious. No doubt other people in Tasavalta might have known that the Sword was being loaned to you?"

"No doubt."

"Then, for the moment at least, this line of inquiry seems unproductive. Let us try another."

Al-Farabi, sitting with his head bowed again, said through his hands: "As soon as we have replenished our supplies and rested, we will return to the desert and try again to track the thief—or thieves. But I fear that the Sword of Siege is lost."

Wen Chang nodded. "And I fear that you may well be right. Still, the situation is not utterly hopeless, even if your pursuit through the desert should fail."

"It is not?"

"No. Not utterly. Consider—what will a thief do with such a treasure when it falls into his hands?"

"He'll most likely want to sell it, I suppose," Kasimir put in.

The narrowed eyes of the Magistrate turned on him again. "Almost certainly he will. And where would anyone go to sell an item of such value?"

Kasimir shrugged. "Why—he'll go to the metropolis, of course, to Eylau. There's no city of comparable size for a thousand kilometers in any direction."

"It would be more accurate to say for several thousand kilometers. Yes, I shall be surprised if our robber has not turned his steps toward Eylau already."

Al-Farabi was frowning. "But such traces of a trail as we

were able to find by moonlight led out into the desert in the opposite direction from the city."

"That, I think, is hardly conclusive."

"I suppose not."

"Certainly not." Wen Chang drank spiced wine. He nodded. "If I am to continue my investigation I shall do so in Eylau."

"By all means—by all means." The Prince appeared to be doing his best to look politely hopeful. "Will you require money for expenses?—but yes, of course you will. And naturally I will provide it, in advance. And in addition a great reward, a thousand gold coins or the equivalent, if you are successful."

Wen Chang raised an eyebrow at the extravagant size of the reward. Then he bowed slightly in his seated position. "Both provisions will certainly be welcome. The expenses because I shall be proceeding as a private investigator, with no official status in this land, and the purchase of information—not to mention a bribe or two—may be essential. I presume that, although you will of course organize a pursuit, a part of your caravan will be going on into the city?"

"Yes. The remaining goods that my caravan is carrying must be delivered there, as well as our passenger. Meanwhile I, with some of my swifter riders, will endeavor to follow the thieves and overtake them—there is nothing else I can do."

"Of course not—how many men are you going to send into the city, then?"

Al-Farabi took thought. "Perhaps a dozen. That should be an adequate guard for my passenger and my cargo for the remainder of the journey."

"Good. When those dozen men have seen your remaining freight—and your passenger, of course—safely to their destination—by the way, I suppose there are no more Swords still with you? Or any comparable treasures?"

"No, nothing at all like that."

"I see. Then, when your dozen men who are going on to the city have seen to the safe disposal of your remaining goods, will you place those men at my disposal? Since I will be unable to call upon official forces in Eylau, it may be necessary at some stage to use a substitute."

"Of course—I shall place a dozen men, with Lieutenant Komi at their head, at your command." The Prince paused delicately. "You realize I cannot be sure of the attitude of the Hetman, who rules the city, toward such a private army. I do not know him."

"Nor do I. But a dozen men are hardly an unusually large bodyguard for a rich merchant, and many such must pass in and out of Eylau. And even if my true mission should become known to the Hetman, well, thieftakers are welcome in most cities."

"Then of course you may have the guard. And for your expenses, all the proceeds for the merchandise when it is delivered—may all the gods help you to recover and retain the Sword!"

CHAPTER 2

S HORTLY after dawn on the following morning, Kasimir stood under tall palms beside the Magistrate, watching while al-Farabi and about two-thirds of his men finished packing up their tents, mounted their rested animals, and rode back out into the desert in the direction from which they had come yesterday.

Wen Chang's pavilion had already been struck, and his temporary servant dismissed. It only remained for him and Kasimir to mount their own riding-beasts and start out in the direction of Eylau, which was still two days' travel distant. Travelers going in that direction followed an obvious and well-traveled road that could hardly lead to anywhere but the great city. Lieutenant Komi, calling orders now and then to his comparatively small detachment of Firozpur troopers, rode a few meters behind Kasimir and Wen Chang. Eleven soldiers, looking fierce and capable, followed their officer today, with the pack animals bearing the caravan's cargo bringing up the rear. Among the cargo were a few latticework crates containing winged messengers, small birdlike creatures used as couriers. Al-Farabi had ordered his officer to let him know immediately of any and all developments affecting the search for his lost Sword in the great city.

18

Wen Chang opened the morning's conversation with his younger companion in a pleasant way, speculating on the nature of the city they were approaching, a metropolis neither of them had ever seen before. Soon Kasimir had been put thoroughly at ease. He found himself telling the older man more of his background, ending with the recent chain of more or less commonplace events which found him now on his way to the White Temple in Eylau, where the temple's usually efficient placement service would more than likely be able to help him find a good place in which to practice medicine.

Their conversation gradually faded, but the ensuing silence possessed a comfortable and companionable quality. Presently, when no words had been exchanged for some time, Wen Chang brought out a folded paper from somewhere in his traveler's robe; he unfolded this paper into a map, and squinted at it between glances at the ascending sun and the empty land around them.

"I suppose you are an experienced traveler, Magistrate."

"Not as experienced as I should like to be. To enter a strange land is to be presented with a vast and intricate puzzle."

By now they had been about two hours on their way. Wen Chang, map still in hand, muttered something and suddenly turned his mount aside from the well-traveled way. Making a detour to his right, he went riding for the top of a sizable hill that rose no more than a hundred meters from the road.

Kasimir turned his mount too, and followed, completely in the dark as to the purpose of this detour. Glancing back, he saw Lieutenant Komi, his expression stoic and incurious, bringing his men and the pack animals along.

At the top of the barren hill the leader halted, and then the whole group followed. From this vantage point there was nothing to be seen but more desert in every direction.

19

Still Wen Chang sat his mount for what seemed to Kasimir a long time, his eyes narrowed to slits against the wind, and shaded under the folded gray hood of his desert robe. He was intently scanning the empty landscape on all sides.

Twice, as the silence lengthened, Kasimir almost broke into it with a curious question, but he forbore. He was for the third time just on the point of yielding to curiosity when Wen Chang spoke at last.

"The place where the Sword was stolen, according to the information given me by yourself and Prince al-Farabi, is a long way from the city. Too far, probably, for anyone to travel without stopping to renew his supply of water. And even if our thief's destination was not Eylau, he would still most likely need to obtain water somewhere in this region." The Magistrate paused. "But he did not come to Abohar Oasis for water while I was encamped there. The people there discussed each new arrival, whether by day or night. Therefore . . ."

"Yes sir?"

"Therefore he sought out another source of water, somewhere in this region."

"May I see the map, sir?" Gripping the paper tightly in the wind when the Magistrate handed it over, Kasimir pored over it for a few moments. Then he announced: "According to this there are no other oases or springs in the area we are considering."

"Exactly. Therefore . . ."

"Yes?"

There was no immediate answer from Wen Chang, who was still staring into the blue heat-shimmer that ruled the far horizon, but now had fixed the direction of his eyes. Following the aim of the Magistrate's gaze, Kasimir was at last able to make out what looked like traces of white smoke, or more likely dust, hanging in the distant air. He thought that if that dust indicated the presence of a body of people or animals, their movement must be very slow. The cloud, as far as he could tell, was remaining in the same place.

Wen Chang turned in his saddle. "Lieutenant Komi, have we reserves of water enough to safely take a side trip? An excursion as far as yon dust cloud?"

Komi, working his mount a little closer to them, squinted into the distance under the shade of a sunburnt hand. "Looks like that little cloud might be half a day's travel from here. But if Your Excellency wishes us to make such an excursion, water is no problem. Our supplies are ample." His tone was neutral, giving away no more than his expression did; it was impossible to tell what he thought of the advisability of taking such a side trip.

"Then we will do it." And Wen Chang immediately urged his mount down the side of the hill away from the road.

Midday gave way to afternoon as they traveled. Kasimir sipped sparingly at his canteen, and chewed on some dried meat and fruit. There was a stop to freshen the animals' mouths with water. In the hours since they had left the direct road to Eylau the country had changed, become more merciless, with smooth desert giving way to low crags and boulders and broken outcroppings of black rock. Here and there the landscape opened before the animals' hooves in a sudden crevice, compelling a detour. But gradually the wisps of white dust in the sky grew closer.

Komi's estimate of half a day for this side journey had been only a little too large. But eventually the source of the dust was near enough for them to identify it: a gang of laborers, several score of them, who toiled like well-disciplined ants in the hot sun, under the direction of whip-cracking overseers.

Before the investigators reached the work site, they came upon the recent product of the workers' labor. It was a road that did not show on the map, obviously newly made. It was a real road, suitable even for wheeled vehicles, as opposed to a mere trail through the landscape, and plainly its making had not been an easy or a pleasant task. As Wen Chang and his party began to follow the road, moving now at increased speed, Kasimir noted where minor crevices in the earth had been filled in, and a steep-sided arroyo bridged with rude stonework, leaving a passage under the bridge for rushing floodwaters when they came as occasionally they must.

The road's winding course among protruding rocks led Wen Chang and his followers inexorably toward the crew who still labored to extend it. But before the road drew very near the place where its creators were now toiling, it had to turn and run patiently along the side of a ridge. The ridge was a mass of sharp rock twice the height of a man, offering no soft spots to cut through, and no gentle slopes to offer a start for ramp-building. Then without warning the road turned again, almost at right angles, cutting straight and level through the obstacle.

Just as the Magistrate was approaching the smooth-sided cut driven through the rock, he stopped suddenly and held up a hand, halting his small cavalcade behind him. By now the workers on the far side of the ridge were so close that their metal tools, probably steel and magically hardened bronze, could be heard clinking against rock. A dozen or more of the laborers were chanting in surprisingly hearty voices as they worked.

So far there was no sign that anyone among the road-building crew had become aware of the approach of Wen Chang and his party.

A moment after Wen Chang reined in his riding-beast he had dismounted, and was closely inspecting the sides of the cut. Whatever he saw made him nod with satisfaction.

In an instant Kasimir had dismounted too, and was

standing mystified beside the older man. But the young physician's puzzlement was only momentary.

"These are strange marks in the ridge," he breathed, with something like awe. "Long and smooth and easy, like those a knife or an ordinary sword might make in cheese or butter. I take these marks to mean that the Sword called Stonecutter has been used on this rock." And he gave Wen Chang a glance of open admiration.

"Exactly so." Wen Chang looked around, and it seemed to Kasimir for a moment that the Magistrate was almost purring with satisfaction. "Lieutenant," Wen Chang ordered, "send a few of your men secretly around to the other side of this work camp. If anyone should attempt to sneak out that way when we enter, detain them, whether they are carrying a Sword or not, and bring them to me."

The lieutenant had made no comment on the discovery of the Sword's marks in the cut rock, though Kasimir thought he could hardly have failed to be impressed. Now Komi saluted and turned back to his small column to deliver some low-voiced orders.

Presently Wen Chang remounted, and, with Kasimir beside him, and Lieutenant Komi, now attended by only seven troopers, supporting him in the rear, rode boldly forth, through the divided ridge, along the just-completed last hundred meters of the road in the direction of the laborers' camp. In a moment the first of the scores of workers had become aware of their approach, and the sounds of labor faltered. But almost at once the whips of several overseers cracked, and the chink of metal on stone picked up again.

From the square of shade produced by a square of faded cloth supported on rude poles, a foreman was now coming forward to receive his visitors. He was a corpulent man of modest height and middle age, wearing over his tunic a broad leather belt with an insignia of the Hetman's colors, gray and blue. He looked worried, not unreasonably, at the sight of all these armed men in the garb of desert warriors, who outnumbered his small staff of overseers. Still, he managed to put a bold tone into his salutation.

"Greetings, gentlemen! Our road, as you see, is not yet complete. But if you are willing to wait a few days, my brave men here and I will do our best to finish it for you."

Wen Chang squinted into the shimmering reach of emptiness extending to the horizon ahead of the road-builders, and allowed himself a smile. "My good man, if you continue to labor to such good effect as you did when cutting your way through this ridge behind me—why then I have no doubt that a few more days should see you at your destination, whatever it may be. What is it, by the way?"

The smile had congealed unhappily upon the foreman's beefy face. "I am given only a general direction, sir, in which we are to extend the road. Beyond that—" He shrugged.

"Of course, of course. It does not matter. My name is Wen Chang, and my companion here is Doctor Kasimir, a physician; and this is Lieutenant Komi, who with his soldiers serves Prince al-Farabi of the Firozpur. And your name is—?"

"I am honored indeed to meet all Your Excellencies! I am Lednik, foreman of this gang of the Hetman's road-builders, and holding the rank of supervisor both of the Hetman's prisons and his roads." Having bowed deeply, Lednik looked up suddenly and slapped both palms upon his leather belt. "Ho, there! Keep those fellows working! No one has told any of you to stop for a vacation!"

These last admonitions were directed at one of the supervisors, and a moment later a loud whipcrack detonated in the air above some workers' backs; the sounds of work, that had once more slackened, hurriedly picked up. Kasimir, looking at the laborers, thought they looked a miserable lot—as who would not, wearing chains and doing heavy labor under the lash?—but still they were better off than some prisoners he had seen, at least well-enough fed and watered. Apparently the Hetman of Eylau and his supervisors were more interested in getting their roads built than they were in mere sadistic punishment.

He realized that Lednik the foreman was looking at him now. With a different kind of smile, and a small salute, the man asked: "Did I understand correctly, sir, that you are a physician? A surgeon too, perhaps?"

"I have a competence in both fields. Why?"

"Sir, a couple of my workers are injured. If it would not be too much trouble for you to look at them—? I appeal to you in charity."

"It would not be too much trouble." Kasimir, grateful for a break in the day's ride, got down from his riding-beast and began to unstrap the medical kit that rode behind his saddle.

"They will be thankful, sir, and so will I. Here, any man who cannot work is useless, and we can spare no food or water for those who remain useless for very long."

"I see. Well, show me where these injured workers are. I will do what I can for them."

Working under another simple shade-cloth that served here as the hospital, Kasimir put a splint and a padded bandage on one man's broken finger. After administering a painkiller he swiftly amputated that of another which looked beyond healing. According to their stories, simple clumsiness had wounded both. With bandaged hands and pain-killing salve, both men ought to be able to return soon to some kind of productive work, and indeed they both got to their feet at once, ready to make the effort.

From some muttered remarks among other prisoners who were getting a drink nearby, Kasimir understood that any injuries perceived as seriously and permanently disabling were treated on the spot with execution. There would be no malingering tolerated in this gang, and no benefit to be derived from self-inflicted wounds. Here, a crippling wound was a ticket to the next world, not back to a shaded prison cell in Eylau.

Meanwhile Wen Chang had accepted the hospitality of the foreman's own square of shade. Seated there in the foreman's own rude chair, sipping at a cup of cool water, he had also engaged the man in casual-sounding conversation.

"Unfortunately," Kasimir heard the Magistrate say when he was able to join him again, "we cannot wait for the completion of this road, however efficiently you may be able to accomplish it."

"Then what can I do for Your Excellency?" Lednik seemed to be doing an imitation of a certain kind of shopkeeper, all anxiety to please.

"You can," said the Magistrate in a soft voice, "tell me all about the man who brought the magic Sword here to your camp a few days ago."

"Sir?"

"I assure you, Lednik, that trying to look like a fish and pretending ignorance will not gain you anything." Wen Chang pointed with a firm gesture. "Those marks on the walls of the cut through the ridge back there testify far too loudly to the presence of a certain magic Sword in which I have an intense interest. I rather imagine that before the Sword showed up you were stymied for some days by that ridge—a piece of rock too long to get around, too steep to readily go over. And much too hard to dig straight through, in any reasonable amount of time—if you had been digging with ordinary tools, that is. So the arrival of the man with the magical Sword was very opportune, was it not? Tell me what agreement you reached with him, and where he has gone now. Come, Lednik, I bear you no ill-will, and if you tell me the truth you need not fear me."

Lednik was now sweating more intensely in the shade than he had been a few minutes ago out in the sun. "Magic Sword? Is that what you said just now, Excellency? Alas, I am only a poor man, and have never heard of such—"

"You will be a much happier poor man in the end, Foreman Lednik, if you do not try to treat me as an idiot. It is true that in this territory I have no official standing as an investigator. But I can go from this spot directly to the Hetman himself, and inform him of the suddenly improved technology of road-building in this portion of his domain. He will, I am sure, be interested to hear of it. And to hear the reasons why you, his trusted foreman Lednik, neglected to inform him of the presence in his domain of one of the Twelve Swords that—"

"I want no trouble, sir!" Lednik was beginning to turn pale under his tan and sweat and road dust.

"Then tell me, from the beginning, the truth about this visitor you had." Wen Chang turned his head to glance at Lieutenant Komi. The officer, Kasimir noticed, was moving closer to the others, to stand inside the square of shade, from which vantage point he was better able to follow the progress of the interrogation.

And now Lednik's story came out. Yes, a man, a complete stranger to Lednik, had indeed appeared at the work site only yesterday. And this man had worn at his side a black-hilted Sword of marvelous workmanship.

"Was there a device upon the hilt?" Wen Chang interrupted.

"A device?"

"A special marking."

"A device. Yes sir, there was such a thing. It was a little shape in white, the image of a wedge splitting a block. I did observe that much."

"Excellent. Continue."

Lednik continued in a halting voice with frequent hesitations, describing how the stranger had been willing to demonstrate the power that he claimed for the weapon, cutting away the rocky ridge as if he were digging in soft clay, or wood.

"No, not even like wood, sir. Like butter is more like it. Like melting butter, yes. And that thing, that tool, that must have come somehow from the gods, why it made a dull, heavy hammering noise all the time that it was working, even though it was just slicing along smoothly. My workers had to scramble to move the chunks of rock away as fast as he could cut them out. He demonstrated the power of his Sword beyond all argument, and then he took it away with him again. I did nothing to interfere with him. No, you may bet that I did not. Who am I to try to interfere with a wizard of such power?"

"His name?"

Lednik looked blank for a few seconds. "Why, he gave none. And I wasn't going to ask him."

"What did he look like?"

Lednik appeared genuinely at a loss. "His clothing was undistinguished. Such as everyone wears in the desert. He was thirty years of age, perhaps. Almost as dark as you are, sir. Middle height, spare of frame. I did not pay that much attention to his looks. I feared his power too much."

"No doubt. Well, be assured that my own powers are formidable too, Foreman Lednik. And they tell me that you have not yet revealed the whole truth. What was the nature of the bargain that you struck with this stranger?"

Eventually the full story, or what sounded to Kasimir like the full story, did come out. As payment for the stranger's help, Lednik had agreed to release to him a certain one of his prisoners.

Wen Chang squinted suspiciously when he heard this answer. "And what were you going to say to your superiors when they asked you about the missing man?"

"It's unlikely that anyone would ever notice, sir, that one

of them was missing. They are all minor criminals here, and no one cares. If someone should notice, it would be easy enough for me to say that the man died, and no one would question it. A good many do die in this work."

"And if someone should question it? And ask to see his grave?"

"Bless you, sir, we keep no record of the burials out here. No markers are put up. They go into the sand when they die, and the sand keeps them. How could we ever be expected to find one of them again?"

"I see." The Magistrate ruminated upon that answer, which had sounded reasonable enough to Kasimir. Then Wen Chang resumed the questioning. "And what was the name of the prisoner that you released, in return for getting your ridge cut through?"

The foreman gestured helplessly. "Sir, I do not know his name. They have only numbers when they come to me."

"I see. Well, had this man been with you long? What did he look like? Who were his workmates?"

"His number was nine-nine-six-seven-seven . . . I do remember that because I looked it up, wondering if it was an especially lucky number, which would be worth remembering next time I visited the House of Chance. But I don't see how that will be of any use to you. He had been here for several months, I think. Yes, he was young and strong, and might have endured a long time yet, so for that reason I was sorry to see him go. And as for workmates, he had no special ones. None of the men do, I see to that. It helps immeasurably, I assure you, sir, in cutting down on escape plots and other nonsense of that kind."

"Young and strong, you say. What else can you remember of his appearance?"

"I'm trying, sir, but there really isn't much I can tell you. Hundreds of prisoners come and go. I believe—yes, he tended to be fair instead of dark. Beyond that there isn't anything I can say. Oh, he and the man who rescued him were well acquainted with each other. They were real friends, I could see that from their greeting when they met."

"But, during the course of this joyous demonstration, neither of them ever called the other one by name?"

"That's right, sir, they were very careful."

"And presumably they left together yesterday, the stranger and his rescued friend?"

"Yes sir, exactly. They didn't want to hang around. Cutting through the ridge with that Sword took that strange wizard no more than an hour, while my workers scrambled to carry away the chunks of rock as fast as he could carve them free. He had brought a spare riding-beast with him, and he and his friend took three filled water-bottles from our supply. They headed out into the desert, sir, that way." Lednik gestured in the direction away from Eylau. "Have mercy upon me, Your Excellency, for I am only a poor man!"

CHAPTER 3

I N response to Wen Chang's continued questioning,
Foreman Lednik assured the travelers that the city of
Eylau lay at less than two days' distance, back along the
winding length of the completed portion of his road. To
travel on to Eylau that way would be a shorter and easier
journey than to go back to their original caravan route and
approach the metropolis by that means.

Kasimir inquired: "And is there any water to be found
on the way?"

"Not directly on the way, sir. The roadside wells are not
yet dug. Of course you may happen to encounter one of
our water-supply caravans outward bound, in fact it's quite
likely, for one comes out almost every day. They will be
happy to fill your canteens for you. Otherwise to get water
it will be necessary to make a short detour to the stone
quarry, where there is a natural supply. You will see the
branching road about halfway to the city."

Presently Wen Chang and Kasimir were remounted and
trotting back along the new road, with Lieutenant Komi
and his full complement of men riding escort behind them
as before.

When they had been riding for a few minutes, Kasimir
asked, "How did you know, sir, that the thief had come
this way with the Sword?"

31

Wen Chang roused himself from deep thought and glanced around him. "I only knew there must be water in this place, if men or animals could stay here raising dust so steadily into the sky. And I knew of course that the thief would almost certainly be seeking water. When I saw the marks left by Stonecutter in the rock, it was a pleasantly unexpected bit of confirmation—and also a sign that the thief had other things than water on his mind when he sought out the road-building crew."

"How's that?"

"Here in the desert, he who has water shares it freely. The thief would not have needed to make such a demonstration, endure such a delay, simply to refill his canteens."

"I see. You think, then, that Lednik told us the truth, after you frightened him?"

"I think so, yes." The Magistrate sighed. "But I suspect he had only a small portion of the real story to tell."

"What do you mean?"

"Whoever stole the Sword of Siege must have had a greater plan in mind than simply freeing a man from that road gang, though the fact that he brought an extra riding-beast along indicates that rescuing the prisoner had been some part of his plan from the beginning. A modest bribe in cash would have accomplished the rescue more simply and quietly. The foreman implied as much, and I believe him on that point . . . no, freeing the prisoner was only a part, though perhaps a very important part, of some greater plan. But the fact that the Sword-thief did it opens up a whole realm of fascinating speculation."

"I confess I am more bewildered than fascinated. If only we knew the identity of the freed prisoner!"

"Yes, who is number nine-nine-six-seven-seven? If Lednik gave us the correct number, we may eventually learn the prisoner's identity. Yes, I think that we are making progress. So far I am satisfied."

And the small party rode on. Kasimir glanced over his shoulder to see Lieutenant Komi riding not far behind, in a position where he might well have overheard at least part of the conversation. The officer's face still showed no real curiosity, but Kasimir thought that his stoic expression had acquired a thoughtful tinge.

That day they encountered no water-supply caravan coming out from the city, or indeed any other travelers at all, and that night made a dry roadside camp. Kasimir, stretching out upon his blanket to sleep, reflected that two days and two nights had now passed since the theft of the Sword. If it was not for the presence of the Magistrate, he would have considered the chances of its recovery zero. But Wen Chang inspired confidence.

Shortly after Wen Chang and his party resumed their march in the morning, they came to the first branching road that they had seen. There were no road signs, but Kasimir supposed this must be the way mentioned by Lednik as leading to a quarry.

Komi asked Wen Chang: "Are we detouring to replenish our water, sir?"

Wen Chang nodded. "I think that would be prudent. It is possible that the thief has visited this quarry too, and that we will be able to learn something to our advantage."

"And shall I send a few men around to the other side of the quarry, as we did at the road construction site?"

"You might as well do it again, Lieutenant, though I doubt the Sword will be here now."

The party proceeded according to this plan, and after they had ridden a few kilometers the quarry came into view; it was the rim of the great almost-square pit, seen from outside, that first defined itself out of the jumbled badlands. The road approached it from above.

At the point where the road began to switchback down a steep slope, to enter the quarry through its hidden mouth below, Wen Chang ordered a detour. While a small detachment under a sergeant moved around the quarry to take positions on the other side, the Magistrate led most of his escort toward a place on the upper rim of rock. From here it was possible to overlook the pit and its swarming laborers, with a good chance of remaining unseen from below. Looking down cautiously, Kasimir observed pools of water, looking clear and drinkable, in the bottom of the deepest excavation. Evidently it welled up naturally from the deeply opened earth.

The Magistrate's attention soon centered on that relatively small part of the great excavation in which the workers were now most active. Soon, in an effort to get a closer look at the area of fresh cutting, he moved over the rim and started climbing down. His goal was an area of huge rock faces, at the feet of which great blocks were lying, evidently having been recently split away.

Wen Chang reached one of the opened vertical faces, and began to examine it closely but had not been long at this inspection job before he was discovered by some workers. There was a shout, and one of the overseers who had seen the tall figure of a stranger moving among the rocks started forward, whip in hand—only to change his mind and withdraw quickly on catching a glimpse of the Magistrate's following escort.

When Kasimir came up to him, Wen Chang, smiling faintly, gestured slightly toward the vertical rock face just in front of them. Having seen similar evidence earlier on the road cut, Kasimir this time was certain of Stonecutter's signature at first glance—those long, smooth strokes were unmistakably recorded here too, their texture plainly shadowed by the glancing angle of the sun.

Now the Magistrate climbed the rest of the way down to the bottom of the quarry, in the process demonstrating a lanky agility, and a disregard of dignity that both pleased and surprised Kasimir. On the quarry's level floor, the two chief visitors, with their military bodyguard still filing downslope after them, confronted another foreman who wore the Hetman's gray and blue.

This man was smaller and younger than Lednik. He was also more openly nervous from the start on finding himself confronted by such a formidable caller as Wen Chang.

This foreman, whose leather belt of rank seemed to have been designed for and once worn by a bigger man, introduced himself as Umar. At first Umar, like Lednik, denied having had any visitors at all during the past few days. Nor had he any knowledge of a magic Sword. But when faced with the sort of pressure that had moved Lednik, Umar too caved in and admitted to a different version of the truth.

Yes, Excellency, two strange men had indeed arrived here the day before yesterday, almost at sunset, bringing with them a magic Sword of great power. They had been willing, even eager, to demonstrate what their tool could do, using it to split enormous stone blocks easily out of the living cliff.

"Yes sir, that Sword was a marvel! Just rest it on its point, under no more pressure than its own weight, and it could bury itself right up to the hilt in the solid stone. And its blade was a full meter long."

Wen Chang nodded encouragingly. "And what bargain did these two men make with you, in return for the work they did in cutting stone?"

"Bargain, sir?" Now little Umar's eyes were popping in apprehension. "No, I made no bargain. We gave them a little food and water, yes, but we would do as much for any honest travelers. What kind of a bargain would such wizards want to make with a simple man like me?"

"That was my question. Perhaps they sought the release of one of your prisoners?"

Umar appeared to find that a preposterous idea. "One of

these scum? I would've given them one for nothing if they'd asked."

"So, they showed you what their Sword could do, purely for your entertainment it would seem, and then they simply went away again?"

"That's it, Excellency. That's just what happened." Umar nodded, glad to have the matter settled and understood at last.

Wen Chang, somewhat to Kasimir's surprise, abstained from pressing the line of questioning further, and apparently lapsed into thought.

Kasimir chose this moment to again identify himself as a physician and surgeon, and volunteered to tend whatever injured might be on hand. He had surmised correctly that here, as on the road job, there would always be at least a few men partially disabled.

The foreman, still smiling as if he now considered the matter of the Sword closed, immediately accepted the physician's offer. Kasimir was conducted into a shady angle of the quarry wall, and shown two patients lying there on pallets. These men had suffered, respectively, a head injury and a broken foot.

Kasimir opened his medical kit and went to work. The man with the head wound complained of continual pain and double vision. His speech came disconnectedly, at random intervals. Usually it was addressed to no one in particular and made little sense. He also had difficulty with his balance whenever he tried to stand. There was nothing, Kasimir thought, that any healer could do for him here, and there would be little enough even in a hospital.

The only attendant on duty in the rudimentary infirmary was a permanently lamed prisoner who handled other odd jobs as well for the foreman. This man stood by while Kasimir bandaged the second patient's freshly damaged foot.

This time Wen Chang had come along to watch the physician work. Leaning against the shadowed rock as if he had no other care in the world, the Magistrate observed to the lame man in a sympathetic voice: "There must be many accidents in a place like this."

The crippled attendant agreed in a low voice that there certainly were.

"And no doubt many of them are fatal."

"Very true, Excellency."

Wen Chang squinted toward the quarry's mouth. "And those who die in these sad accidents are of course buried in the sandy waste out there."

"Yes sir."

"And how long has it been now since the last fatal mishap?"

"Only two days, sir."

"Oh. Then it occurred upon the same day that the two strangers paid their visit?"

The attendant said no more. But under renewed questioning the little foreman Umar, who had also come along to the rude hospital, admitted that that was so.

"A very busy day that must have been for you." Then Wen Chang looked up at Lieutenant Komi, who was standing by alertly, and announced in a crisp voice: "I want to take a look at those bodies."

"Yes sir!" Komi turned away and started barking orders to several of his men.

Umar began a protest and then gave it up. He had more overseers under his command than the foreman of the road-building gang, and these were somewhat better armed. Still, they did not appear to be a match for the Firozpur occupying force.

Within a couple of minutes some of Komi's soldiers were making the sand fly with borrowed tools, at a spot out in the sandy waste about a hundred meters from the quarry's mouth.

They had encountered no difficulty in locating the two-day-old burial site—the grave had been shallowly dug, and from a distance flying scavengers were visible about the place. At closer range tracks in the sand were visible, showing that four-legged beasts had been at the bodies too. Kasimir as he walked closer to the grave saw that a pair of human feet and legs had been partially unearthed by the scavengers and gnawed down to the bones. He opened the pouch at his belt containing things of magic, and began to prepare a minor spell to help disperse the odors of death and decay.

The first body unearthed by the soldiers was naturally the least deeply buried, the one with the gnawed feet, that proved to be clad only in a dirty loincloth. Undoubtedly, Kasimir thought as he began to brush the last dirt away from the inert form with a tuft of weeds, it was that of a quarry worker. In this dry heat, decay might be expected to move slowly; a few whip-scars, not all of them fully healed, were still perfectly visible on the skin of the back. The head had been badly injured, perhaps by falling rock, so that not even a close relative would have been able to recognize the face.

Kasimir was about to ask what else there was to look for when Wen Chang, who had squatted down beside him, grabbed the body by an arm and turned it over. A moment later the Magistrate nodded minimally and let out a tiny hiss of satisfaction.

It still took the physician a moment longer to take notice of the thin, dry-lipped blade wound entering between the ribs. If that wound had any depth to it at all, the edged weapon that made it must have found the heart, or come very close to it.

The physician nodded in acknowledgment.

The Magistrate stood up, and with an economical gesture ordered the first body dragged to one side. "Keep digging!" he commanded, and the soldiers did.

In only a few moments a second body, which had been buried right under the first, had come into view. Again the only garment was a loincloth. The back of this man had also been permanently marked with the lash, and his head too had been virtually destroyed, by some savage impact that had well-nigh obliterated his face.

This time Kasimir was the first to discover blade wounds; there were two of them in this corpse's back, and they might have been made by the same weapon as the wound in the first man's chest.

Wen Chang, showing little reaction to this discovery, stood with hands clasped behind his back, nodding to himself. "Keep digging, men," he ordered mildly.

The third corpse, found almost exactly under the second, was paler of skin than the first two, and showed no visible evidence of beatings. As if, thought Kasimir, this was not the body of a quarry laborer at all—though who else would be buried here? But the third body like the first two was clad only in a single dirty rag around the loins.

The face of the third man also had been obliterated, in a way that might be the result of the impact of heavy rocks. And there, under his left arm, was the entry wound of what might have been a sword.

Wen Chang lifted one of the limp arms, relaxed past rigor now, looked at the hand, and let the arm fall back. "A somewhat unusual accident," he commented dryly. "Three men killed in virtually the same way. I suppose that a number of very sharp objects, as well as heavy ones, fell upon them as they were laboring in the quarry?"

Umar had been hovering nervously near the resurrection party, alternately approaching and retreating, and Kasimir could not have said whether the foreman was aware of the discovery of the blade wounds or not.

However that might be, Umar chose not to understand the Magistrate's comment. "You see? These are just dead prisoners, we have them all the time. Who are you looking for? I will summon all my workers to stand inspection for you if you like. Maybe the man or men you want can be found among them."

"I will tell you presently who I am seeking." Wen Chang sighed, and shot a glance at Kasimir that seemed intended to convey some kind of warning. "But first, the two men with the magic Sword—which way did they go when they left here?"

"That way," said Umar immediately, pointing out into the desert, toward nowhere.

"I rather suspected as much. You may rebury these poor fellows now." He seemed about to add some further remark addressed to Lieutenant Komi, but then simply let the order stand.

Wen Chang, Kasimir, and Umar walked slowly back toward the foreman's shaded observation post, while the officer stayed behind to supervise the reinterment.

"I would offer you hospitality, Excellencies," Umar was beginning, "I would bring out refreshment for you, had I any worthy of the name to offer. But as matters stand—"

"You were wondering who I seek," Wen Chang broke in. "They are two men. The name of the leader, or the name I know him by, is Golovkin. I had information that he was foreman here. And that he was the man the Sword-bearing strangers came to visit."

Kasimir, who had never heard of any such person as Golovkin before, shot his mentor a curious glance. But the Magistrate ignored him and continued: "This Golovkin is about forty years of age, tall and powerful, black of skin and hair. Missing an eye. Unless I am badly mistaken, he is the man who wore, before he gave it to you, that foreman's belt that fits you so poorly. I intend to track him in the city of Eylau. Well? Have I described your predecessor in the office or have I not?"

Umar shook his head emphatically. "Not at all, sir, not at all. The man who wore this belt just before me was promoted two weeks ago, and transferred to the other end of the Hetman's domain. He is red of hair. His skin is not black, but freckled, and he had two good eyes when last I saw him. He couldn't possibly be this Golovkin or whatever his name is—you can ask anyone here!"

"His name?"

"His name is Kovil. Ask anyone here!"

Wen Chang blinked as if in disappointment. "Then it appears he cannot be the man I seek . . . when Kovil left, did not another man go with him? The second man I am looking for is some years younger than the first. Not red-haired, but light of skin, and jolly of face and manner, though not always so jolly upon further acquaintance. His—"

"No, no." Umar appeared to have taken renewed alarm. "Nothing like that. I mean no other man went with Kovil when he was transferred. Nor with the two strangers when they left. No, not at all."

The Magistrate tried again, in his best soothing manner; but Umar's latest fright was not going to be soothed away. Eventually Wen Chang expressed his regrets for having wasted the foreman's time, and signed to his companions that they were ready to leave.

In a matter of only a few more minutes, Wen Chang was leading his small party away from the quarry in the direction Umar had indicated, almost directly opposite from that where the city of Eylau lay.

Kasimir could hardly wait until they had got out of earshot of the quarry to begin his protest. "Why didn't you challenge the man, tell him we knew he was lying about those bodies? That they were all stabbed, and that one of them at least, the most deeply buried, was not that of a quarry worker!"

"I have my reasons for not challenging the man," Wen Chang assured him mildly.

Since they had left the quarry the Firozpur lieutenant had been riding close enough to Kasimir and Wen Chang to be able to join in their conversation. "That third body," Komi put in now, "could have been that of a newly arrived worker, one who had not been on the job long enough to acquire calluses on his hands, or even to be lashed."

"You are quite right," Wen Chang assented. "It could have been. But I am morally certain that it was not. For identification we must consider other evidence than the appearance of the body itself. Doctor Kasimir, how long would you say those men had been dead?"

"Two or three days would be about right, I'd say. Though it's hard to tell in this dry heat. Corruption and mummification fight it out and like as not the latter wins. They're slowly turning to stinking leather."

"He was wearing," said Lieutenant Komi stubbornly, "only a loincloth, like the other two. As for the stab wounds, perhaps the foreman—either the new one or the old one—grew angry, or went mad, and stabbed some of the workers. Perhaps one of the overseers went mad. Or perhaps there was a rebellion among the prisoners that had to be put down."

Wen Chang signed agreement. "Admittedly those are possibilities. But the cloth was not a new one—did you notice that? It was dirty, even more so than would result from the mere proximity of his decaying body. The fabric of it was creased and frayed, as if from long usage, while at the same time the skin of that third man's back was pale, not sunburnt as it would be if he'd worked even an hour here. The dirty loincloth was put on him only when he was buried, just in case there should someday be an investigation."

Komi fell silent, frowning. Kasimir asked the Magistrate: "All right, then, sir. If the third man in the grave was not a quarry worker, who was he?"

"I believe he was one of the two men who came to the quarry carrying the Sword. In fact, he was the thief, the man who three nights ago took Stonecutter from the tent where you were sleeping."

Kasimir sat back in his saddle, trying to digest it all. Looking at Komi, he saw with faint surprise that the lieutenant had been jarred out of his stoic calm at last.

Komi was shaking his head. But all he said was: "And then, the second body in the grave—?"

The Magistrate spoke gently. "Very probably it is that of the man who had just been rescued from the road-building gang—I hope he enjoyed his brief day of freedom. The third body, the last killed, the one buried on top, was most likely that of the man the other two were intending to set free from quarry labor.

"Using the Sword once, at the camp of the road gang, was a mistake on the part of our unfortunate thief, that might have been his downfall once I took up his trail. But he survived that blunder. Using the Sword again in the quarry proved fatal."

Kasimir thought aloud for a couple of sentences. "So, the thief and his newly released comrade came here from the road-building site. They demonstrated the Sword here as the thief had done there—and then they were both murdered?"

"We have just seen their bodies. Men have been killed for far less than a Sword. Of course the foreman here must have been their murderer—I mean the real foreman, the man his replacement was good enough to describe for me, and name as Kovil."

"You told Umar you were looking for two men."

"And so I am, now. Kovil, however self-confident he may be, would have preferred not to carry the Sword into the city alone to try to sell it. He would have chosen someone as a companion, a bodyguard perhaps, if possible someone who knows Eylau and its ways . . . and possibly someone Umar fears even more than his old foreman. Umar was on the verge of describing that second man to us, but then he realized what he was doing and closed his mouth.

"I think we may rely, however, on his description of Kovil, the old foreman. Kovil has not been transferred peacefully away. Kovil is instead the chief instigator of the Sword-thief's murder. No one else in the small dictatorship of that quarry could very well have arranged it. It is easy to imagine. A few smiles, apparent agreement—then treachery. A surprise attack, a double killing—then the prisoner who had been the object of the rescue attempt slain also, for good measure."

"So, this man Kovil—and his companion if he indeed has one—they are now—?"

Wen Chang nodded in the direction of Eylau. "They left here two days ago. I presume that they are already in the city, doing their best to sell Stonecutter. Of course Kovil has also promised his assistant Umar a share in the profits. Probably the other overseers in the camp are also to get something for their silence."

"We can still arrest Umar."

The Magistrate shook his head. "Only on our own authority. The removal of the foreman from the quarry would very possibly create turmoil among the overseers and prisoners. This might result in escapes or even an uprising. We would very likely get ourselves into trouble with the Hetman—I do not know him, nor perhaps does he know me. And it is more than likely that at least one of the whip-carrying overseers still in the quarry is in on the plot also. And as soon as we were out of sight with our prisoner he would contrive to send a warning ahead to the man we really want, the one who took the Sword away. No, let them think that we are fooled. Come, we are out of sight of the quarry now. Let us turn back toward Eylau."

CHAPTER 4

THERE was still half a day's light available for traveling, and Wen Chang set his party a good pace upon the road to Eylau. Calling Lieutenant Komi up to ride beside him, while Kasimir remained close on his other side, he took pains to rehearse both of his chief associates in what he wanted to do when they reached the city.

The Magistrate intended to appear there in the character of a wealthy merchant, one who was particularly interested in buying and selling antique weapons. It would be quite natural for such a merchant to travel with a large, heavily armed escort. That the members of his escort were men of the tribe of Firozpur ought not to arouse suspicion, for the people of al-Farabi's tribe had a reputation as reliable mercenaries, and hired out fairly often in that capacity.

Both men agreed that their leader's plan sounded like a good one, and the ride went on, largely in silence. Now there was a faint smell of water in the air from time to time. The fierce aspect of the landscape gradually moderated. Birds became plentiful, tree-covered hills could be seen in the distance, and irrigated fields began to appear at no great distance from the road. The Tungri could no longer be far away.

Now other roads intersected the main one. Gradually

traffic increased, and there were other signs that a large city was near. It was near sunset when the party at last came close enough to see the stone-built walls of Eylau, topped with blue-gray banners, rise against the fading sky. Those walls were high, and extended for what seemed an unreasonable distance to both right and left. Even in the diminishing light they were impressive.

"It is said," the Magistrate mused, "that the walls of Tashigang are even higher than these. And in the south I have seen cities even larger than this one. But this is an imposing sight, nevertheless."

Wen Chang would not entrust the choice of an inn to anyone else, and so the whole party entered the city together as dusk approached. The busy gate through which they passed was manned by the city Watch, officers and men wearing the Hetman's livery. These guardians took note of those who entered—in this case the merchant Ching Hao and his party, fourteen men in all—and urged the peace of the city upon the wealthy trader's Firozpur bodyguard.

Once inside the walls the Magistrate's party split in two. While Komi and his troopers found their way to the warehouse where the caravan's cargo was to be delivered and the payment due thereon collected, Wen Chang led Kasimir expertly through the masses of would-be guides, beggars, and passersby of every description who clogged the streets in the vicinity of the great gate through which they had entered the city. The two men inspected, one after another, most of the inns which clustered in this area. After looking over several hostelries quickly but carefully, the Magistrate selected one whose sign in three languages—one of which Kasimir had never seen before—described it as the Inn of the Refreshed Travelers.

This inn was quite a large establishment, having as Kasimir estimated a hundred rooms or more. It was a fairly expensive one as well. When Komi rejoined them at the agreed-upon meeting place, and handed over the purse of his master's money, Wen Chang had to lighten that purse by a good many coins to make the required advance payment to the innkeeper.

Even before entering the city, the Magistrate had disguised himself in a subtle way, putting on some different clothes chosen from his own wardrobe, so that he even appeared a little shabbier than before, as would be expected of a wealthy merchant traveling through unknown and possibly dangerous territory. And he had adopted a slightly different speech and manner. He was still speaking the common tongue of the region, but now with a different accent.

As for Kasimir, he had been mostly quiet during the past few hours; he had been thinking deeply about his immediate future. It was now time for him to make a decision.

Wen Chang had evidently been aware that some such process of reassessment was under way. He had waited patiently for its conclusion, and realized that a moment of decision had now arrived.

He surveyed the younger man appraisingly. "So, Kasimir—is this the point at which we two part company?"

The physician shook his head. "I must admit that the White Temple holds no great attraction for me at the moment, and I am willing to delay going there indefinitely if you think I can be of the least help to you in your search for the Sword. I still feel . . . well, not exactly responsible for the loss of Stonecutter; but concerned in it. I wish I could do something to help Prince al-Farabi, who has treated me, a stranger to him when we met, with such great kindness."

"Then it is settled!" Wen Chang grabbed him by the right hand and shook it warmly. "You will share accommodation here at the inn with me. There is plenty of room in the quarters I have chosen. And I will be greatly obliged if you would undertake to assist me in one or two points regarding the investigation."

Kasimir knew a sudden sensation of freedom. "Thank you for the invitation, sir. That would suit me very well indeed, and I accept gladly."

The young physician when he inspected the chosen quarters agreed at once that they were adequate. The supposed merchant and his traveling assistant were to share a two-room suite on the third floor of the main building of the inn, while their military escort was quartered in a large room just below them. Their riding animals and loadbeasts were to be housed in a stable immediately under that. The suite on the third floor had a small balcony with a view, not too offensive, of nearby streets and the buildings that lined them. These were mainly other inns, taverns, and two-story houses with narrow fronts. A grillwork of wrought iron defended the balcony against at least the casual attentions of thieves and prowlers. The only regular entrance to the upper suite was by means of a stairway that came up through the room in which Komi and his troops were bivouacked.

Kasimir found that by putting his face almost against the grillwork on the third-floor balcony, and looking out over lower rooftops at a sharp angle, it was possible to see, in the distance, a conspicuous tall building faced with red stone. This, the innkeeper informed them, was the Red Temple of Eylau, now undergoing a remodeling. It was an imposing structure upon which a good deal of new, white stone-carving had recently been completed. More work of a similar nature was obviously in progress. Some larger-than-life-size statues had already been set in their places on the high cornice, and empty pedestals at several levels on the front of the building awaited others.

From his first sight of this temple, Wen Chang's attention was strongly engaged by it, so that Kasimir wondered briefly if his new associate was contemplating a serious debauch. But the Magistrate was content to remain in the inn, and nightfall soon blotted the details of the building from sight—the outline of the temple remained glowingly visible after dark, because of the torches and bonfires kept going at its corners. By such means a Red Temple commonly called attention to its existence, and sought to attract its devotees.

The process of their settling in at the inn was soon accomplished. Whatever money Wen Chang had brought with him, together with the expense money from al-Farabi, went into a small strongbox, and this box was put under Wen Chang's bed in the innermost of the two upper rooms. Kasimir kept his own modest funds with him on his person. A comfortable couch in the outer room offered him a softer rest than any he had had since setting out in al-Farabi's caravan many days ago, and with the door at the top of the stairway bolted his rest was undisturbed.

In the morning, breakfast was brought to the two professional men in their quarters by servants of the inn, while Komi and his troops were fed by turns in the ground-floor kitchen below. Over mugs of tea and plates of fruit and eggs and roasted strips of meat, with sunlight and cheerful street noises coming in the window, Wen Chang discussed his plans with Kasimir.

Discussion in the strict sense was short-lived. The Magistrate was ready to give orders. "The remodeling activity at the Red Temple leads me to believe that an excellent stone-carving tool, such as the one in which we are interested, might well find a ready purchaser in that establishment. I have never yet seen an impoverished Red Temple in any city, so it is quite possible that they would be able to pay enough for the Sword to obtain it from a thief.

"Your assignment, therefore, will be to present yourself

50

at the House of Pleasure, and inquire whether they currently have any opening for a physician. It is highly possible that they will: Devotees who exalt the pleasures of the senses above all else frequently find themselves in need of medical attention."

Kasimir sipped hot breakfast tea. "Often, sir, a Red Temple will have an arrangement with the White Temple in the same city, by means of which the needs of medical care are met."

"I am aware that such arrangements are common. But it is not essential that you actually be given a job, only that you are able to spend enough time inside the Temple, away from the rooms usually frequented by customers, to conduct an investigation. That should not be too difficult; every large Red Temple has in it constantly a number of young men, particularly those from rural areas, applying for one kind of a job or another. I see no reason why you should be conspicuous among them."

"I am not from a rural area," Kasimir protested, somewhat stiffly.

His mentor smiled joyfully. "Splendid! Insist vociferously that you are not, employing just such an expression and tone. Thereby you will convince most of your hearers that you are. So you ought to be able to appear to dawdle aimlessly all day in those precincts without arousing any great suspicion. I say 'appear to dawdle.' Of course you are actually to use your time to good advantage, and obtain any scrap of evidence available bearing on the possibility that the chief sculptor there may have just acquired Stonecutter."

Kasimir frowned thoughtfully. "It is not obvious to me just what sort of evidence that would be, unless I should be able to catch sight of the Sword itself."

"That would be desirable, but I fear very unlikely. There are several other possibilities. Perhaps some workers in stone, no longer needed now that their work can be done faster without them, have just been told that their services no longer are required. Strike up an acquaintance with any employee you can, especially one who appears dissatisfied. Or perhaps you will be able to discover discarded scraps of stone bearing marks similiar to those we observed at the quarry and the road-construction site. It is really hard to think of every possibility in advance. At a minimum, you must learn who is in charge of doing the stonework for the temple; I feel sure it must be an artist of some stature."

Kasimir was still pondering the best way to go about this projected investigation of an unknown artist when Lieutenant Komi came up the stairs and looked in at the open door to ask about his orders for the day. Kasimir, while passing through the second-floor room last night before retiring, had observed that the officer had arranged a semiprivate sleeping chamber for himself by enclosing one end of the room with a couple of hanging blankets, while his men sprawled everywhere else upon the floor and furniture. Now Kasimir thought that the lieutenant, definitely an outdoor type, looked ill-at-ease here inside four walls, even such rough walls as these of the inn.

After routine morning greetings had been exchanged, Wen Chang first instructed the officer to follow Kasimir's orders at any time when he, Wen Chang, was absent. Next he urged him to keep his eleven men under sufficiently tight discipline, and to enforce moderation upon them in their patronage of the local taverns and brothels.

"You must also see to it that they speak and act always as if they were in fact mercenaries, in the service of a merchant who is in the market for fine weapons. Whether that tactic will bring us into contact with the current possessor of the Sword, I do not know. But we must try. That is all I require of you today. Stay—I suppose you will soon be making a report to your prince?"

Komi turned back from the stairs. "Yes sir, though I was hoping for something more to report beyond the fact that we have found lodgings. I have taken the cages with the flying messengers up to the roof of the inn, and one of my men is looking after them."

"Very good."

The officer, upon being dismissed, saluted and went downstairs, where Wen Chang and Kasimir could hear him speaking firmly to his men upon the subject of their behavior in the city.

Now it was time for Kasimir to make the few preparations he thought necessary for his own assigned mission. He would leave off his desert traveler's robe, and wear instead the street clothes of a professional man. He would carry with him only the small medical kit worn on his belt, not the large one that had occupied his saddlebags. And he would use his own name, as it seemed impossible that anyone in this city would yet have any reason to associate Kasimir, the obscure physician, with the famed investigator Wen Chang.

On stepping through the gate of the inn's courtyard into the street, the young physician began to walk with a certain sense of pleasure through the morning crowds. Around him thronged peddlers, shopkeepers, servants of the Hetman, beggars—no doubt there were thieves and pickpockets—busy people of every description. It had been a long time since he had traveled freely along the thoroughfares of a great city. And there could be few cities in the world greater or more exciting than this one.

Kasimir spent the better part of an hour making his way gradually closer to the Red Temple. Frequently he lost sight of his goal in the maze of narrow streets that intervened, but he persevered, relying on a good sense of direction. At last he emerged from the maze on the western side of a great tree-lined square, whose eastern edge fronted directly on the temple he sought. Seen at this closer range the structure looked even larger than it had at a distance.

The Red Temple in Eylau was perhaps six stories high, somewhat broader than its height, and proportionately deep. The façade of the building, following the usual Red Temple style of architecture, was marked by columns, most of them frankly phallic in design, and some as much as two stories tall, going up the front of the building in tier above tier. Between the columns the statues Kasimir had seen last night as distant white specks, and had heard described by the innkeeper, were now visible in detail. They were finely and realistically carved, and larger than life. Distributed in archways and niches at all levels of the façade, they were almost exclusively of human bodies, generally nude. Most of the bodies portrayed were beautiful, with a few of calculated ugliness to provide comic variety.

The activities depicted among the statues were for the most part sexual, but involved as well the prodigious consumption of food and drink, and the amassing of wealth in games of chance. The ingestion of drugs also engaged the attention of certain of the figures, particularly in one frieze whose carven marble people appeared to float on marble clouds. Whoever had done that carving, thought Kasimir, was indeed an artist of more than ordinary talent.

Behind its new façade, the building must have been recently enlarged. New timber showed in several places, and the color of structural stonework on the upper floors was slightly different from that on the lower. Again the job was not yet finished. Kasimir reflected again that this was indeed a very logical place to begin a search for the stoneworking Sword.

CHAPTER 5

K ASIMIR had just started across the square—a hec-
tare and more of tesselated pavement studded here
and there with fountains and obscure monuments—in the
direction of the temple, when his attention was drawn by a
noisy disturbance to his right, at the border of the paved
expanse.

Some kind of official procession was making its way
along that edge of the square. A modest crowd, quickly
formed from the people in the busy square, lined the procession's route. Now mounted guards in the Hetman's colors of blue and gray were using cudgels and other blunt
weapons to beat back a minority of the crowd who were
trying to stage a chanting, arm-waving protest. The protesters, who were fewer in number than the troops and certainly not organized for resistance, promptly gave way.
They had dispersed among the rest of the people on the
plaza before Kasimir could get any idea of who they were
or what they wanted.

His curiosity aroused, Kasimir moved toward the place
where the demonstration had flared up. The procession itself, he saw as he drew near, was quite small. It consisted
of an armed and mounted escort, twenty or so troopers,
surrounding a single tall, lumbering vehicle. Loadbeasts

pulled an open tumbrel, carrying a single figure bound upright—a man, presumably some object of the Hetman's wrath, who was thus placed on display for all the city to behold.

The progress of the cart was deliberately slow, and Kasimir had time to walk closer without hurrying. When the cart finally passed him, he was quite near enough to get a good look at the prisoner. The bound figure was dressed in baggy peasant blouse and trousers, both garments dirty and torn. He had an arresting face—people who didn't know a man might elect him their leader on the strength of a face like that—and he was paying no more attention to the modest crowds around him than he was to those orgiastic statues looming across the square. His eyes instead appeared to be fixed upon some unattainable object in the distance.

A placard had been fastened to the front of the cart, but one corner of the paper had been torn loose; it was sagging in a deep curl, and Kasimir could not read it. Turning to a respectable-looking man who stood nearby, he asked what was going on.

The sturdy citizen shook his head. The corners of his mouth were turned down in disapproval. He said: "I have heard something of the case. The man is called Benjamin of the Steppe, and they bring him out of his cell every few days for a little parade like this. I believe he was engaged in some treasonable activities in the far west, at the very edge of the Hetman's territory. Something to do with organizing the small farmers there over water rights and taxes."

"Organizing them?"

"To form local legislative councils. To vote, and govern themselves." The citizen made a gesture expressing irritation. He obviously didn't know, couldn't remember, exactly how those farmers had intended to organize themselves, but it was an activity which he opposed in general. "They're going to hang him on the first day of the Festival; it's traditional in Eylau, you know, to execute one prisoner then, and set another free. It's hanging, drawing, and quartering, of course." The prospect of that extremely gory spectacle didn't please the townsman either.

The cart had rumbled past; Kasimir cast one more glance after it. Then he thanked his informant and turned away, reflecting that such public executions were probably rather routine events in a city of this size, even though, as far as he knew, the Hetman had no particular reputation for ferocity. Kasimir supposed that very few rulers would be willing to let people, even remote farmers, start governing themselves. Once started, where would that end?

Still walking at a moderate pace, he now turned his steps again in the direction of the main entrance of the Red Temple.

He approached the establishment with mixed feelings. In general Kasimir considered the White Temple, devoted as it was to healing and the worship of beneficent Ardneh, morally superior to any other, particularly to either the Blue or the Red. But in his opinion other forms of religion, including both Red and Blue Temples, had their places in society too. The Blue, at best, served the rest of the world as bankers, offering—for a price, of course—investments that were sometimes sound, and a secure depository. As for the Red—well, Kasimir liked to think that he enjoyed sex, food, and drink as much as the next man. Perhaps even a turn of the gambling wheel now and then. But he had grave doubts about the wisdom of worshipping the gods of those engrossing activities—or any other gods, for that matter. And as a physician he knew too much about the drugs that were so popular among Red Temple worshippers to feel any temptation along that line himself.

The main entrance archway of the temple was draped in red, with scarlet curtains hanging in long folds over the duller masonry. Through the gap between those curtains there came out of the dim interior a hint of crimson light, along with a taste in the air of some exotic incense. The pulsebeat of a drum was throbbing somewhere deep inside that doorway. As Kasimir delayed outside, making his last mental preparations, another man hurried past him and inside. And then a second customer. Business was not bad, even this early in the morning.

Having done his best to put on a businesslike mien, Kasimir followed. Just inside the curtains, as he had expected, a physically impressive attendant waited to exact a small fee from each person entering; a greater contribution would be required of each worshipper later, depending upon the form that his or her devotions might take today.

Today Kasimir managed to avoid paying the nominal entrance fee. In answer to his question, the attendant pointed to a small sign, so inconspicuous that Kasimir almost missed it even as he looked for it. This sign directed the business-minded visitor to the offices, which were up a narrow flight of stairs.

Ascending these stairs, and pushing his way through a double set of sound-deadening curtains at the top, Kasimir found himself in a moderately large room well lighted by several windows, and occupied by a minor episode of bedlam.

A clerk who looked as if he had been born to sit at a desk was on his feet and trying to stand taller than he was, while shouting instructions and vague warnings to a room full of men and women. Meanwhile all the people in this small throng, most of them young and physically attractive, were waiting restlessly, even anxiously—for what? So far Kasimir was unable to tell. While they waited they argued with one another, or waved their hands trying to get the clerk's attention.

Before Kasimir could decide how best to approach someone and ask for a job in a dignified and professional manner, a couple of assistant clerks entered the fray, just in time to keep their leader from entirely losing control of the crowd. Kasimir found himself taken by the arm by one of these assistants, and pushed into a line along with the rest of the job-seekers. He considered making an effort to establish his dignity as a physician, but then decided it would be wiser not to draw too much attention to himself. His first objective, after all, was not really to get a job but to spend as much time as possible within these walls. He relaxed, resolving to let himself be processed along with the rest.

"You," cried a clerk, pointing at someone in the line—randomly, as far as Kasimir could tell—and then pointing again and again. "And you! And you! Come with me now!"

The last jab of the clerk's finger had been aimed at Kasimir. With an unreasonable feeling of satisfaction at having been so promptly singled out—though he had no idea what the pointing clerk might have had in mind—he elbowed his way forward. Behind him, as he followed the red-clad fellow by whom he had been selected, the remainder of the line was quickly collapsing into a minor mob once more.

With the two who had been selected with him—both of them, Kasimir now realized, were sturdy, chunky young men of average height like himself—he was directed on up yet more stairs, and then still more, until he began to wonder whether they were going to come out on the roof.

But the termination of this stairway was not on the roof, but rather within a great open, well-lighted loft-space one or two stories below that ultimate level. It was a loft, or great room, whose high walls consisted mostly of draped canvas, like barriers meant to block off the sights and sounds of some process of construction. Indeed, other signs of new construction were all around, in the form of raw timbers and unfinished stonework.

Overhead was mostly more fabric, shades or awnings of translucent cloth now partially opened to the morning sky, which had turned gray. Kasimir supposed that treatment with oil, and perhaps magic, would serve to keep that cloth roof waterproof.

Ordered to stop where he was and wait without moving, Kasimir stood and looked about. A score or more of agitated people, including artisans, priests, and others less easily identifiable, were milling about the L-shaped loft, some of them shouting at each other in anger or excitement. In the middle of one of the long sides of the L, an open freight-elevator shaft yawned dangerously; above it a system of pulleys creaked in slow motion, and the taut chains and cables going down into the shaft vibrated. A man standing at the head of the shaft yelled something down into it, and presently an unhappy answering shout came back.

Half a dozen statues of gigantic nudes, most of them looking nearly finished, stood about the great room, surveying the scene with pallid marble gazes that passed above the people's heads. Some of these statues were still being worked on, and the rough boards underfoot were gritty with powdered stone. A background sound of chipping and hammering testified to the presence of more workers around the corner of the L, invisible from the place near the top of the stairs where Kasimir was standing.

Even amid all the confusion among the several dozen people present, there was no doubt, thought Kasimir, as to who was supposed to be in charge here. Or, rather, the number of candidates for that honor could be quickly reduced to two. Both of these were men, and one of them, garbed in glossy black richly trimmed in red, could hardly be anyone less than the Chief Priest of the temple. The second candidate for dominance was a man garbed in rougher clothing, as tall as Wen Chang, but unlike the Magistrate in having cold, pale eyes, and a blond beard trimmed with such fanatical neatness that it managed to look quite artificial.

This layman, who wore a sculptor's apron whitely powdered with ground stone, was moving about energetically, passing judgment upon a number of the other people present, who, as Kasimir now realized, were models or would-be models and had been brought up here for his consideration. The prospective models were being ordered to appear nude, two or three at a time, on low platforms or pedestals crudely built of packing crates.

The black-and-red-garbed priest, who kept following the sculptor tenaciously as the latter moved about, was in something of a temper. Evidently his anger had nothing to do with the prospective models, but a great deal to do with the sculptor himself, upon whom the priest's attention was unwaveringly fixed. Nor was the Chief Priest accustomed to being argued with. Especially not—so Kasimir gathered—by a mere artisan who earned his living by carving stone.

On the other hand, neither was the artist much impressed by ecclesiastical authority, at least not the one by which he was currently confronted. At one point the tall blond man interrupted his talent search to stalk over to a cluttered desk at one side of the huge workroom. There he rummaged in the litter of paperwork until he could come up with a sheaf of sheets that his shouts identified as a contract. This document he waved under the priest's nose as the two men resumed their peripatetic argument.

The burden of the argument, as Kasimir had by now determined, was twofold; first, whether or not the sculptor was going to meet his deadline for finishing his work in this room and clearing out of it so it could be returned to its original intended purpose of a gambling casino; and secondly, what was going to happen if he failed to meet the deadline. The deadline was the first day of the Festival—Kasimir had recently heard that mentioned in another connection—and for several reasons it was very important to the Red Temple that all the statues be finished and in place by then, and the gambling tables be opened.

The artist, while listening—or perhaps refusing to listen—to these arguments, went on in a coolly professional way about his business, inspecting one nude prospective model after another as they appeared upon their little sets of elevated stands, male on one side of the center of the room and female on the other. Most of the models were rejected as quickly and decisively as were the protests of the priest, with quick, curt gestures and a few well-chosen words.

And still the argument between the two men went on, the priest trying to convince the artist that it was all very well to be a perfectionist and have artistic scruples, but right here and now the important idea was to produce the contracted number and type of statues, so that the grand official reopening of the remodeled temple could go on as scheduled, in time with the Festival.

The blond man sneered over his shoulder. "You mean so that the passersby in the square will stop having doubts as to whether you're completely open for business, and will rush in to spend their money without hesitation."

It was not that at all, said the man in black and red, outraged at being thrown momentarily upon the defensive—it was important that the consciousness of all the people be awakened to their full sensuous potential!

Meanwhile, another model had just stepped up on a recently vacated stand, where she attracted Kasimir's attention. She was a graceful young woman, really only a girl he thought, not yet out of her teens. Her face was unprepossessing and her hair, worn in awkward braids, the approximate color of used washwater. But her body was striking, tall and strong without being either fat or in the least unfeminine, and he found himself immediately distracted from trying to follow the argument, or even thinking about the Sword.

Kasimir's appreciative gaze was at once tempered with sympathy; even worse, he supposed, than having everyone in a roomful of people stare at you when you were undressed might be to have the same roomful ignore you almost completely. That was what was happening to the young woman now, and she did indeed look a little faint.

Kasimir was jolted out of his contemplation when one of the many clerks in this room grabbed him by the arm again and hustled him, along with the two men who had been chosen with him, across the floor of the great room and into a small antechamber lined with benches. Here and there on the benches were little piles of clothing.

The clerk snapped orders at them, in the tone of one who enjoyed being able to snap orders. "All three of you, get your clothes off, quick. What are you waiting for? Hurry, hurry!"

"But I'm applying for a job as—"

The clerk was already gone; and anyway, as Kasimir kept reminding himself, the purpose of his coming here was not to defend his dignity or even to get a proper job, but to discover as much as possible about this sculptor and his operations. So, in company with his two rivals, all three of them casting wary looks at one another, Kasimir removed his clothes and piled them on a bench.

In a moment the clerk—or another clerk who looked very much like the first one—was back, to shepherd the three sturdily built men, all now naked as infants, back into the great studio. Here each was urged to mount, like a trained circus beast, on his own small stand. Then they stood there waiting. From his new position of vantage on this modest pedestal Kasimir could get a better look than before into the far recesses of the vast room, and see a little farther into the other end of the shallow L. Over there, right under some windows where the light was particularly good, a number of workers were laboring industriously, chipping and sawing away at blocks that were not statues but doubtless would be part of the stonework out on the façade. Kasimir saw no indication that any of those workers were using magic tools.

Glancing back in the direction of the other set of little pedestals, he saw that the young woman who had attracted his attention was now gone, her place occupied by another, more voluptuous, more classically beautiful, but somehow less interesting.

And the argument was over, or at least in abeyance. The Chief Priest had retired, as if between rounds of a contest, into a far corner of the room, where he was now in conference with other red-clad figures. But his opponent was not resting. In another moment the domineering sculptor was standing directly in front of Kasimir, staring at his body with wildly urgent and yet abstracted eyes, as if Kasimir were a piece of stone that might or might not be of just the proper size and shape to meet some emergency need. It came to Kasimir suddenly that he had seen physicians who looked at their patients in a very similar way. He hoped he would never be one of them.

The sculptor, having examined Kasimir's physique from hair to toes, at last stared him straight in the eye.

"Who are you?" the artist demanded.

Kasimir gave his name, though not his profession. But to be snapped at in this discourteous way was very irritating. "Who are *you*?" he demanded right back.

One of the sculptor's assistants, hurrying after the great man with a scroll of notes and a pen, blanched when he heard that. But the artist himself accepted the question—as if it would take a lot more than an uppity model to upset him.

"I am Robert de Borron," he replied in a cold voice. "And this is my work you see all around you. I see no reason to believe that you are going to fit into it."

With a jerk of his head the artist signaled to his aides that Kasimir should be removed. In a moment the physician found himself making his way back to the dressing room, still naked amid a throng of indifferent people.

His clothing and his small medical kit lay on the bench just where he had left them, apparently untouched. He had begun to worry that his modest purse would be stolen, or perhaps some of the drugs taken from his kit. But apparently he need not have worried. Maybe the folk who worked in an artist's studio—or who wanted to work here—needed no other drug than the hectic conditions of their employment.

Kasimir dressed quickly. He supposed he could now return to the second-floor personnel office, and try to convince someone there that he was really applying for a physician's job. But he felt a need to regroup mentally, to get out of the temple for a while, before he tried again. Then in an hour or less he would come back.

Kasimir had just stepped out of the front entrance of the temple, under a sky whose gradually growing promise of rain was beginning to come true, when he caught sight again of the strongly built and graceful young lady with the faded braids. She was sitting on a bench not far from the front entrance, and she did not look well.

Perhaps she was poor and hungry—her blouse and trousers looked rather shabby—or perhaps the experience of posing in the nude had been too much for her. In a moment Kasimir had stopped beside her.

CHAPTER 6

"IF I may intrude for a moment upon your thoughts? I am a physician, and you do not look well. Can I assist you in any way?"

"Oh." The young woman sitting on the bench turned up her face to Kasimir. Again he was struck by the plainness of her face. But her greenish eyes, seen at such close range, were unexpectedly impressive.

Her voice had an intriguing quality too, low and throaty. "It's a long story. But I expect I'll be all right." Then she frowned. "Didn't I just see you somewhere inside the temple?"

"No doubt you did, I was looking for a job. I noticed you in there too." Kasimir was about to add that it would have been difficult not to notice her in the circumstances, but he had approached her as a physician, and it was a little too soon to alter that.

The girl was still frowning up at him. "You were trying out as a model? I thought you said just now that you were a physician."

"I was. I am. There were a series of misunderstandings—originally I was supposed to be applying for a physician's job in the temple. Do you mind if I sit down?"

"No." She moved over slightly on the bench, adjusting

66

her baggy peasant trousers. "Except that I have things to do, and I ought to get up and do them—did the sculptor hire you, then?"

Kasimir sat down. "No. It seems that something about my attitude displeased the great artist, Robert de Borron. Perhaps he didn't like my shape any better than my attitude. What about you?"

"Did you deliberately displease him?" Her frown vanished. "I'm glad, I would have liked to do that too—but I couldn't afford to. So he hired me. I'm to start modeling for him tomorrow."

"I'm pleased for you, if you are pleased. You don't sound exactly overjoyed about it."

"Oh, I am, though. Getting this job was absolutely essential for me." It was said in a tone of heartfelt seriousness.

"Then I can rejoice with you." At this point, inspiration came to Kasimir. "By the way, I missed my breakfast this morning—would you care to join me in an early lunch? We could at least get in out of this drizzling rain somewhere."

Her greenish eyes appraised him thoughtfully. She stood up from the bench. "That sounds like an excellent idea, thank you."

They went into a nearby wineshop, where sights and aromas provided an intriguing menu. Sausages were hung invitingly from the rafters, and cheese and fresh, crusty bread were displayed on a counter.

They sat at a table, and ordered wine and food. The young woman's name, she told Kasimir, was Natalia. As he had surmised, she was originally from a small village. But she had visited Eylau several times before moving here a few months ago. Economic conditions at home were poor. She ate hungrily—though not like one actually on the verge of starvation—of bread and cheese, but sipped sparingly at her wine. She also persisted in turning the conversation around to him.

"Have you been a physician long?"

"About five years. How long have you been a model?"

She smiled at him. "My experience in that line is very limited. I expect the hardest part will be just holding still for a long time. Well, the hardest part besides . . ."

"I understand."

Natalia tossed back her awkward braids. "I did study at a White Temple for a while. Not modeling, of course, but medicine."

"Really? Then we might have been colleagues."

"I never had the chance to finish."

"Sorry. Where did you study?"

She named a small city that Kasimir had barely heard of, hundreds of kilometers to the west.

Kasimir chewed a mouthful of his sandwich. "It's easy to tell that you're well educated."

"Thank you."

"But short of money just now."

Her green eyes questioned him. "I might have landed a different kind of job in the Red Temple, without too much trouble. But I'd like that even less than posing."

"Of course, of course. I sympathize."

During their lunch Kasimir, sounding out his companion as gradually and carefully as he could, at last admitted to her that he had had an ulterior motive in trying to get a job inside the Red Temple. Yes, he was really a physician—but his main occupation at this time was a partnership with the well-known dealer in antique and special weapons, Ching Hao.

Natalia blinked her green eyes, as if she had never heard of the famous Ching Hao—small wonder—but wasn't quite ready to admit the fact, because she realized she ought to be impressed.

Ching Hao, Kasimir went on to relate, was particularly interested just now in locating and buying a certain special sword, an ancient and very valuable weapon. There was reason to suppose that this sword might have come into the possession of the Red Temple, or perhaps even the hands of Robert de Borron, for whom Natalia would presently start modeling. It would be worth some money to Ching Hao and his partner—more money than a model was likely to get paid—if an insider at the temple could find some evidence that the sword was really there.

Natalia didn't respond at once, except to look at Kasimir thoughtfully.

He pressed on: "We wouldn't be asking you to take any risks. And it's not a matter of getting anyone in trouble. It would just be a matter of keeping your eyes open and reporting to me."

"How would I know this sword if I saw it?"

Kasimir drew in a deep breath. "It's an impressive-looking weapon, to begin with. The blade is a full meter long, of mottled steel. The hilt is plain black, with a simple white image on it, depicting a wedge splitting a block." He hesitated briefly. "Most importantly, the blade has the magical ability to cut stone, any stone, very easily."

The greenish eyes were wide, really impressed at last. "The magic must be very powerful, I suppose. Does this sword have a name?"

Probably out there in the remote lands to the west they weren't altogether caught up on what happened out in the great world. Evidently their ignorance extended even to the history of the Twelve Swords.

"Yes," said Kasimir. "Some people call it Stonecutter. Or the Sword of Siege."

Natalia, thinking the matter over as she finished her lunch, eventually agreed to act as Ching Hao's agent. She would receive a small advance now, an additional payment every time she reported to Kasimir, and a substantial reward if she could provide some useful information about Stonecutter. They made arrangements for their next contact, which would be in the White Temple.

When he left the wineshop, Kasimir, taking what he considered rather ingenious precautions against being followed, returned by a somewhat indirect route to the Inn of the Refreshed Travelers.

He felt reasonably well pleased with himself for what he had managed to get done today. He might, he thought, possess a hitherto undiscovered knack for this sort of thing. It hadn't taken him long to conclude an arrangement with a young woman who was going to be one of Robert de Borron's models. Of course it would still be possible for him to go back to the temple and try again for the physician's job. But now it seemed to Kasimir that that would probably be unnecessary; with Natalia in place inside the temple he would be free to help Wen Chang in some other way.

Nor was that all he had accomplished today, Kasimir thought with satisfaction. He had discovered also that the sculptor, Robert de Borron, had a large reputation, and the ability to justify it. Also that de Borron was under intense pressure from the Red Temple authorities to complete his work; it seemed highly probable that he would suffer financial and other penalties if he failed to do so in time. When it came to business matters, Kasimir had observed, the Red Temple was likely to be as grasping and unyielding as the Blue. And sometimes, if the truth be told, the White could hold its own with either.

The day was getting on toward midafternoon when Kasimir returned to the inn. The place was busy, but as far as he could tell everything was peaceful. Lieutenant Komi and a few of his men were on guard in their second-floor room, seated around a table near the stairway where they played at some tribal card-game. A couple of the other troopers slept on cots. Three or four were absent, and Kasimir assumed that these were off duty, enjoying whatever they might be able to afford of the delights offered by the big city.

Komi looked up as Kasimir walked in. The officer appeared glad to see him, and tossed a casual salute without rising from the table.

"Ching Hao has not yet returned," Komi announced, giving the name of the supposed merchant a slight emphasis, as if he thought the physician might need to be reminded of the alias. "He left this note for you. Also there is a man waiting out in the courtyard now, who says he wants to see either the merchant or his assistant."

Kasimir accepted the casually folded square of paper but did not immediately open it. Close under the windows of the inn a street vendor screamed, hawking his dried fruit. "A man waiting? Who is he?"

"An elderly fellow who looks to me as if he might possibly have money. Beyond that I have no idea who he is— that is why I insisted he wait in the courtyard and not in any of our rooms. But he says that he is interested in possibly purchasing antique weapons from you."

"If he wishes to buy weapons then he can hardly be trying to sell Stonecutter." Kasimir spoke freely in front of the card-playing soldiers at the table; all the members of Komi's squad had been informed of the essentials of their mission. "Still, for the sake of appearances, I suppose I'd better see him."

"I'll point him out."

Looking out one of the small windows that opened on the inn's interior courtyard, Kasimir studied the figure the lieutenant indicated—a gray-haired man, garbed in the drab clothing of a desert traveler, sitting on the rim of one of the courtyard's two fountains, and talking to someone

71

who might be another merchant. At this distance it was hard to get any very distinct impression.

Before descending to talk to the caller, Kasimir opened the note Komi had handed him. The message was recognizably in the writing of Wen Chang and seemed innocuous.

> Kasimir—if you have no urgent reason to go out again, remain at the inn until I return, which will probably be before dark.
>
> Ching Hao

Yes, it might very well be a communication from a merchant to his assistant. There was no hidden meaning that Kasimir could detect. He tossed the note carelessly on a table, almost hoping that some spy might find and read it—though he really doubted that any spy would be watching them at this stage of affairs.

In a moment he was going downstairs again.

When Kasimir came out into the courtyard, the man who waited by the fountain was alone, sitting patiently with folded arms. He got to his feet as Kasimir approached. Despite his gray hair and lined face, he was still erect and hale, of average height and build. The two men bowed, in the approved manner of polite strangers unsure of each other's exact status. Kasimir was wishing silently that he had been able to learn something about antique weapons before undertaking to play the role of a dealer in them.

"I am Kasimir, secretary to the merchant Ching Hao. Can I be of service to you?"

"It may well be that you can, young man." The elder nodded in a benign way; he had a gravelly voice, and a vague accent that Kasimir had trouble trying to define. "I am Tadasu Hazara—few in these parts know me, but in my own region I have something of a reputation of a collector of fine weapons. Having heard that your master was here, I decided to find out if he might have any of the specialized kind of weapons upon which my collection is centered."

"And what kind of weapons are those, sir?"

"My chief interest lies in jeweled daggers of the Polemonic Epoch; also, if they are of the first quality, mail shirts of the bronze alloys made by the smiths of Aspinall." The hands of the elder gestured; they were gnarled but strong, those of a man who had at some time done a great deal of physical work.

Kasimir assured the other, in perfect truthfulness, that Ching Hao had nothing like that in stock just now.

"Ah, that is too bad." After considering for a moment, the gray-haired man announced that he was also unfortunately under the necessity of parting with one or two very old weapons that had once belonged to his father. Was the merchant thinking of purchasing anything just now?

"What sort of weapons are they?"

When it turned out that none of them was a sword, Kasimir, feeling that whatever more he did was likely to be a blunder, pronounced himself unable to make decisions on such matters. Tadasu would have to wait for the return of Ching Hao himself.

The visitor seemed annoyed at having spent his waiting time in the courtyard for nothing. After expressing his formal good wishes to Kasimir and his absent master he bowed again, more lightly this time, and walked on out of the courtyard, through the main entrance of the inn.

The rain had ended some time ago, the day was growing hot and muggy, and Kasimir would have returned to the comparative coolness of his upper room. But before he could leave the courtyard another prospective customer had appeared, forwarded to him by the helpful innkeeper. This latest potential customer was actually carrying with him a bundle in rough cloth that looked very much like a wrapped sword.

This man was much younger than the first, and appeared considerably more nervous. "You buy weapons?" he demanded tersely.

"That is our business."

"I have a sword here."

"Very good." Kasimir attempted to sound confident. "If I may see the merchandise?"

The other man's fingers hesitated on the wrappings. "If you like this weapon—it's really something special—then you can give me cash for it this moment?"

Kasimir had to suppress his excitement. He had never seen any of the Twelve Swords, but he had no doubt of being able to recognize one of them if it should come his way.

Carefully he said: "I do not carry large amounts of coin on me, but still cash is readily available. If your sword there should prove to be something that I really want, then you may have money in hand for it before you are an hour older."

After another few moments of cautious hesitancy, the potential customer unwrapped the sword he had brought with him. Kasimir knew bitter disappointment. When the weapon was at last shown it did not look spectacular—the hilt was not even black, nor had the steel of the blade the finely mottled look that everyone who had seen the genuine Swords remarked upon.

Then a thought struck the young physician. Having heard tales of magical alterations in the appearance of things, and having once, years ago, had actual experience of such a trick, he thought he had better apply one more test. Taking the cheap-looking weapon in hand, he made a trial of it against the stone edge of the fountain. The only result of this was an angry protest from the seller. What was Kasimir trying to do, ruin a fine blade?

By the time Kasimir had succeeded in soothing the angry man, and sending him on his way with his precious sword, sunset was near. Leaving the courtyard that was already deep in shadow, Kasimir looked in on the innkeeper and gave orders that a warm bath be brought to him in his upper room, with dinner to follow. Then he went plodding up the stairs. Over the past several hours, his earlier feeling that the investigation was making progress had gradually faded into a sense of impatience and futility.

The bathtub had been taken away again and he was just finishing his solitary dinner when the sound of feet ascending briskly on the stairs made him turn his head. But instead of the familiar countenance of Wen Chang or Komi, there appeared in the doorway, just at the top of the stairs, the visage of a scowling beggar.

Kasimir immediately reached for his dagger, and was about to bawl an oath downstairs at Komi for having allowed this stranger to get past him when the beggar called out a greeting in the voice of Wen Chang.

Kasimir's hand holding the dagger fell to his side. "You! But—is this magic?"

"Only a touch of magic, perhaps, here and there." The figure of the beggar doffed its ragged outer coat.

"Why such a marvelous disguise?"

"It is sometimes necessary to gather information on the streets," the Magistrate said, his voice a little muffled in the process of pulling off the shaggy gray facial hair that had concealed his own neat mustache along with most of his lower face.

"I never would have known you!"

"I trust not." With another muffled grunt the older man now tugged off a sticky something that had altered the shape of his nose and cheekbones, and tossed this flesh-colored object on the table along with his wig and beard. Now undeniably Wen Chang again, he straightened his back and stretched.

"Now," the Magistrate continued in a clear tone of satisfaction, "we must exchange information. My day has been a long and trying one. The beggars' spaces at the Great Gate are considered most desirable, but they are too jealously guarded and fought over for an outsider like myself to have any chance of forcing his way in. The same situation obtained in Swordsmiths' Lane, and again behind the Courts of Justice, where there was much rumormongering over the matter of the execution two days hence. But as it turned out, all those difficulties were undoubtedly for the best. When I finally found a place to put down my begging bowl, in the vicinity of the Blue Temple, I learned something that may prove useful to us indeed."

Kasimir could readily understand why there was no surplus of beggars near the Blue Temple, whose priests and worshippers alike were notoriously stingy. He asked: "And what was this most useful thing you learned?"

"Have you ever heard of the famous diamond, the Great Orb of Maecenas?"

"I admit that I have not."

"If you, Kasimir, were a lapidarist, or a jewel thief, or a priest in the Blue Temple, you would certainly give a different answer to that question. Know, then, that such a diamond exists, that it has recently been brought to the Blue Temple of Eylau in secret, and that it is there to be carved into several smaller stones in the hope of thereby increasing its total value. This is obviously a matter of concern to us, for it is certain that the Sword can be used in the precise cutting of small stones as well as great. But before we discuss that any further, tell me of your day. What did you discover at the Red Temple?"

As Kasimir began his tale with his arrival at the Red Temple in the morning, the feet of servants were heard on the stairs. Soon they entered once more bearing a tub and buckets of hot water. The physician delayed his story until the tub had been set up behind a screen and the servants had departed.

Faint splashing sounds issued from behind the screen as Kasimir detailed his adventures in the vicinity of the Red Temple, and Wen Chang listened. The young man's story of recruiting the girl model to act as a paid spy elicited only a momentary cessation of splashing.

Not until Kasimir described his leaving the temple area to return to the inn did Wen Chang comment aloud. "And you did not persist in your attempt to obtain employment there yourself?"

"No sir, I thought I had explained that. What I had managed to achieve at the temple seemed to me at least enough to deserve reporting—and of course when I reached the inn your note was waiting for me, asking me to remain here."

The Magistrate grunted. "And I suppose there have been no callers at the inn wishing to sell us Stonecutter?"

As Kasimir began to describe the first man who had come asking to buy weapons, there sounded a louder splash than before from behind the screen; a moment later the face of Wen Chang, staring narrow-eyed above the folds of an enormous towel, peered fiercely around the edge of the screen. "And you simply let him go?"

"But the man told us, both Komi and myself, at the start that he wanted to *buy* weapons—"

"Did it not occur to you that he may have begun that way simply as a precaution? That he wished to see if our merchant operation was a legitimate one before he approached us with his real treasure? What did he look like?"

Here, at least, Kasimir had not failed, and could supply a fairly complete delineation. But the description of the elderly would-be client did not tally with that of anyone Wen Chang was able to recognize.

Wrapped from shoulders to knees in his great towel, his bath for the moment forgotten, the Magistrate paced impatiently. "Well, well, it is impossible for me to tell now whether he had any connection with our real business here or not. Did he give you the impression that he was coming back?"

"Frankly, he did not. Though I fear that also is impossible to know with any certainty."

"Then it is useless to speculate upon these matters any longer. Here comes my dinner up the stairs if I am not mistaken, and when I have eaten I intend to sleep. Tomorrow we must arise early. Unless there is some new development, we are going to interest ourselves in the gem-cutting project at the Blue Temple."

CHAPTER 7

W EN Chang declined to discuss his plans for approaching the Blue Temple until morning. Even then he remained silent on the subject until, over breakfast in their rooms, Kasimir questioned him directly.

"How are we going to approach the authorities in the House of Wealth? If, as you say, this fabulous diamond is being kept there secretly, they are not likely to admit its presence, or that any special gem-cutting is about to take place."

"True, they will not admit such things to the merchant Ching Hao. But if they are approached directly by the famous Magistrate Wen Chang, their response might be more favorable—especially if I bring them information of a plot to steal the gem."

Kasimir paused with a tea mug halfway to his lips. "You said nothing to me last night of such a plot."

"Nor did I learn anything of one during my investigations yesterday. But today it strikes me as a very useful idea."

"I see. And who am I going to be today?"

"The very well-known Doctor Kasimir, of course. We shall both be surprised—raise our eyebrows politely, so—if any of them admits that he has never heard of you. You are my assistant—or my associate, if you prefer—and a specialist in forensic medicine."

Kasimir thought about that. "It is not a common specialty. In fact I have never heard of it. But I suppose the very fact that it is unknown makes it sound prestigious. Very well. And I think I do indeed prefer 'associate.'"

"So be it, then."

There was not a single shabby thread in any of the garments in which Wen Chang arrayed himself this morning. Before starting for the Blue Temple with Kasimir, the Magistrate left orders with Lieutenant Komi to maintain the fiction of the merchant Ching Hao against any suggestion to the contrary, and to take careful note of any potential customers.

"In particular I am interested in the elderly man who was here yesterday and said he wanted to buy weapons. If he should return, send one of your men riding to the Blue Temple at once to let me know. And meanwhile detain this fellow merchant of ours, forcibly if necessary, until I return."

"It shall be done, sir." Komi saluted. His salutes meant for the Magistrate always looked more serious than the ones he gave Kasimir.

"Good. Have you been sending reports to the Prince?"

"I dispatched a flying messenger yesterday, sir, bringing him up to date. There has been no reply as yet."

Wen Chang had decided to go to the Blue Temple on foot; a riding-beast carried more prestige, but only if you were assured of a place to put it safely when you had reached your destination, and they had no assurance of being offered such hospitality. A good walk lay before the two men, for the Blue Temple was in a different quarter of the city. Wen Chang, who had observed it while in the guise of a beggar yesterday, reported that it, like the Red Temple, bordered upon its own vast square.

Their route took them close to the Hetman's palace, which like the great temples had its own plaza; in the case of the palace, the plaza surrounded the building completely. Wen Chang detoured slightly so that they should go right past the palace, crossing the surrounding open space. About all they were able to see of the great house itself were the formidable outer walls of gray stone, several stories high.

At one place on the pavement, no more than thirty meters or so from those walls, a few men and women in country garments were conducting a protest demonstration. Kasimir was reminded at once of the public exhibition he had seen as the tumbrel passed bearing the unfortunate Benjamin of the Steppe. Whether these were the exact same people or not he couldn't tell, but he supposed it likely. Here they were crouched, facing the high gray palace wall, which in this area was pierced by a few high, small, heavily grilled windows, appropriate for prison cells. All of the demonstrators were slowly and rhythmically pounding their heads—fortunately with no more than symbolic force—upon the plaza's paving stones.

Kasimir stopped, joining a few other passersby who had taken time out from their own affairs to stare at this bizarre behavior. Wen Chang paused too, to stand with his arms folded, observing. As moments passed, a few more gawkers gathered.

The crouching head-bangers were all dressed in loose peasant clothing. The loose braids of the women swung as their heads moved up and down. When one of the men, perhaps sensing that by now a sizable audience had gathered, raised his head and looked around, Wen Chang called to him, asking the reason for these actions.

Eager to tell his story, the man abandoned his symbolic head-banging and jumped to his feet. He spoke in an uncouth accent.

"Oh, master, the prisoner who is to be so unjustly and horribly executed on the first day of the Festival, Benjamin of the Steppe, is even now held captive in a cell inside this building!" Raising a quivering arm, the protester pointed at the palace. "All the people of Eylau should be here now, petitioning the Hetman for his release!"

The reaction of the small crowd was not generally sympathetic. Many jeered and made threatening gestures. Some looked over their shoulders and hurried away, lest they be seen by the Watch associating with these mad treasonous folk who seemed to criticize the government.

The Magistrate did not answer the speaker but turned away. Kasimir followed silently. They had other matters to discuss besides these hopeless protests, and were talking in low voices about the Sword again when at last their goal came into sight.

The Blue Temple of Eylau, like most of its kind elsewhere, was practically devoid of exterior decoration, and sported no statuary at all on walls or roof. To most of its clients as well as its managers, such ornaments would have indicated a tendency toward frivolous waste. Whenever Kasimir looked at the outside of a Blue Temple in any city he got the impression that an effect of shabbiness if not actually dirtiness, the grim opposite of frivolity, was what the proprietors were striving to achieve.

Nor was the style of architecture accidental either. This particular Blue Temple, true to type, was reminiscent of a fortress; even more, perhaps, of a miniature mountain, though the total bulk of this structure was somewhat less than that of the Red Temple across town, which looked less like a mountain than like a giant hive. Undoubtedly this fortress, the Blue Temple, would be an extremely good place in which to leave your money and keep your valuables on deposit. Nothing, not even an earthquake, was ever going to budge or threaten this building and its contents—that, at least, was the impression meant to be conveyed by the massive walls and foundations, and reinforced by the iron bars, each thick as a strong man's arm, that guarded all the windows.

Wen Chang confronted all this majesty of strength undaunted. He marched majestically forward, straight across the square in the direction of the main entrance of this formidable edifice. Kasimir, walking half a step behind him, observed that here as at the Red Temple the majority of worshippers entering were men.

There was no difficulty about entering, for men so respectably dressed. Once they were inside the lobby, all cool white and pale blue, the Magistrate did not delay to look around. As if he knew exactly where he was going, he made his way straight to one side of the marble counter where a massive and yet somehow discreet sign promised information. Already, here in the outer lobby, the impression of penuriousness was beginning to fade.

The imposing manner of Wen Chang's approach did not appear to make the least impression upon the well-dressed clerk behind the counter, who doubtless dealt every day with equally imposing folk.

Nor was the clerk shaken when the Magistrate fixed him with a narrow-eyed glare, and announced in a firm voice: "I wish to see the Director of Security."

The expression on the clerk's face remained perfectly neutral as he looked this grand visitor up and down. "And may I tell the Director who wishes to see him?"

The tall figure that stood in front of his marble counter became, if possible, even a little taller. "You may tell him that his callers are the Magistrate Wen Chang, and his associate Doctor Kasimir."

The expression on the clerk's face achieved something—not quite a real change, thought Kasimir, more like a greater intensity of neutrality. In a moment, speaking in a voice that now admitted a certain grudging courtesy, the man behind the counter invited: "Step this way, if you please, gentlemen."

Wen Chang, with Kasimir remaining more or less half a step behind him, followed the clerk through a curtained doorway behind the information counter. On the other side of the doorway, solid steps led up. As he climbed Kasimir observed, in the materials of walls and stairs themselves, that they were now definitely entering the plusher precincts of Blue Temple administration.

The information clerk conducted them up only one level, and into a small office where he left them standing in front of the desk of another functionary. This woman, upon hearing the Magistrate's identity, welcomed him and his associate with something approaching warmth. Then she promptly left her small office to escort the visitors on up to a higher level still.

This process repeated itself, with subtle variations, on several levels. In each new office Kasimir and Wen Chang encountered a pause in front of a new desk, new introductions, and a brief conference. All this was conducted in an atmosphere of cordiality tempered by suspicion, palpable though never openly voiced, that this imposing man might not really be who he claimed to be.

Early on in the game it became evident to Kasimir that the higher up you went in the Blue Temple, the closer you penetrated toward its center, the plusher, more luxurious, everything became. Inside this fortress it was no longer frivolity to display wealth. Instead it had become a duty to show it, or at least enough of it, to suggest how much more treasure must be available.

There was a great deal of affluence in sight already, and still he and Wen Chang had not penetrated to their goal. The Director of Security, Kasimir was thinking, must be a very important part indeed of this establishment.

But at last Wen Chang, with Kasimir at his elbow, was

standing in the office of the Director himself, who came around from behind his enormous ebony desk to greet them with a moderate show of warmth, that somehow did not include revealing his name if he had one apart from his office. No great sensitivity was needed to detect a certain wariness in the Director's manner as he pressed his callers' hands, one after another. Inside this man's fine robes of blue and gold his body was very lean, as if perhaps the guardianship of such mind-boggling wealth as had been entrusted to his care left him with no time to eat.

The words of the Director's greeting, at least, sounded perfectly sincere.

"To what does our poor establishment owe the honor of this visit? Everyone has heard of the wise judge Wen Chang, whose eye is capable of penetrating with a glance to the very heart of wickedness. But I confess, Your Honor, that somehow I had pictured you as an older man."

Wen Chang bowed, lightly and courteously. "And I, even in lands far distant from this one, have heard of the Director of Security in the Blue Temple in the great city of Eylau. But we have not come here for an exchange of compliments however pleasant. Instead we are upon a matter of the most serious business."

"I am all ears. Please, be seated."

Wen Chang and Kasimir helped themselves to ivory chairs, while the Director resumed his place behind his desk of ebony. Then the Magistrate continued: "It was another matter entirely that brought myself and my associate, Doctor Kasimir, here to Eylau. But in the course of our investigations in this city there has come to our attention the existence of a plot to steal from this temple the jewel known as the Great Orb of Maecenas."

The Director blinked once, and then his face went totally blank. "What reason have you to believe that jewel is here?"

The Magistrate shook his head. "Come, come, sir, we are going out of our way to do you a favor. Do not waste my time or your own."

At this crucial moment there was a confused bustling and whispering at the door of the Director's office. In a moment a man entered, a fat and oily-looking man wearing a cape of almost pure gold, touched only with a little blue.

The two visitors got to their feet, and a fresh round of introductions began, this time with more ceremony than before. The new arrival was actually Theodore, Chief Priest of the Blue Temple in Eylau.

From the moment of his arrival in the room, the Chief Priest's manner indicated that he was at least somewhat mistrustful of everyone else, including his own Director of Security.

When all were seated again, Wen Chang repeated, for Chief Priest Theodore's benefit, his statement about the discovery of a plot to steal the jewel.

Theodore did not trouble to deny the presence of the Orb inside his establishment. Instead he asked Wen Chang bluntly: "How do you know this?"

"The circumstances in which I gained the information are closely connected to the original investigation upon which my associate and myself were engaged. More than that I cannot tell you at present. You will appreciate that I extend to all my clients the same confidentiality I would extend to you, were I retained by you personally, or by the Blue Temple."

This speech did not go down well with either of Wen Chang's priestly hearers, who exchanged grim looks. Then the Director still attempted to deny the presence of the Great Orb, and even disclaimed any knowledge of its whereabouts.

The Magistrate was growing impatient with them. "Come, come! I know that the gem we are speaking of is in this city, and I am almost certain that it is within the walls of this very building."

At this point the Chief Priest asked Wen Chang and Kasimir, politely enough, to step into another room while he had a private discussion with his Security Director.

Wen Chang signed agreement and got to his feet. "Of course, gentlemen. But I advise you not to take too long to make up your minds to listen to me. In this matter time is of great importance."

The Director glared at him. "It seems to me that we could all save time if you would condescend to tell us the source of your alleged information."

The Magistrate appeared to be maintaining his patience only with an effort. "Even if I was willing to break confidence with my client—which I am not—nothing I could tell you about the source would help you in the least to prevent the theft. By the way, I suppose you are perfectly sure that the stone is secure at this moment?"

This question threw the two high authorities into a state of considerable confusion, impossible to conceal. As an open argument began between them, Wen Chang and Kasimir were conducted away by an underling.

They were deposited in a comfortable anteroom and left alone with the door closed. They glanced at each other, but neither had anything to say. It was obvious to both of them that any conversation they held would almost certainly be overheard.

The duration of their wait dragged on, to a length that Kasimir, at least, had not expected. Wen Chang waited with newly imperturbable patience, hands clasped in his lap, his weathered face impassive as a mask. But Kasimir was bothered by mounting apprehension. Had they somehow unwittingly precipitated a real crisis in the local Blue Temple leadership? Had they—but such speculations were pointless.

Eventually a silent attendant brought them refreshment on a tray, tea and cakes in portions of hardly more than symbolic size. Both courteously declined. Following that they were again left alone for almost an hour, when a group of temple officials, including the High Priest and the Director of Security, suddenly entered the anteroom. They brought with them a newcomer, an outsider to the temple, a man attired in the uniform of an officer of the city Watch, in the Hetman's colors of gray and blue. This was a large grizzled veteran of about forty.

As soon as this man's eyes fell on Wen Chang, he stepped forward and opened his arms in greeting.

"Magistrate!" His voice was a bass roar. "They told me there was someone here I might recognize, but they never gave me a hint that it was you. It's years since we have worked together—how are you?"

Wen Chang, smiling, had arisen to return the greeting heartily. "I am healthy and busy as you see. And how are you, my friend Almagro? It is indeed too long a time since we have seen each other, but you do not appear to have changed much."

After Kasimir had been duly introduced to Captain Almagro, the two veterans spent a few moments more in private conversation, most of it reminiscing about a particularly filthy gang of bandits they had once succeeded in luring into an annihilating ambush. In this exchange of memories they must have removed from the minds of their priestly hearers any lingering doubts of the Magistrate's true identity.

The discussion turned away from the bandit gang. Almagro mentioned how, after several unlikely sounding adventures, he had come to be now in the employ of the Hetman.

"And a good thing I am here, too, for now I may be able to return the great favor that you, Magistrate, once did for me."

Wen Chang made a dismissive gesture and objected mildly. "It was a matter of no consequence."

"On the contrary, I consider my life to be a rather significant component of the universe. So tell me, what brings you and your friend to Eylau, Magistrate? A job of thieftaking?"

"I thank you for your generous offer of help, Captain, and it may be indeed that my associate and I will want to call upon you in the near future. As to the exact nature of our mission in Eylau, I must tell you that I am bound by an oath of secrecy. Just at the moment, however, our problem concerns the Orb of Maecenas. What can you tell us about its current safety?"

At this point in the conversation the Director of Security appeared to be trying to say something urgent, while at the same time wanting to avoid the disclosure of any information at all. He was rescued from this self-strangled state by the Captain of the Watch, who shook his head at him ruefully.

"I'm afraid the presence of the gem here in the temple is no longer a secret," Captain Almagro told the official almost apologetically. "One hears about it these days in the streets."

The Chief Priest, a vein outstanding in his forehead, was fixing a baleful glance upon his Director of Security.

"I am going," Theodore said, "directly from this room to the lapidary's workshop, there to see for myself whether the Orb is still in our hands or not at this moment." His eyes swept fiercely around the little group. "I want all of you to come with me!"

A moment later, with Chief Priest Theodore in the lead, the whole party was tramping through a series of elegant corridors, traversing one after another a series of doorways, each doubly guarded by warriors cloaked in blue and gold, the Blue Temple's own security force. At every doorway the guards saluted and stood aside at a gesture from the Chief Priest's chubby hand.

The party with Theodore at its head had not far to go before it reached its goal, a set of unmarked heavy doors. Here too guards stood aside. Then the doors were opened a crack from inside in response to an impatient tapping with the Chief Priest's heavy golden ring, and then they were thrown wide as soon as he was recognized.

The party of visitors filed into the room. It was a workshop, much smaller and cleaner, Kasimir noted, than the studio of Robert de Borron across town. This place was also much quieter than de Borron's studio, and it had not been at all crowded until their group arrived. Here, instead of noise and confusion, was a sense that great logic and precision ruled.

There were three people in the room already when Theodore entered with his entourage. The person in charge here was a short, intense, black-skinned woman of about thirty years of age, who was soon introduced to all who did not know her as Mistress Hedmark, the famed lapidary. It was one of those fields like forensic medicine, Kasimir supposed, in which one could be famous and at the same time almost totally unknown to the world at large.

The other two people already present were the famous woman's assistants. The Mistress, despite her lack of size, looked to Kasimir quite as hard and tough as the sculptor at the other temple. The physician got the impression that she would be quite capable of murder and robbery to get something that she really wanted.

Under a broad, heavily barred window, where the best light in the room obtained, an elaborate workbench had been set up. In response to a question from Wen Chang, Mistress Hedmark explained that she and her helpers had been busy practicing the techniques that they would use when the time came for the actual cutting of the priceless gem.

The surface of the workbench was largely covered with a framework of jigs and supports. Kasimir saw that there was a fine revolving grindstone along with other tools, some doubtless more magical than technological.

Having given a concise explanation of her work, the Mistress had a query of her own. "And now, gentlemen, I must insist on knowing what you want here. I don't like all these people in my workroom."

"Nor would I, ordinarily." Chief Priest Theodore shook his head. "But I want to see the Orb for myself, to make sure that it is still safe. And if it is I want to show it to them."

"Of course it is quite safe," said Mistress Hedmark automatically. Then she looked at Theodore for a moment, and then at his chief of security. Then she shrugged and drew a cord from around her neck and inside her clothing. It was a leather cord with a small key hanging at the end of it.

The Director of Security produced a similar key from somewhere. Meanwhile others in the party were making sure that the outer doors of the room were closed. Then Mistress Hedmark, together with the Director, went to a great metal box in one corner of the room. Kasimir had enough sense of magic to sense the immaterial barricades surrounding it, forooo that ouboidod only whon tho Dirootor whispered a secret word.

It was necessary for the custodians to use their two keys simultaneously. Then they were able to open the box and swing back the heavy lid.

Mistress Hedmark reached inside. The Orb of Maecenas was brought out and held up in her fingers for everyone to look at.

It was only the size of a small, faceted egg; somehow this came as a faint disappointment to Kasimir, who had unconsciously been expecting something the size of his fist. But then he had never found wealth in any of its manifestations overwhelmingly interesting.

"Are you satisfied, then?" Mistress Hedmark demanded of the delegation that had burst in on her.

"Yes, for the moment." Much of the tension was gone from Theodore's voice. His gaze had softened, resting on the gem, and he allowed himself a little sigh.

The lapidary asked in her sharp tones: "Has there actually been a plot to steal the Orb?"

The Magistrate spoke soothingly. "We have had an alarm. So far as I know there has been no more than that as yet. Has anything untoward happened here? Or to you or any of your assistants?"

The attention of the group focused on each of the aides in turn: No, none of them had anything like that to report. Kasimir found the denials credible.

Mistress Hedmark discoursed briefly to the others on the art of the diamond cutter, and the problems inherent in trying to cut so very hard a stone, the hardest substance known. The discussion sounded quite open and innocent to Kasimir.

He could see or hear nothing to indicate that this woman might already have the Sword of Siege in hand to help her with her work, or that it had ever entered her mind to try to get it.

CHAPTER 8

B OTH the Chief Priest of the temple and his Director of Security were considerably relieved when they were able to verify with their own eyes that the almost priceless Orb was still in their possession. They were both ready now to consider what Wen Chang wanted to tell them.

The Magistrate, after a quick consultation with Captain Almagro, had several recommendations to make. The first was that arrangements should be made to station officers of the city Watch—not the Captain himself, he could not be spared—here in the lapidary's workshop as long as the gem was present. The Watch people would serve in shifts, so that at least one should be on duty around the clock.

The second recommendation made by Wen Chang was that an entire new squad of Blue Temple security people be brought in, to replace all those who were currently engaged in protecting the stone.

"I emphasize," Wen Chang continued, "that I have no reason to think any of the old crew are implicated in the plot to steal the diamond; no, I make this suggestion purely as a precaution."

Chief Priest Theodore exchanged glances with his chief subordinate in security matters. Then the chubby man shrugged. "Very well. A sensible precaution, I think. It shall be done as you say."

Mistress Hedmark was not happy, though. She complained that these changes would entail further disruption of the routine of technical practice and ritual in which she was engaged with her assistants. Peace and tranquility were necessary for her work.

The Chief Priest heard her out, then overruled her. "Now that the whole world knows the gem is here, we can take no chances."

Wen Chang tried to soothe the lapidary too. Then he said: "Now, Doctor Kasimir and myself must be on our way. Captain Almagro, if you could withdraw with us? There is much we have to discuss with you in the matter of how potential jewel thieves should best be taken. And these gentlemen of the temple, and Mistress Hedmark, will also have much to discuss among themselves."

As the three of them were escorted out of the temple, Kasimir marveled to himself at the smoothness with which Wen Chang had been able to accomplish several objectives during their brief visit. First, they had determined with a fair degree of certainty that the Sword was not in the Blue Temple now. Next, to have an officer of the city Watch continuously present in the diamond-cutters' workshop ought to make it practically impossible for Mistress Hedmark and her crew to use the Sword secretly in their work, assuming they might have the chance to do so—and any efforts to get the Watch out of the way would signal that they were up to something clandestine. Finally, the priests of the Blue Temple were now convinced that Wen Chang was trying to help them.

There was little conversation among the three men as long as they were still inside the temple. When they had passed out through the front entrance, and were halfway across the fronting square, Captain Almagro muttered something that Kasimir did not entirely catch, but that made the physician think the Watch officer did not really care for the place they had just left.

Wen Chang's reply at least was clear: "Hot work in there, old friend, trying to get the moneybags to believe us. I think it might be time for us to ease our throats with a mug of something cool."

The Captain brightened immediately. "My idea exactly, Magistrate. And I know just the place, not far away."

"Lead on."

After making their way through several blocks of the activity that occupied the streets of the metropolis at midday, the three men were soon seated in the cool recesses of a tavern, a large, old building of half-timbered construction. The main room was filled with the delicious smells of cooking food, and occupied by a good number of appreciative customers.

One of the barmaids, who was evidently an old acquaintance of the Captain, served them swiftly. Wiping his mustache after his first gulp of ale, Almagro expressed his doubt that there was any real plot to steal the Orb at all—though he referred to the matter only indirectly. He bewailed the increasing tawdriness of crime in these newly degenerate days. Not only the times and the crimes, but the modern criminals themselves, suffered from degeneracy. By and large they were far from being the bold brave rascals that their predecessors of a decade or so ago had used to be.

"Hey, Magistrate? Am I right?"

"You are almost invariably right, old friend. And there is much truth in what you say now." Wen Chang groomed his own slim mustache with one finger.

"Damned right, very much truth. Want an example? Look at those people who're demonstrating in front of the Hetman's palace now, pounding their stupid heads on the pavement. If they choose to damage their own thick skulls, so what? What kind of a crime is that? And yet we've orders now to make them stop it."

The Magistrate made a gesture indicating resignation. "The subject of their protest—this Benjamin of the Steppe as he is called—he would not seem to me to be a very great offender either. To ask for a few local councils, voting on local matters, deciding such things for themselves. And yet it seems that he must pay with his life for his offense."

"Ah, that's politics. There's always that, and when it comes to politics the police must just do what they're told. If we had a different ruler, politics would go on just the same, only with different faces in the dungeons. Different feet climbing up the scaffold."

"I fear you are right."

"Damned right I'm right." The Captain belched, and drank again.

Wen Chang murmured something properly sympathetic, and Kasimir, taking his lead from his chief, did likewise.

"Not like the old days," Almagro summed up, and drank deep from his mug. "No, not at all."

"I wonder if you could do me a favor?" Wen Chang inquired.

"Glad to," was the automatic response. But then the Captain blinked in hesitation. "What is it?"

"I know the prisoner's number of a man who was sentenced, probably several months ago, to the road-building gang that is now working between here and the Abohar Oasis. "I would like to discover as much as possible about the man himself—his name, his crime, whatever else you can find out."

"Is that all?" The Captain was relieved. "Sure, I can look that up. What's the number?"

"Nine-nine-six-seven-seven."

Almagro pulled out a scrap of paper and laboriously made a note to himself. "Nothing to it."

"But I suppose," said Wen Chang after a moment's silence, "that in this huge city, despite the degeneracy of these modern would-be criminals, and the futile protesters, there remain a small number of real thieves, and also some genuinely dangerous individuals."

"Ah yes, of course. If you say so, it's possible you're really onto something about a plot—to swipe the Orb." The Captain looked around him cautiously before uttering those last words. And now conversation was briefly suspended while the barmaid placed in front of each of them a bowl of steaming stew.

"Only place on the street where I'd order stew," Almagro muttered, taking up his spoon with energy. "But here it's good."

"Indeed, not bad," said Wen Chang, tasting appreciatively. Kasimir, who would have declined if he had been asked whether he wanted stew or not, tried the stuff in his own bowl and had to agree.

Half a bowl later, Wen Chang prodded the Captain: "You were saying, about the present elite of real criminals—?"

"Yes, of course. Well, in this city there are naturally lawbreakers beyond counting. But very few of this modern bunch would have the nerve, talent, or resources even to think of undertaking any job like the one you suspect is being planned at the Blue Temple."

"And I suppose that once such a gem was stolen, it would be difficult even in Eylau to arrange to sell it, or dispose of it in trade for lesser gems."

The Captain smacked his lips over the stew, and tore off a chunk of bread from the fresh loaf the barmaid had deposited in the middle of the table. "Difficult, yes. But in Eylau nothing is totally impossible. No matter how rare and unique an object of value may be, there'll be someone in this city who can buy it—paying only a small fraction of the real worth, maybe, but—"

"Naturally." Wen Chang nodded. "And it is part of your job to know who these folk are."

"I know most of them. And there are not many who'd want to handle something like the Orb—today there are even fewer, in fact, than there were just yesterday morning."

The Magistrate's hand paused, supporting a mug of ale halfway to his lips. "Oh? And what is responsible for this diminution in numbers?"

"I'd say it was the result of a disagreement between buyer and seller, of just what property I don't know." The Captain went on to relate how, only yesterday evening, one of the city's most rascally merchants and most celebrated dealers in stolen valuables had been found dead, his body drifting in a backwater of the Tungri, near the lower docks.

Wen Chang had set down his mug again without drinking. "And have you turned up any clue, old friend, as to who killed this man or why?"

"Interests you, does it, Magistrate? I should have realized it would. No, I'm afraid that there's no such clue. Apart from the fact that whatever happened was a bit more than your ordinary little squabble. Two other bodies were also found nearby, of men who must have been killed at the same time, in the same fight. Don't know who they were."

"And there is no clue as to who killed them, either."

"Just so. Ah, we do our best, Magistrate. Whenever there's a complaint of robbery or assault in the city we in the Watch will do what we can to get the miscreants taken into custody, and hold them for trial before the magistrates of this city."

"I am sure that you do your best."

"We do. But as you can well imagine, in a city of this size it would be hopeless to expect to solve very many of the crimes."

Wen Chang drained his tankard. "It would interest me very much—and I am sure it would interest Kasimir too—if we could see those bodies, of the men killed yesterday."

"Ah? And maybe your interest is a little more than purely theoretical?" The Captain's eyes, suddenly shrewder than before, probed at both of his companions from under shaggy brows. "Well, the gods know I owe you a bigger favor than that, Magistrate. We'll see what we can do, though the family of our late prominent merchant may not welcome any more attentions by the Watch."

"It is the other bodies, the unidentified ones, that I find more particularly interesting."

"Oh? That's all right, then. Except that they may already have been exposed on the northern walls. We'd best go right away and take a look."

Kasimir and the Captain finished their drinks.

In Eylau, as Captain Almagro explained while they walked, the disposal of paupers' bodies, and any other unidentified or unclaimed dead, was carried out atop a section of city wall, a tall spur of fortification about a hundred meters long, which currently went nowhere and protected nothing. This section had become disconnected from the main walls of the city as a result of the destruction of some ancient war, and the subsequent rebuilding according to a different plan. Here, barely within the city's modern walls, and four or five stories above the ground, the remains were set out in the open air to be the prey of winged scavengers. Many of these creatures were reptilian; others, originally the product of experiments in magic and genetics, were hybrids of reptile and bird.

There were no human dwellings very near the isolated section of wall now called the Paupers' Palace, except for a few huts of the poor and almost homeless, who from their doorways could contemplate what their own final fate in this world was likely to be.

When the investigators arrived at the base of the mortuary wall, Captain Almagro sought out and spoke to a particular attendant. This man bowed and murmured his respect for the Captain, and passed the three visitors along to another man. This fellow conducted the three investigators up a stone stairway, dangerously worn and crumbling, to the wall's top.

Here, under the leaden sky, filling the broad strip of pavement between the parapets, was a scattered litter of more-or-less dried human bones, with here and there a more recent arrival. The older bones, pulverized and scattered, crunched underfoot; if you moved about at all there was no way to avoid stepping on some of them. Kasimir understood from a few words of explanation offered by the attendant that the bones finally rejected by the scavengers were gathered periodically and burned or buried somewhere.

By now it had begun to drizzle again in Eylau, and Kasimir had heard people talking about the fierce windstorms out over the desert. Up here atop the Paupers' Palace the drying-out of corpses was undoubtedly being set back by the wet weather. The smell here at the moment was rather worse than at the last opened grave, out in the quarry, and Kasimir once more pulled out an amulet from his pouch of magical equipment. Presently a scent of fresh mint began to dominate.

At a word from Almagro the attendant who had escorted them upstairs pointed out the two bodies that had been brought in with knife wounds yesterday afternoon.

Whatever the losers of that fight might have possessed in the way of clothing or valuables had of course been stripped from them already, either before or after they arrived at this last stop. By now, Kasimir noted, their eyes were missing as well, evidently the first gourmet morsels to be claimed by the scavengers. One of these reptilian beasts, the size of a large vulture but with iridescent scales, was in attendance now, and flew up heavily with a squeak of protest as the men approached.

But certain items of important evidence remained, and it might be possible to learn the essentials, thought Kasimir, even without making a very close examination of these bodies.

One of them was that of a red-haired, freckled man whose stocky build and thick limbs indicated that he had been strong, before someone's narrow blade had opened those thin fatal doorways in his chest.

"The treacherous foreman," Kasimir commented, almost at first glance. He chose to disregard the fact that his words could be heard by Almagro, who was standing back, watching intently to see what his old friend would be able to make of this evidence. There would be no keeping the Captain out of the matter now.

Wen Chang, kneeling by the first body, nodded abstractedly. In a moment he had concluded his own examination, and stood up, brushing off his hands.

"Treachery is a powerful medicine, and those who rely upon it are likely to die of an overdose. It is easy enough to imagine the scene yesterday. A meeting, somewhere near the river, between the murderous foreman Kovil, and the equally dishonest Eylau merchant, with each principal supported by at least one retainer. From the beginning, an enlightened distrust on both sides, who are strangers to each other. Then, the display of the stolen treasure—a vaster prize than even avarice had imagined—and then the sudden flare of treachery and violence."

In a moment he had turned his attention to the second body. It was that of a stranger to Kasimir, though it ought to have been identifiable, he thought, by anyone who had known the man in life. This fellow too had died of blade wounds, and these wounds were larger, as if made by a full-sized sword, perhaps Stonecutter itself. By all reports eleven of the Twelve—all except Woundhealer—were fine weapons apart from the magical powers they possessed.

"This one has been neither prisoner nor overseer at a quarry in the desert," Wen Chang muttered after a minute, standing up again. "His skin is everywhere too pale for that. I assume he is some minor criminal of the city." Then he turned to Almagro and asked: "I would like to see the place where the bodies were found."

"Of course."

They descended from the wall, and Kasimir was able to put away his magic scent. Next Almagro conducted them back into the center of Eylau. Standing on the bank of the river, he pointed out the place where the bodies were said to have been found, drifting in a pool or large eddy on the left bank of the river.

The Magistrate looked up and about, slightly upstream. "I see dark stains," he announced, "upon that windowsill."

Kasimir could see very little at the distance. But along with the Captain he followed the Magistrate into an old building whose empty windows gaped out over the Tungri.

The three investigators entered the building and climbed to an upper level to find that there were still bloodstains on the worn floor.

"There is no doubt that the fight took place here," mused Wen Chang. "And whoever survived took the trouble to dump the bodies into the river, hoping thereby to postpone their discovery. Ah, if only I had been able to inspect this place sooner! Clues have a way of vanishing quickly with the passage of time."

But Wen Chang soon gave up his lamenting and went to

work, examining every centimeter of the scene with a thoroughness Kasimir found surprising—not so Almagro, who had evidently seen similar performances in the past.

Soon the Magistrate was able to discover, on an inner wall of exposed brickwork, a place where Stonecutter had left its distinctive marks. Kasimir could easily imagine the great Sword, swung in combat, taking a small chunk neatly out of the solid wall—and then, its energy unslowed, going on to cut down someone.

Almagro, scowling, looked at the place. He said: "I think you'd better tell me the whole story."

"We shall," Wen Chang promised.

Kasimir asked, "But then who has the Sword now?"

"Someone who was strong and fierce and cunning and lucky enough to survive that meeting yesterday. It seems that our task may be only beginning."

CHAPTER 9

STILL standing in the room where the fight had taken place, Wen Chang and Kasimir completed the job of taking Captain Almagro into their confidence regarding the true nature of their mission in Eylau. The Captain, naturally anxious to hear the whole story, listened eagerly.

He had of course heard of the Twelve Swords, and was naturally impressed with the value of such a treasure. "Small wonder, then, that these scum are killing each other over it. And you say the dead man with the red hair was really a foreman on one of the Hetman's stone quarry gangs?"

"I have no doubt that it is the same man. He and a companion brought the Sword here to the city. Doubtless Kovil—that was the foreman's name—expected that his absence from his post would not cause any problems until they had completed the sale—and once he had his fortune in hand it would no longer matter."

The Captain shook his head. "As a rule those convict-labor places are not very well supervised. Not even the ones with the really dangerous people in them. I don't doubt he thought he could get away with it."

"And is the quarry in question populated with really dangerous people, as you call them?"

"Ardneh bless you, Magistrate, that one gets some of the worst. The worst in the line of ordinary, nonpolitical crooks, I mean. I heard a judge tell a convict that hanging was too good for him, and then send him there for ten years—which in the quarry is the same as life."

"And where, I suppose, even the worst offender may be almost forgotten, and ignored." Wen Chang looked worried. "Almagro, I want you to arrest Kovil's hand-picked replacement, Umar, now, and bring him into the city. Preferably to some quiet place where I may be able to question him in privacy, and no one else will pay too much attention. Meanwhile it might be a good idea to preserve the body of the red-haired man, so that Umar can be confronted with it, and shown that at least he has nothing to fear from that quarter any longer. Then, perhaps, he will tell us who Kovil took with him as a companion from the quarry. If Umar still hesitates to tell us the truth about that, a matching of the records at the quarry with the prisoners still actually there may be necessary to tell us who is missing. I want to know the identity of the second man."

"Because he's most likely the one who has the big knife now."

"Exactly. And, by the way, there is something else that you should know, my friend. A large reward has been promised me if my search in this city can be brought to a successful conclusion. You will remember from our past dealings that I am inclined to share such rewards generously."

"I remember that fact very well, Magistrate! And I'll certainly see what I can do about fulfilling all your requests. But reward or not, remember that I can promise nothing."

On leaving the riverside building, the three separated. Almagro had plenty of official work to occupy him. Kasimir had an appointment in the afternoon to meet Natalia, and he did not want to miss it. And Wen Chang was now rather anxious to get back to the inn, fearing that in his absence the elderly caller of yesterday might return, and Lieutenant Komi would after all not detain him.

Kasimir, hearing this fear expressed as the two walked toward the inn, remarked: "You have little faith in Komi, then?"

"I admit that I have some doubts about him." The Magistrate refused to elaborate on that.

As soon as Kasimir and his mentor arrived at the Inn of the Refreshed Travelers, Wen Chang fired questions at Lieutenant Komi, but the replies were disappointing. The Firozpur officer said he had seen nothing of yesterday's elderly visitor. There had been a couple of other people in today asking about antique weapons, but when Wen Chang had heard the details of these inquiries he judged neither of them to be of any importance.

When Kasimir asked Komi a routine question about his men, the lieutenant responded in a satisfied voice that almost all of them had so far kept out of trouble—the one exception was of small moment, involving as it did only one trooper, and a minor altercation in a tavern, which fortunately had been resolved before anyone had called in the Watch.

Wen Chang put in a question: "I don't suppose it had anything to do with the sale or purchase of antique weapons?"

"Nothing whatsoever, sir."

"I thought not. You are continuing to send out winged messengers to your prince?"

"I've dispatched a couple, sir."

"Have any yet returned?"

"No sir." For the first time in Kasimir's experience, Komi looked worried. "They say that there are sandstorms over the desert. Flyers going either way might have trouble getting through."

"Too bad. And are your men all present and ready for duty now?"

"Yes sir. With one exception." The lieutenant went on to assure the Magistrate that the one exception was only a trooper—not the same one who had had the fight—who had relatives in what was called the Desert Quarter of the city. It was called that because of the high proportion of former nomads among its population. That trooper had gone, with Komi's leave, to pay his relatives a brief visit.

Wen Chang ordered the officer to grant no more leaves for the moment—the one already authorized could remain in force—and turned to gaze out the third-floor window. The intermittent rain had now stopped for the time being, leaving picturesque puddles in the courtyard. Now, as the sun emerged briefly from behind a cloud, some of these puddles turned to rainbow pools, stained with spilled dye from the cargo of some merchant's loadbeasts.

Without turning from the window, the Magistrate said to Kasimir: "So far we have observed three different groups in the city, any one of which in my opinion is likely to have the Sword in their possession now, or to very shortly gain possession of it from our mysterious former quarryman. For the time being I intend to concentrate our investigation upon these groups."

Already the sun was gone behind clouds again, and already rain had once more begun to fall, making a steady drip from eaves and gutters just outside the window. Kasimir said: "The first group, I take it, are the authorities at the Red Temple."

"If you wish you may count them as the first—if you include with them the sculptor Robert de Borron."

"Then is it true that you don't think the Red Temple are really the most likely candidates?"

"I did not say that."

Kasimir sighed. "Well, I shall of course find out all that I can about them—and about the sculptor—from Natalia when I see her today."

"Do so by all means. But if she tells you nothing of interest, we may have to institute some stronger measures there—you see, I am interested in the Red Temple. Where and when are you going to meet her?"

"Inside the White Temple, in about an hour and a half." Kasimir at the window tried to judge the height of the clouded sun. "It seemed a good place to arrange a casual encounter."

Wen Chang nodded his approval. "No doubt it will serve."

"So, then, we come to the second group under suspicion. I presume them to be the people at the Blue Temple?"

"Yes. Naturally their leaders would want to gain such a treasure if they could. They have probably already convinced themselves that their organization has an inherent right to possess anything so valuable. And I am sure that Mistress Hedmark would seize any opportunity that might arise to use the Sword in her work. Whether she knows that it is nearby and might be available . . ." Wen Chang shrugged.

"I suppose there's no doubt that Stonecutter would carve a small stone as neatly and easily as a great one?"

"In my mind there is none. It is my understanding that the god Vulcan forged that blade to cut stones, and that is precisely what it will do, with divine power. Though neither of us has ever seen the Sword or handled it, we have now seen enough of its work to feel confident on that point."

"I agree with you that Mistress Hedmark will be trying to get her hands on it if she can."

"Yes . . . Kasimir, I am of two minds about going public with our search. I mean spreading the word as widely as possible that the Sword is lost, and that it is definitely the property of Prince al-Farabi—which is close enough to the exact truth for our purposes. There are certainly difficulties, but still it will be well to have made that point, so that when the Sword is recovered the Prince's claim will be well established."

"You said 'when the Sword is recovered,' Magistrate. I admire your confidence."

Wen Chang smiled dryly. "It is a useful quality."

Kasimir paused for a moment, cleared his throat, and shook his head. "So, after the Blue Temple we come to the third group of suspects, who, I take it, must be the gang— if that is the right word for an organization some of whose members must be quite respectable—associated with the crooked merchant, lately deceased. Judging by what we have heard of them so far, they would cheerfully try to steal the wings off a demon, if they thought they had even the remotest chance of getting away with it."

"You are probably correct. On the other hand, the professional criminals might be easier for us to deal with in one respect at least. They might be willing to collect a ransom and return their loot to al-Farabi or his representatives. And they might even be disposed to be reasonable about the price, considering that the alternative would be severe prosecution—perhaps I mean persecution—by the authorities. We could certainly collaborate with our friend the Captain in an effort to provide that." Wen Chang fell silent, regarding his younger friend attentively, as if waiting for his reaction.

Kasimir considered. "So, the question becomes, which of these three groups actually has, or is most likely to get, Stonecutter? If Kovil's mysterious bodyguard carried it away from the scene of the fight by the river, has he yet managed to sell it to one of them? Or possibly to someone else altogether?"

The Magistrate's eyes were even narrower than usual. "It

would not be wise to dissipate our energies too widely. We will concentrate upon the three groups that I have named."

Kasimir found himself a little irritated by the dogmatic tone of that last sentence. "Of course, you are in charge of the investigation. Though I suppose it is possible that the Sword of Siege *is* really with someone else altogether?"

"Yes, many things are possible." Wen Chang's tone was even; if Kasimir had hoped to provoke an explanation he was disappointed. "Nevertheless, I repeat, we are going to confine our attentions to those three groups, at least for now. So you had better prepare yourself for your meeting with the agent you have recruited to spy on the Red Temple."

The physician needed only a few minutes to complete the few preparations he thought necessary. When he was ready to go, he paused on his way out. "There is one other matter that I cannot stop wondering about: the identity of our original thief, whose body we found buried at the quarry. Perhaps it is only because I actually saw him in the act; I suppose that it hardly matters any longer who he was."

The Magistrate hesitated. Then he said: "On the contrary, I should say that it matters a great deal."

"Eh? Why?"

Wen Chang leaned back in his chair. "There are several interesting points about that man. To begin with, there is the fascinating fact that, as you describe the event, he found it necessary to slit the wall of your tent twice."

"I admit that I puzzled for some time over that detail. But I could see no good reason for it."

"Perhaps you are not approaching the question properly. Of course your attitude may be justified—people sometimes do unreasonable, inexplicable things."

"Yes, they do. You said you found more than one point about the man to be interesting?"

"I consider it also very interesting that the thief was

110

working from the start in accordance with a plan, that the theft was not the mere seizing of an opportunity."

"Well, the only real evidence for his having a plan, it seems to me, is the fact that he brought along an extra riding-beast. Indicating, of course, that he intended to rescue the first prisoner from the road-building gang. But he did not bring along two extra mounts. So we may deduce that the second rescue, that of the prisoner at the quarry, was not planned from the start. It was an improvisation, undertaken perhaps only at the suggestion of the first prisoner to gain the freedom of someone else."

"Very good, Kasimir! We will make an investigator of you yet. What else have you been able to deduce from these facts?"

"Well—nothing as yet."

"As you continue your efforts there are a couple points you ought to keep in mind. First, no one is likely to steal one of the Twelve Swords with the *sole* object of using it to free a prisoner from that road-building gang. That could be accomplished much more easily . . ." Wen Chang's voice trailed off. His eyes appeared to be gazing at something in the distance, over Kasimir's shoulder.

"Magistrate?"

"A thought has struck me. Never mind, go to your meeting. Learn all that you can from the interesting Natalia. What you learn may be of great importance."

Kasimir set out, pondering the situation as he walked. He had to pay careful attention to where he was going, because his goal this time was in a different part of the city from those which he had previously visited.

The White Temple of Eylau, like most of its kind around the world, was a large, pyramidal building. This example was faced with white marble, while a good many others Kasimir had seen were only painted white. And in this building, as in almost all White Temples everywhere, a good part of its sizable volume was devoted to hospital facilities. Here no one who came seeking food or medical care or emergency shelter would be turned away. Nor would anyone be absolutely forced to pay, though donations were solicited from all who appeared able to give anything at all.

Kasimir's appointment with Natalia was in the Chapel of Ardneh, also a standard feature of most White Temples. Here the chapel was located about halfway up the slope-sided structure. It was a white, large room, well lighted by many windows in its slanting outer wall. The room held a number of plain wooden chairs and benches. Above the altar an Old World votive light burned steadily, a pure whiteness without flame or smoke. The altar itself was dominated by a modern image of the ancient god Ardneh. Images of Ardneh as a rule—this one was no exception— were almost always at least partially abstract, in keeping with the idea that the eternal foe of the archdemon Orcus was essentially different from all other gods.

This particular image was an assemblage of bronze blocks and slabs, looking eerily bluish because of some quality in the perpetual glow of the votive light above.

Kasimir took a seat near the middle of the simply furnished chapel and looked around him, at the few others who had come to this place for worship or meditation.

There was one more statue in the chapel, this one of the god Draffut. Carved of some brown stone, it stood in its own niche or grotto off to one side. In this image, as tall as a man, the popular Lord of Beasts and of Healing looked like nothing more, Kasimir thought, than a dog standing on his hind legs. During the last few years a rumor had swept across the land to the effect that Draffut was recently dead; of course a great many people held that the Beastlord, like the other gods, had been dead for many years. Meanwhile considerable numbers of folk continued to insist that some of the gods or all of them were still alive, and would come back one day to call people to account for what they had been doing in the divinities' absence.

Natalia entered the chapel shortly after Kasimir had arrived, and came quietly to take a chair beside his. She was dressed in a skirt and blouse and sandals with narrow straps, more citified clothing than when Kasimir had seen her last, though hardly of any higher quality.

"Hope I'm not late," she whispered demurely.

"Not at all." Actually he had rather enjoyed the interval of waiting, the chance for peaceful meditation. He might not want to work all day in a White Temple, but they were good places to visit, havens where you could sit as long as you wished and not be bothered, unless it might be by one of your fellow visitors. Street people now and then came in to take up collections for this or that, or frankly as beggars. None were ejected, as a rule, unless others complained about them to the White Guards.

But, back to business. "How did the modeling go?" he asked.

"Not as embarrassing as I had feared—and actually they paid me a trifle more for it than I had expected."

"That's good. But I suppose you've seen nothing of what I wanted you to look for?"

"Nothing, I am sorry to say."

"And you go back there tomorrow?"

"That's right. He says he'll want me for several days yet at least. It's the master himself I'm posing for."

"De Borron, then. Good. What kind of tools is he using to work the stone?"

She blinked at him solemnly as if she understood this question must be important but could not think why. "A hammer and a chisel. Several different chisels actually. Nothing like the special item that you described to me."

"All right. And you haven't mentioned that special item to anyone else—hey?"

"Not at all. Of course not. You told me not to." Natalia's new lowcut upper garment showed a lot of pale skin below the former neckline of the old peasant blouse. Her hair was now worn in a new style too, Kasimir realized vaguely, though it still looked like strings of dishwater.

He asked her: "Who else is present in the studio?"

"It's about the same as when you were there, people coming and going. Did you want me to try to keep track of them?"

"Not necessarily. No, you'd better just concentrate on the important thing."

Their conversation about conditions in the Red Temple meandered along, pausing when a stooped old priest in white robes moved close past them on his way to light a candle at the altar.

Kasimir was coming slowly to the realization that he found himself attracted to this woman. Somewhere in his mind, not very far below the surface, he resented the idea of the sculptor and all those red-robes staring at her body. The truth was that he wanted to stare at it himself.

But the purpose of this meeting of course was business. Instead of inviting Natalia to his room, he asked her if she would like something to eat or drink. As before, she accepted, and they moved to a nearby tavern where they enjoyed some food and drink. He also passed over the coins due her for her day's observations and report.

Telling himself it was his duty to become better acquainted with his agent, he justified somewhat prolonging the meeting; and the truth was that they each enjoyed the other's company. They exchanged some opinions upon art, and medicine, and life.

But soon Natalia was growing restless; she had other things to do, she said, and didn't volunteer any hint of what they were. Kasimir didn't volunteer any questions. Instead he went back to the inn alone.

It was near dusk when he arrived again at the sign of the Refreshed Travelers, and he felt somewhat tired. It had been a long and busy day, beginning with his and Wen Chang's visit to the Blue Temple in the morning.

But the long day was not over yet.

As soon as he entered the stable below their rooms, he discovered Lieutenant Komi and his men, fully armed and mobilized. Wen Chang was there too and they were waiting for Kasimir, in fact almost on the point of mounting up and leaving without him. Komi and his men looked ready and willing to say the least; the days of boredom were evidently beginning to tell on them.

Wen Chang said: "Word has just come from Captain Almagro. He has located one of the men who was in the fight yesterday, in which our foreman Kovil was killed. The man we want is hidden in an infamous den of thieves, and Almagro would like our help in digging him out."

The clouds of sleep were cleared in a moment from Kasimir's brain. "Then I am ready!"

CHAPTER 10

IN a city with a population the size of Eylau's there would always be large numbers of folk awake and wanting light, and the city would never know total darkness as long as lamps and torches could be made to burn. But night was on the way to enfolding Eylau as completely as it ever did before Wen Chang and Kasimir were ready to mount their riding-beasts. As soon as they were mounted, and Lieutenant Komi and his troop of Firozpur soldiers were in the saddle behind them, their small force set out from the inn. The soldiers' uniforms and some of their weapons were effectively concealed under their desert capes.

Riding close beside Wen Chang at the head of the little column was a sergeant of the city Watch. This was the man who had been sent by Captain Almagro, to inform Almagro's partners that he was about to launch the raid, to request their help, and to guide them to the site as quickly as possible.

Kasimir, riding just behind Wen Chang and their guide, was wide awake now, not tired at all; the excitement of the chase was growing in him. So far their mounts were able to maintain a rapid pace; at this hour the darkened streets of the city held comparatively few people, and those who found themselves in the way of the silent, businesslike procession quickly moved aside.

Streets in the vicinity of the Inn of the Refreshed Travelers were comparatively broad. But it soon became apparent that their guide was leading them into a very different portion of the city. As they approached the district where the raid was to take place, the streets grew narrower and their windings even more convoluted.

This gradual constriction continued for some minutes, during which time the party, now often riding in single file, made the best speed possible. Then their guide signaled them for even slower movement, and less noise.

They had now come in sight of distant lamps, sparkling on a broad expanse of water. Kasimir realized that they were now once more near the bank of the Tungri, which here as elsewhere in the city was lined with docks and warehouses. He had no way to tell how far this site might be from the place where the bodies had been found. Boats bearing lights were passing in the night. Though the sea was thousands of kilometers distant, the river here evidently bore a great volume of local freight and passenger traffic.

In this section of the metropolis the residential area closest to the docks and warehouses was obviously a slum. On both sides of the street, tenements leaned against each other. Few lights showed in these close-packed, ramshackle buildings. The torches carried by a couple of the Firozpur troopers made a moving island of light in the narrow, dusty street.

In this neighborhood the people who appeared in the street were losers, the Emperor's children if Kasimir had ever seen the type. These slum-dwellers were quicker than people in other neighborhoods had been to scramble out of the way of the advancing column. Anonymous voices hidden on roofs and in windows above called out oaths and comments against the mounted men below, whom they took for a patrol of the Watch.

Presently the sergeant who was riding beside Wen

Chang pulled his mount to a halt. Close ahead, two figures, one of them carrying a small torch, had just emerged from the mouth of a dark alley. In a moment Kasimir was able to recognize the man holding the torch as Captain Almagro.

The Captain came forward on foot and greeted his two chief colleagues eagerly but quietly as they swung down out of their saddles. Then he led them just inside the mouth of the alley, where he introduced them to his companion, a middle-aged man who tonight would be nameless in the line of duty, a wizard in the employ of the Watch.

"Before we discuss anything else," the Magistrate murmured to his old friend, "tell me whether you have managed to take care of the items I requested at our last meeting."

"I have set things in motion," said Almagro. "That is all I have been able to do so far."

"Then that is all that I can ask."

Next the Captain conducted a low-voiced briefing for the new arrivals, on the subject of the coming action.

The building he meant to raid had been abandoned as a warehouse several years ago, and was now notorious as a den of thieves and cutthroats. On looking out of the mouth of the alley where they now stood they could see it, just visible at the end of the street, less than a hundred meters away. The old warehouse was four or five stories high— depending on how you counted certain irregular additions—and contained perhaps as many as a hundred rooms. Almagro's basic plan was to break into the place through several entrances at the same time.

The Captain had assembled a dozen of his own men here in the alley, and with the reinforcements provided by the Firozpur he planned on being able to conduct the raid with overwhelming force. An attack on such a scale would surprise whatever criminals were in the building, and with any luck at all none of them would be able to get away.

The official wizard followed the Captain's briefing with a reassuring prediction that the gang in the building would be able to mount little or no magical resistance to the raid.

After Wen Chang had approved the plan of attack, the Watch sergeant who had served as guide took over the job of showing Lieutenant Komi exactly where his dismounted men should be deployed. More than a score of feet went shuffling off into the darkness. A couple of other Watch patrolmen were going to remain in this alley, keeping watch over the riding-beasts.

Almagro announced that he himself, with the Watch-wizard beside him, was going to direct operations from street level, while the Magistrate and Kasimir were to accompany the party attacking through the roof. Wen Chang approved this proposal too.

Before leaving his two unofficial colleagues, the Captain cast a worried glance at Kasimir, then shook his head and pronounced a last-minute warning.

"Doctor, there are a good many people in that building who aren't exactly going to welcome us with open arms when they see us. So mind yourself. In fact it might be a good idea if you stayed here, with the men who'll be watching our riding-beasts, until the fighting's done."

"Nonsense, I can take care of myself." Kasimir's tone was a little stiff; perhaps more than just a little. "I carry a dagger. And if one of your men will loan me his cudgel, I am quite prepared to answer for my own safety."

Almagro glanced at Wen Chang, shrugged, and turned to one of his own men nearby to give a quiet order. Kasimir accepted with thanks the oaken cudgel that was handed to him. The weapon was half a meter long, and weighted at one end. At the other end was a leather thong by which the club could be secured to its wielder's wrist. Kasimir had observed that cudgels like this were standard Watch equipment in Eylau, though tonight of course the men embarking upon the raid had equipped themselves with heavier weapons, including swords and axes.

Kasimir tucked the club into his belt, where it rested between two of the bulging pouches of his augmented medical kit. Then he signed that he was ready.

Wen Chang before leaving the inn had buckled on a lovely rapier, and now he was making sure of the fit of this weapon in its sheath. Kasimir had once or twice seen this sword among the Magistrate's belongings, though he had never seen him wearing it until now.

With everything in readiness, Almagro's two unofficial allies followed him through the alley, which was pitch-black except for his small, guttering torch. But the Watch officer seemed to know his way as well as a blind man on a familiar route.

Pausing after they had gone about a hundred meters, the Captain whispered to his companions that they were about to enter a building, another next door to the one they were about to raid. They stood in a doorway of this building, another abandoned-looking warehouse, on the side opposite their target structure. A ruined door on the level of the alley offered a sinister welcome, and once they were inside the building they confronted a tottering, treacherous stairway that Almagro whispered would bring them all the way up to the roof.

The darkness immediately surrounding their torchlight as they climbed was quiet, while crude music and drunken laughter sounded from a few buildings away. The night air smelled of the nearby river, an odor half fresh and half polluted. Kasimir listened in vain for any sounds from elsewhere in the building they had entered, or from the other assault parties, which ought to be getting into position at this moment. If all was going according to the plan Almagro had hastily outlined, two groups would be approaching at street level, and two more through windows on upper floors, one reached by a ladder, one by a low roof. This assault upon the roof would complete the encirclement, and if everything went well the wanted people should be trapped with their loot inside.

The group approaching the front door had the most delicate task. They were mostly Firozpur, on the theory that no one inside would be likely to recognize the desert troopers; but the group included one sergeant of the Watch. It would be his responsibility to raise a loud outcry at the proper moment, signaling the other assault teams that the time had come for them to make their moves.

Meanwhile, Wen Chang, Kasimir, and their group had reached the roof of the warehouse. A moment later they had gained the roof of the target building, equally high, by the simple expedient of stepping over to it across a gap of space less than a meter wide.

The moon had come out clearly now; probably, thought Kasimir, it would soon be obscured again by fast-moving clouds, but meanwhile it was a very useful source of illumination on the open roof, above the narrow, twisting canyons of the streets. Kasimir could see that there were two or perhaps three trapdoors in the roof, which was basically a tarry surface under a layer of light boards. Its contours formed a wilderness of little peaks and gables and ridges, pierced here and there by a skylight. Probably all the skylights had once been covered with oiled skin or paper, but the ones that Kasimir could see were now broken open to the weather. Iron bars, rusted but formidable, still defended these openings against human entry.

Two of the Watch troopers among the assault party on the roof, working under a sergeant's direction, blocked two of the three visible trapdoors closed, wedging them shut with pieces of lumber pulled from the top of the ruined wooden parapet. Then they prepared to break in through the remaining entrance.

Placing themselves one on each side of the third trapdoor, the burly patrolmen hefted their axes and waited for a signal.

Presently it came, in the form of raucous voices raised from street level, loudly demanding to be allowed entrance.

The axes poised over the rooftop fell together. Almost simultaneously there sounded from several directions, near and far, a crashing and splintering of wood, a rending of thin metal. The other entrances to the building were being attacked on schedule.

Kasimir saw now that the onslaught against the roof entrance was being directed not against the trapdoor itself, which was reinforced with metal bars and perhaps with magic as well. Instead the axes fell in a rapid rhythm upon the roof just at one side of the designed entrance. Under their repeated blows a hole had already appeared and was growing rapidly. Doubtless the basic construction of this building had not been particularly sturdy to begin with, and decay had weakened some of the structural members.

While the choppers plied their tools Kasimir, holding one lighted torch, was busy lighting others from it, and handing them out to the members of the attacking party who stood by in readiness.

The roof was quickly pierced, and in a few more moments the hole had been enlarged to the size of a man's head. The sergeant barked an order, and when the axemen paused he went down on his belly beside the hole. Sliding an arm through it, he was able to release the bar that held the trapdoor closed. It fell inside the room below, with the crashing of some homemade alarm system to add to the noise. Only the one fastening had secured the trapdoor, and now it swung up easily.

There were no stairs or ladder inside, but Wen Chang was ready. While others held torches for him, he dropped lithely through. A moment later he called for the others to follow, and the Watch poured in after him, one man at a time. Kasimir, as he had reluctantly agreed, was last. Left alone for a moment on the roof, he sat on the edge of the opening, hung for an instant by one hand from the edge, then let go and dropped.

Landing easily on the bare floor, he found himself still alone. The other members of his party had already hurried ahead, leaving the small unfurnished room through its only other door. Raising his torch, Kasimir saw that this stood at the head of a narrow stairs that led down to the floors below.

Cries of alarm and anger, accompanied by the clash of arms, were resounding from down there now. Holding his torch aloft in his left hand, his right ready to draw a weapon, Kasimir hurried after the Watchmen and Wen Chang.

The stairs went down only one flight, to a flat space with unpromising darkness on every side. Nearby a hole in this floor, with the top of a ladder protruding through it, offered a way to continue the descent. As Kasimir approached the hole he could hear the voices of his comrades, along with other noises, coming from down there. It might be that only the lower levels of this building were inhabited tonight.

When he reached the foot of the ladder, Kasimir could see dim passageways leading off in three directions. At the far end of the passage to his right, he could see torches in rapid motion, as if their holders might be dancing. Kasimir caught a single glimpse of Wen Chang, cloak wrapped around his left arm and rapier active in his right hand, before a door slammed in between, cutting off the physician's view of his partner.

Kasimir ran recklessly toward the action, stumbling through darkness. He burst into the room in which he had seen the Magistrate, to find Wen Chang gone but the situation now well in hand. A lantern burning on a table illuminated the room, and doors in the other walls were standing open. In this room three people remained, two of the Watch having one of their prey boxed into a corner. The man had a blade in each hand, and both were active. But in a moment, after a brief flurry of action, the man resisting arrest was cut down.

Kasimir picked up the lantern from the table and brought it close to the fallen figure. No lengthy examination was needed; the man was obviously dead.

Hurrying on, Kasimir entered a large room where loot that must be the product of a hundred robberies was stacked in several piles. Here were stolen golden candlesticks, over there a collection of silver plate, on the far side of the room a pile of drinking vessels of horn and wood, inlaid with gold and silver, and small open boxes that glinted with precious metals. When he held his torch closer to another pile nearby he could see the wink of gold from the covers and edges of finely bound books. Whether the Sword finally proved to be in this building or not, the Watch would have a goodly profit from their raid, in the form of a haul of loot, at least some of which would presumably find its way back to its rightful owners.

And still shouts and the uproar of conflict sounded from somewhere below. Kasimir found a way down and descended yet another level, estimating as he did so that he must now be very little if at all above the level of the street outside. Here, amid a labyrinth of rooms, torches and lanterns were plentiful. It was obvious that the main drama of the raid was being enacted here.

When the physician entered the next room, it appeared to him for a moment that he had just missed all the excitement. The people here had apparently surrendered just before he entered. Four or five men and a couple of women, one or two of them well-dressed and all of them looking sullenly enraged, were being herded together in preparation for their being searched; one of the women was still screaming insults at the invaders, warning them to keep their hands off her.

Kasimir looked around quickly, then demanded of the room in general: "Where's the Magistrate?"

One of the patrolmen answered with an economical motion of his head. Moving down another passage in the direction indicated, Kasimir felt a momentary sensation, the plucking of some fading defensive magic, a moment of disorientation as he passed through a doorway. It must, he thought, have been only a third-rate defensive spell to begin with, because the moment weapons were drawn it had faded like some night-blooming flower. There would be no point in calling upon Almagro's wizard to deal with anything so trivial.

Looking for the Magistrate, the physician found himself momentarily alone, out of sight of anyone who had come with him.

A faint sound from a dark side passage made Kasimir turn his head. The warning had come just in time; he found himself confronted by a wild-faced man, who struck at Kasimir with a desperate blow. Turning with a simultaneous thrusting motion of the torch in his left hand, Kasimir did his desperate best to parry. The assailant flinched away from the torch at the last moment, and his first stroke at Kasimir missed.

Kasimir swirled his cloak, which was partly wrapped round his left arm, and continued with thrusts and feints of the torch in his left hand to do his best to distract the enemy. The man, who had a long knife in his hand, fell back.

A moment later Kasimir had drawn the cudgel from his belt with his right hand.

The two men stalked each other. Kasimir, doubly armed, felt stoutly confident of being able to hold his own.

In this situation time was on Kasimir's side, and he called out for help. As soon as he did this the other man lunged at him again. Kasimir parried with the torch as best he could, stood his ground and swung his club, hitting his assailant on the shoulder. The long knife went clattering to the floor.

A moment later, two Firozpur troopers had materialized in response to the physician's yell, destroying the local darkness with their torches and taking charge of the howling prisoner.

Resenting the time consumed by the scuffle, Kasimir pushed on. He was still trying to locate Wen Chang.

Sounds of another scuffle, in a dim alcove, distracted him. When he held up his torch in that direction, its light gleamed on an arc of startling brightness, the flash of a long blade in deadly motion. One dark figure with a long sword in hand was contending against two others, members of the Watch, more lightly armed. One of these two went down even as Kasimir watched, and the other one dove to the floor a moment later, trying to get out of the way of the long blade.

Could the full-sized sword be Stonecutter? The light was too poor to tell. Shouting again, Kasimir moved forward. The floor here was worse than the stairway, rotten, weakened, and unsafe; suddenly it bent and crackled under his additional weight. The man with the long Sword—Kasimir was suddenly convinced it was indeed Stonecutter that he saw—turned toward him, for the moment sparing his last opponent.

When the stroke of the long blade came Kasimir could do nothing but throw up his right hand holding the cudgel in a sort of defensive reflex, at the same moment casting the rest of his body backward. He felt an impact, but realized that he had survived.

Meanwhile the other surviving opponent, the one who had fallen to the floor unhurt, was not willing to give up the fight. The figure on the floor writhed up to strike at the swordsman with some kind of club.

Before the holder of the Sword could react, the whole treacherous portion of the floor had given way. The people on it, living and dead, were plunged down to the next level, amid a cloud of dust and debris. The collapse was relatively slow, the impact at the end of it somewhat moderated, but it scattered the combatants and put an end to the fight.

Coughing and spitting dust, getting back to his feet as quickly as possible, Kasimir got his back against a wall and looked around for the man with the Sword; but as far as he could tell, he was now quite alone.

The borrowed truncheon in his own hand felt strangely weightless, and he looked down at it. At that point he began to understand how lucky he had been not to lose a hand, or at least several fingers. He had felt the jarring impact between oak and steel, and when he looked down at the club still held to his wrist by a thong he saw that only a wooden stump remained of it. Most of the length of the tough oak had been sheared off neatly, only about two centimeters above his thumb and forefinger.

As far as the physician could tell no magical power had been involved in the blow. Nor had any been needed. Kasimir stood for a moment looking dazedly at the result, understanding now on a deeper level than the intellectual what must be the almost supernatural keenness of a Sword's blade. He could appreciate also the determined strength of the arm that had driven the weighty steel behind that edge.

Undamaged except for a few bruises, he scrambled about on the reassuringly solid surface of the level where he now found himself, looking for any sign of the Sword, or the man who had been carrying it. But both were gone.

More men of the Watch joined him, as well as some Firozpur troopers, and in response to Kasimir's questions reported that the building was being satisfactorily cleaned out.

Not wishing to be delayed by their questions, he said nothing to them about his last skirmish. Instead he asked: "Where's the Magistrate got to now?"

"He's downstairs, sir."

Again Kasimir plunged on, finding a ladder and going down, angry beyond words at having the object of his search almost within his grasp, then seeing it whisked away again. He had risked his life but achieved nothing, nor was he at this moment a centimeter closer to gaining final possession of the Sword.

He had reached what he thought was almost certainly the lowest level of the building—at least it was partially below the level of the ground outside, as he could tell by the view through a barred window—before he again caught sight of Wen Chang. This time he was able to reach the Magistrate's side before anything happened to keep them apart.

He seized him by the sleeve. "Magistrate, I have seen the Sword! For a moment I almost—"

"I, too! The man who has it is down here now. Quickly, go that way! Carefully, for he is deadly dangerous."

With gestures and a few hurried words the Magistrate, rapier in one hand and torch in the other, directed Kasimir down one dim corridor, then turned away and plunged down another himself.

Kasimir, his own torch fallen and extinguished somewhere behind him, moved into dimness as silently as he could. Then he paused, holding his breath to listen.

He could hear only the drip of water somewhere. And farther off, out of sight of the hidden desperation of this struggle, some slum-dweller plunking a stringed instrument.

And now, another sound, also faint, muffled by walls and angles of walls. A muffled pounding . . . Kasimir stalked forward through the dim, half-buried cellar.

Then he was once more taken almost completely by surprise. He caught one bright glimpse of a long blade lifted high, in an energetic arm. In an instant, it was going to swing down directly at him.

In the rush of movement the hood covering the head of this new opponent fell back, momentarily revealing the face. Kasimir had barely the space of a heartbeat in which to recognize that the figure brandishing the sword—or Sword—at him was definitely Natalia. The light was bad, and he had only a brief glimpse, but still the physician felt certain that he was not mistaken.

Again Kasimir could only try to throw himself out of a weapon's path. He might not have succeeded, except that when the blade came swinging at him there was a hesitation, a hitch in the swing that allowed Kasimir to survive.

The enemy rushed past him, and a moment later a heavy door had slammed behind the fleeing figure.

Kasimir allowed himself to remain dazed only for a moment. Then, just as he was scrambling to his feet, a shout in the Magistrate's voice sounded from somewhere behind him.

Let Natalia go—he could not be certain that her weapon was the Sword. In a few moments Kasimir had scrambled halfway across the cellar to join Wen Chang and Captain Almagro, who with some of their men were holding a torchlight meeting in front of a closed and very substantial-looking door.

The Captain appeared to have relaxed a little.

"We've got him, and the Sword too! That's a blind wall

on that side of the building. There's no other way out of that room."

But Wen Chang was already stepping back, shaking his head even as he sheathed his rapier. His eye met Kasimir's.

"Come, quickly!" the Magistrate rapped out, and in a moment was running for a stairs that led up to the level of the street.

Kasimir ran after him immediately, ignoring the Captain's startled, querulous call behind them. Already Kasimir thought he understood Wen Chang's haste.

Wen Chang in the lead, with Kasimir continually a step behind him and unable to catch up, the two of them negotiated the tortuous passages of the main floor, and burst out at last into the night. Wen Chang as he ran was able to gather with him a half-comprehending reinforcement of Watch and Firozpur warriors, a group whose footsteps pounded after Kasimir. The moment they were outside, Wen Chang looked back over his shoulder, beckoning to Kasimir.

"The wall of that basement room must give on this alley to our right—quick!"

Kasimir and the Magistrate, a small mob of followers just behind them, thundered around a corner of the building into an alley. There was a heavy thudding sound from somewhere ahead, as if someone, Kasimir thought, were still battering on a door and trying to break it down.

But before they had run halfway down the alley, Kasimir realized that they were already too late. A moment later they had come to the smoothly carved hole in the lower stone portion of the wall. The cut-out pieces of heavy stone were still lying where they had fallen from the touch of the hurrying Sword.

Now someone was coming through the hole. Kasimir stepped back and raised his cudgel. But in a moment the light from the torch he still held in his hand was falling upon the furious, bearded features of Captain Almagro. Understanding had come to the Captain too late, and rage had come with it. He now had a better understanding of Stonecutter's true nature.

But the Sword had now vanished in the night, along with the mysterious person who now possessed it.

CHAPTER 11

THE fighting in the old warehouse was over, the last sullen spasms of physical resistance crushed. Now Kasimir the physician was called upon to tend the wounded.

There were not so many of these as he had begun to fear there would be; he estimated now that there must have been about fifteen people in all in the building when the raid began, and more than one had probably escaped, but the great majority had given up without a fight as soon as they became aware of the strength of the attacking force.

Two of the small handful of occupants who had elected to fight, both of them men, were beyond the help of any surgeon, while another had suffered a badly gashed arm. This last man could be expected to live, and even to use his arm again, once Kasimir had stopped the bleeding and administered some stitches. On the other side, one of the Watch had been run through with a long blade and was dying; another had sustained a knife cut on the hand. Casualties among the Firozpur troopers were limited to one, who had hurt his leg, not too badly, falling through a trapdoor between floors in the darkness.

Before Kasimir had finished doing what he could for these people, the swift runners sent out by Captain Almagro in pursuit of the unknown person carrying the Sword had returned to the scene of the raid, reporting that they had failed even to catch sight of their quarry. No one was surprised at their failure. There had been no real hope of overtaking the fugitive in darkness, particularly not in the warren of streets and alleys making up this neighborhood, in which the forces of law and order were at best unwelcome.

The Captain cursed his luck, and went on to the next thing. As part of his preparations for the raid, Almagro had arranged to have a couple of heavy wagons, cages on wheels, brought up to the building at the appropriate time. These had now arrived on the scene, and all of the prisoners were bundled into them. Wen Chang gave the catch of captives a cursory looking over, but, having done so, showed no particular interest in any of them.

Kasimir had not yet mentioned to anyone the fact that he had recognized Natalia. But he made the identification now, as soon as he had the chance to pull the Magistrate aside, and make sure that the information reached his ears alone.

Wen Chang stared at him intently in the dim light obtaining in the street. "You are sure?"

"Yes. I am certain it was Natalia."

"The light inside the building was very bad. You say you cannot be sure that the weapon she was holding was Stonecutter."

"True. Nevertheless, I am sure that it was she who held it." Again the moonlight came and went around them, with the passage of a cloud.

"All right." Wen Chang sighed. "Let me call Almagro over here and we will tell him alone before we separate. But say nothing about this identification to anyone else just yet."

"I won't."

In a moment Almagro had joined them. The Captain,

not surprised that the Magistrate had chosen to be suspicious of his subordinates, went through the same routine of questioning the certainty of Kasimir's identification. Kasimir went through the same routine of giving reassurances.

Wen Chang suggested in a low voice: "A matter that calls for thorough questioning of all your prisoners, old friend. To find out which of them might know her."

"Indeed, they shall be questioned. Though most of them may have to wait until tomorrow—I am going to need some sleep."

"And so are we. Good thought is impossible in a condition of great fatigue."

Having seen Almagro off with his pair of cage-topped wagons and their unhappy cargo, Wen Chang, Kasimir, and their mounted Firozpur escort returned to their inn, where they found that the landlord had successfully guarded their quarters in their absence.

As they were mounting the narrow stairs to their third-floor rooms, the Magistrate suddenly turned to his younger companion and demanded: "Did she say anything to you?"

"Natalia? No. Nor I to her."

When they had entered their suite and closed the door, Wen Chang asked in a low voice: "Do you think she knows that you were able to recognize her?"

Kasimir considered the question very carefully. "I'm not sure," he said at last. "But I don't think so. But I believe that she knew me."

"Why so?"

"Because she might have been able to kill me. But she didn't really try."

"Ah. I see. And you still have, or thought you had, another meeting with her scheduled for today." The time was now so far past midnight as to be obviously morning.

Kasimir sighed wearily. "That is correct."

Wen Chang yawned, and shook his head as if he were now too tired to think effectively.

"What am I to do about the meeting?" Kasimir asked.

"I expect you should try to keep it. But not until you have had some sleep."

Kasimir did not awake, stiff and tired, until well past midmorning. At some time while he slept a screen had been put up in front of his couch, and from beyond this ineffective shield he could hear the energetic voice of the Magistrate. Wen Chang sounded like a man who had been up and about for quite some time as he gave orders to the hotel servants who were just delivering breakfast.

Sitting opposite Kasimir at the breakfast table a few minutes later, Wen Chang reported that more news had just come in from Almagro, who had apparently spent a sleepless night after all. Some of the prisoners who had been taken last night had been persuaded to provide some information about the person who had fled the old warehouse with the Sword.

"Good!"

"I am not so sure it is. There is considerable disagreement among their stories. One prisoner confirms that the person he last saw with the Sword was a woman, another insists he saw a man getting away. But both agree on one thing: that certain criminal elements within the city are developing a plan to rob the Blue Temple. Captain Almagro says he has already sent this information on to the Director of Security there."

"Well," said Kasimir, "that at least ought to confirm your status as a prophet in the eyes of the Blue Temple. But I wonder if the prisoners are just telling the Captain what they think he wants to hear."

"It is quite possible. But there is more. The final element in the Captain's latest communication to us has nothing to do with the interrogation of last night's prisoners, but still I find it the most interesting. It concerns instead prisoner nine-nine-six-seven-seven, the man who was freed from the road gang by the original Sword-thief. Almagro informs me that nine-nine-six-seven-seven was a rural agitator, convicted of minor political offenses—nothing as egregious as those of Benjamin of the Steppe, we may suppose, or he would have been hanged, drawn, and quartered too."

Kasimir waited, but there seemed to be no more. He asked: "And what does that tell us?"

"Do you not find it interesting too? And the squad that is to arrest Umar goes out this morning. By the way, I suppose you are still intending to keep your appointment with the Lady Natalia today?"

"I think I must try to do so, though after last night I have the most serious doubts that she will be there. I suppose you are intending to have the White Temple surrounded, and arrest her if she does show up?"

"On the contrary. If we did that we would have her, but we would not have the Sword. Nor, I think, would we be any closer to getting our hands on it. No, I am willing to gamble on finding a better way."

"Well then, if she appears I will try to open negotiations to get back the Sword, assuming she got away with it last night."

"Do so. And let your behavior be guided by this fact: She will not risk coming to the meeting unless she hopes to gain something of great importance from you."

"What could that be, Wen Chang? In the beginning she must have recognized me as an investigator, and made an agreement with me simply to be able to keep an eye on the course of our investigation. What a fool I was!"

Wen Chang did not dispute the assessment. "Perhaps you should have been a trifle more suspicious of her all along."

"But now what can she and her people hope to gain of great importance? From us?"

"We can hope that she—and the people who are in this

with her, as you say—would like to make a deal. An arrangement, whereby we would come into possession of Stonecutter—for a suitable price, of course—after it has filled its purpose in their hands."

"What purpose are they likely to have for it, except to sell it? And why should she not sell it to the highest bidder?"

"With the backing of Prince al-Farabi, we can make our bid sufficiently high."

At this point the conference was interrupted by a tap at the door, followed by the appearance of Lieutenant Komi at the head of the stairs. The officer announced that the Blue Temple's head of security had just arrived at the inn, and was insisting that his business could not wait for even a few minutes. The Director was demanding to see the Magistrate and his associate.

"He'll wait, though, if you tell me that's what you want," Komi added hopefully. No one outside the ranks of its outright worshippers liked the Blue Temple. And even within those ranks, Kasimir had observed, feelings about the upper hierarchy tended to be mixed.

"Keeping the gentleman waiting will serve no purpose." Wen Chang sighed. "Let us hear what he has to say."

Komi saluted and retreated to the room below. The Director's heavy-footed tread could soon be heard climbing the stairs, and in another moment he was in the upper suite. He entered talking loudly, insisting in a domineering voice that something more had to be done to guard the Blue Temple's few remaining assets. He hinted that the Eylau branch at least now tottered upon the brink of bankruptcy; and if such an institution were to be forced into financial failure, the damage done the whole community would be incalculable.

Kasimir noted that here, in a more or less public place,

the Director made no direct reference at all to the Orb of Maecenas.

Wen Chang, for the moment all diplomacy, adopted a soothing manner. He suggested the posting of extra guards around the perimeter of the Blue Temple, and also in any of the rooms that were at or below ground level, where thieves armed with the Sword of Siege should be most likely to effect their entrance.

The Director was not soothed, nor reassured. He protested that such measures were easy enough to suggest, but they cost money, a great deal of money. He demanded to know who the Magistrate thought was going to pay for them.

The Magistrate at last allowed some of his disgust to show. "Considering what miserable pay you give the enlisted ranks of your security forces, the men and women who would actually stand guard, such measures would certainly cost you much less than the fee I would charge you, were I willing to act as your consultant."

Kasimir considered that this was a good moment to apply some diplomacy himself. He interrupted to announce his departure, and Wen Chang came partway down the stairs with him to offer a final word of friendly caution.

Today Kasimir had not been sitting for long in Ardneh's chapel before a ragged street urchin approached, tugged at his sleeve, and asked if he were Kasimir the physician. As soon as he had admitted his identity, the boy handed him a folded note.

The physician unfolded the grimy scrap of paper and read its message while the boy stood waiting.

> Kasimir—I am not going to model any longer at the Red Temple. Yet I would like to see you once more. If you would like to see me again, follow the

bearer of this message. Believe me, I will be sorry
if we can never meet again.

> In friendship,
> Natalia

Kasimir read the note through twice, then folded it and
put it in his pocket. It seemed to him that the wording of
the message gave no indication as to whether Natalia knew
that he had recognized her last night—or even whether or
not she had been able to recognize him.

He asked the urchin: "Who gave you this?"

The child returned no answer, but turned away silently
and walked out of the chapel. Kasimir got to his feet and
followed, staying close behind his guide.

They descended from the chapel and walked straight out
of the White Temple complex. Without ever looking back
the urchin entered the bazaar nearby, and moved through
it on a zigzag path. Still following, Kasimir suddenly wondered if someone, Wen Chang or an agent of the Watch,
might now be following him in turn. If so, it would be easy
for anyone loitering in the bazaar to see them and call of
the scheduled meeting. Of course if it was Wen Chang himself on Kasimir's tail, he was said to have the capability of
making himself invisible . . .

After a few more unhurried and apparently random turns
through the marketplace, the ragged child turned suddenly
down a side street, one even narrower than most, where he
continued to move unhurriedly along. Still the boy did not
look back, and Kasimir remained five or six paces behind
him.

At last his guide did turn. Stopping at a doorway, the
urchin indicated with a brief gesture that Kasimir was to
enter it. Then he darted away to vanish in the crowded
street.

Kasimir looked the place over; at first glance it appeared quite innocuous, a cheap tearoom three-quarters full of customers. He went in. Seeing no one he could recognize, he took a chair at one of the empty tables and waited for what would happen next.

A waiter came and he ordered tea. Then somehow, before he had any clue that she was near, Natalia was standing at his table, pulling out a chair and sitting down.

She was dressed approximately as he had seen her at their last scheduled meeting, and today she looked tired but still energetic. When their eyes met, Kasimir did his best to look as innocent as he must have been when they first encountered each other.

Natalia's expression was one of calm alertness, which told him nothing. There was a moment of silence, which threatened to stretch out to an awkward length.

"So," Kasimir began at last, clearing his throat. "You have ceased to be a model?"

"I posed this morning. But in another day or two I am going to quit." She paused. Her remarkable eyes flickered, and her husky voice changed. "Kasimir—when did you last see me?"

"At the same moment that you saw me last." His tea had arrived, and he took a deliberate sip, his eyes not leaving hers. "Would you like to order something?"

Natalia's total control of her expression lapsed. "All right. I am very sorry that I almost killed you last night. The moment I realized it was you, I gave up trying to kill you and ran away instead."

"For which I am grateful," Kasimir said. "We both survived last night, and I am glad of it. Where is the Sword now?"

"First I would like some tea." She put out a hand to detain a passing servant, and placed her order. Then she turned back to Kasimir and spoke in a low voice. "I came here today, taking a considerable risk, to talk to you about that."

He said briskly: "It seems we are both accustomed to taking some risks in the course of our jobs. How much do your people want for Stonecutter?"

Natalia shook her head. "I wish you wouldn't be in such a hurry. It's not that easy."

"Why not? This is your business, isn't it? Stealing things and selling them for the best price you can get? Or it's a good part of your business anyway, I should think."

"The idea seems to make you angry, Kasimir."

"Well, I suppose it does. I'm angry that you made a fool of me. But that's beside the point, isn't it?"

"I suppose it is. Well, as for selling you the Sword, I can't quite do that yet."

"What does that mean? We haven't even started haggling about the price."

She turned her head to right and left, as if trying to make sure that they were not being overheard. It seemed highly unlikely that anyone could eavesdrop in the noisy room. Then she said: "It means that the organization I work for has concluded an agreement with the Red Temple. According to the agreement, de Borron must be allowed to use the Sword to finish his work there—he has until the first day of the Festival to complete it. Then the Sword comes back to us, and we are free to make some other disposition of it."

"The Red Temple doesn't mind it being known that they're using stolen property."

"You won't be able to prove it, or do anything about it."

"The Festival begins day after tomorrow."

"Exactly. So you won't have long to wait."

"So in my view right now shouldn't be too soon for us to begin our bargaining."

"It is a little too soon." Her voice was firm.

"I see. Perhaps you'll be able to get in a quick robbery or

two, at the Blue Temple, say, before you'll accept our ransom."

Natalia's face was becoming totally unreadable again. "I won't insist on anything like that."

"And when do you want to discuss price? I assume there will be others bidding against us."

"I will tell you when the time has come to discuss price. And now you had better go."

"Just answer me one question first—"

"Now you had better go."

This, he thought, was Natalia's territory. He pushed back his chair and went.

CHAPTER 12

IT was a tribute to his sense of direction, Kasimir thought, that he was able to reorient himself, and make his way out of the quarter of extra-narrow streets near the White Temple after making no more than one false start. In a few moments he was in half-familiar thoroughfares again, and heading back in the direction of the Inn of the Refreshed Travelers. He was angry, and thinking furiously as he walked.

When he tried to examine the reasons for his anger he understood that it had several causes. Part of it, he supposed, was a delayed reaction to his being nearly killed, probably by the very weapon he was supposed to be recovering, in the hands of a young woman who had made a fool of him. It did not help a bit to realize that he still found her attractive. And part of his anger was a result of his still being manipulated, largely by the same person— made to attend upon her, until it should be convenient for her to talk business. He was not really in control of anything.

Immersed in gloomy meditations of this kind, he was still at some distance from the inn when he heard his name called, jarring his attention back into focus on the world around him. Looking up he saw one of the Firozpur troopers of Komi's squad, who was standing lounging in front of a tavern as if he had been stationed there simply to watch the street. When Kasimir approached, the man informed him that he was wanted inside the tavern.

When Kasimir demanded an explanation, the trooper only shrugged. Leaving the man in the street, Kasimir entered the tavern, pausing for a moment just past the threshold to allow his eyes to accustom themselves to the relative dimness. The general layout of this place reminded him strongly of the teahouse he had just left, except that here the windows were somewhat smaller and the room as a result notably darker.

Presently Kasimir caught sight of the Captain and the Magistrate, who were established at a table toward the rear of the large room, from which vantage point they were able to observe almost everything that went on inside the tavern, and something of the street outside. The two older men both waved to Kasimir. When he reached their table and pulled out a chair, they both expressed their pleasure that he was still alive.

"You sound surprised to see that I am," he said grimly as he sat down.

Wen Chang shook his head. "Not really that. Come, sit down and tell us of your meeting with the fair Natalia."

"We already know," put in Almagro, "that she arranged for you to be escorted out of the White Temple and through the bazaar. It was there that my people lost sight of you."

"Perhaps," said Kasimir, "it was just as well that they did." He ordered a mug of beer from a passing barmaid, and began to tell his mentors as concisely as possible the details of his meeting with the woman in the teahouse.

The Captain, listening intently, scowled and squinted and tugged at his beard. "So, the lady implies she's willing to make a deal with us—but not just yet, if I understand her. And she's some kind of leader in her gang, or wants to be."

"That was certainly my impression," said Kasimir.

"I'd say she must be fairly new in town, or I'd have run into her somewhere before."

"A most reasonable deduction," agreed Wen Chang. "Though most likely she has associates who are very familiar with the city."

The Captain scowled at him thoughtfully, then faced back to the young physician. "So then, neither of you got down to the real business? I mean, mentioning any specific sums of money?"

"She refused to do so. And I couldn't very well open the bidding, not knowing how much Prince al-Farabi might be prepared to pay to get back his Sword. Also I am generally unfamiliar with this business of paying ransoms."

Wen Chang nodded. "It had seemed to me that the time was ripe for negotiation. But perhaps not. I wonder . . . is it possible that the young lady does not have the Sword in her possession at all?"

"If one of the gang carried it away from the warehouse—"

"One of 'the' gang, you say. But what if there is more than one gang involved?"

The Captain had been listening silently to this last exchange, but it was plain from the expression on his face that the more he thought about the situation, the less he felt he understood it.

"Don't know how much of her story we ought to believe, about an agreement with the Red Temple and all that. It would seem to contradict this talk of a move being planned against the Blue Temple by the people who have the Sword."

Wen Chang took a sturdy draught from his mug, then delicately stroked foam from his black mustache. "The contradiction does not necessarily arise. The more times these enterprising criminals can profit from their loot, the happier they should be. First they rent the Sword to the Red Temple for a high fee; a few days later they use it to break into the Blue Temple; and then lastly they sell it back to its rightful owner for a high price."

"You really think they intend doing all that, Magistrate?" The Captain squinted as if the thought pained him.

"It is certainly a possibility. But what I think most strongly now is that we must contrive somehow to find out whether the Sword is really being used in the Red Temple as the lady said. Is Stonecutter actually there, and under what circumstances? Is it on loan from some gang of criminals? Is it in the hands of Robert de Borron, and is he actually using it in his work?" Wen Chang paused. "If so, what are the chances of our taking it away from him?"

Here the Magistrate broke off to order another round of drinks. As soon as it arrived the two experienced investigators began planning their next move.

Almagro was not optimistic. "If it comes down to our getting into the Red Temple, maybe being able to take the Sword right out of there with us—well." The Captain shook his head and began to spell out some of the difficulties as he perceived them. "If we were just to try to push our way in there, like we did at the old warehouse—well, this is a very different situation. To begin with, there's not much chance that we'd ever get a look at the Sword before it was spirited away somewhere. It'd take an army to search that place—the Red Temple—properly, and I can't order up an army without letting my superiors know what I'm about.

"For another thing, they have their own security force there in the temple—such as it is." Here he paused, and the three men exchanged faint smiles, as at a joke familiar to all. It was received wisdom that Red Temple security people could be counted on for very little, and were more likely than not to show up for duty drunk, or stoned on other drugs than alcohol.

Almagro's smile faded quickly again as he continued. "One thing they do have that works is plenty of political influence. It would probably be more than my badge of office is worth to go barging in there on my own."

Kasimir asked: "Even if you were sure of recovering the Sword of Siege by doing so?"

Almagro rubbed his forehead doubtfully. "Well. That'd certainly make a difference. But I can't be sure of anything like that, can I?"

Wen Chang thought a little, and sighed, and shook his head reluctantly. "No, my friend. Whatever plan we concoct, no one can assure you of its success."

"Well, then." The Captain drank, and ran his fingers through his hair, and drank again, and thought. The impression he gave was that the more he thought about his situation the worse it looked to him. "I wonder if I ought to go to the Hetman himself and tell him at least that the Sword of Siege is here in the city somewhere, and that we're looking for it."

"You know him better than I—"

"Aye, that's why I'm wondering."

"—but it occurs to me that it might be best to tell him only if—or when—Stonecutter has actually been recovered."

"There is something in what you say."

The two older men lifted their mugs simultaneously, as if they were toasting each other, or perhaps harking back to old times, sharing some private joke or ritual.

Then Wen Chang was abruptly serious again. He took the merest sip from his mug, leaned back in his chair again, and said, "Yes, I think we must get someone into the Red Temple to take a look around for us, and do it as soon as possible. Tonight, if we can."

"Tonight?"

"If the sculptor is as desperate to complete his work as

everything indicates, then he will be working late, with or without the help of the Sword we are looking for."

"Sculpting after dark?"

"I have no doubt that the Red Temple can provide him with some kind of effective light. I suppose you, the Watch, have no regular agents in place within the temple upon whom you can rely?"

"Hah. The Watch has no agents at all in there that I know of. I wish we did. More likely than not it's working the other way around. Red Temple has a lot more money to spend on bribes than I do."

"Well, then. Do you have anyone available to be sent in? Preferably someone who knows his or her way around inside the temple?"

"Hah! I'd say that most of my men know the public parts of that building only too well. But as for the rest of the place, no, I don't think so. And now that the temple's being remodeled, the layout will be changed anyway. Especially in the parts we most want to see, upstairs where the statues are being carved. No, I can't say that I have anyone I'd want to try sending in there."

Both of the older men turned their heads to gaze at Kasimir. He had been expecting this development for some time now. He drank from his mug and quietly set it down.

"Then I suppose it is up to me to go in again," he said. "If I can. Well, I'm willing."

Wen Chang studied him through narrow appraising eyes.

Almagro looked relieved. "As to simply getting into the place," he offered, "I can be of some help there. I can get the names of some of their security people who are more than ordinarily amenable to bribes, and probably I can find out when and where some of those people are likely to be on duty. I'm afraid, though, that if I were to try to send one of my own people in there the Red priests would know about it before he ever arrived."

* * *

Returning to the inn ahead of the others, Kasimir tried to get some rest, and made what other preparations he and Wen Chang thought necessary. Near sunset he held a final conference with the Magistrate, and with Captain Almagro who had come to give him some final directions. Then Kasimir was on his way.

The sun had set before Kasimir arrived in the square in front of the Red Temple, whose façade was aglow with the red of firelight from its numerous torches and iron fire baskets. As usual, nightfall meant an increase in business at the Houses of Pleasure, and as he approached the building he fell in with an almost steady stream of customers, the great majority of them men.

He was within a few meters of the entrance when his eye was caught by a stray gleam of light, coming from above, somewhere within the building, that proceeded from no ordinary fire. When the realization struck him that the source of the peculiar light must be in or very near the artists' studio on the fifth or sixth floor, Kasimir stepped aside from the stream of customers to stand for a moment near the entrance with his head craned back.

He had to find the precisely correct position before he could see the light again. But at last there was the tiny gleam: very steady and bright, pale as daylight. Extraordinary. Even, he thought, unearthly looking. Perhaps, Kasimir thought, the illumination was being produced by some kind of magic. Whatever its ultimate source, the light must be leaking out of the studio through a crevice between some of the draped canvases and drop cloths that shrouded the walls of the sculptor's temporary workshop. And whatever the source, it certainly looked bright enough to allow Robert de Borron and his crew to continue working after dark. Suddenly it occurred to Kasimir that this light had a strong resemblance to the Old World votive lamp on Ardneh's altar in the White Temple.

The intermittent stream of men around Kasimir, intent on thoughts of what they were going to do once they got inside the temple, were ignoring him and the strange light alike. Now more than ever determined to make this mission a success, he rejoined the stream of customers.

Shuffling through the line of impatient customers at the entrance, Kasimir paid his small coin there like everyone else, and as a member of an anonymous throng entered the interior of the temple. At night the public lobbies, lighted by fire, were even redder than during the day. The fires made this part of the building somewhat too warm. Cheerful music throbbed here, played in a rapid tempo by concealed musicians.

On Kasimir's previous visit he had not penetrated this deeply into the public areas. But nothing here was very much different from any other Red Temple that he had ever visited. Signs, well lighted and elaborately designed, relying heavily on iconography as a courtesy to clients who had trouble with their letters, indicated the way to the various Houses contained within the establishment.

Every Red Temple—at least every one Kasimir had ever seen from the inside, admittedly a comparatively small selection—was divided according to the same basic scheme, into interconnected domains devoted to various pleasures. Here as elsewhere there were the Houses of Flesh, of Food, Wine, Chance, Sound or Music, and Heavenly Vapors. The last was a catch-all category for various entertainments, mostly chemical. Kasimir had heard that in other regions of the world the arrangement varied somewhat, but as far as he knew a Red Temple was basically a Red Temple the world around.

Every time you entered a different House you had to pay another fee, though otherwise it was easy and convenient to pass from one to another. The House of Flesh was on the third floor here, the highest level currently open to the public, and for that reason Kasimir had made it his official goal. As soon as he had paid the rather hefty entrance fee, he was free to climb the winding, recursive stairs, liberally provided with landings and chairs for the benefit of the unsteady devotee who might be coming this way from the House of Wine on the ground level. Kasimir's was a popular choice tonight, and he had plenty of company on the stairs.

Once having attained the third level, he entered and passed through a large, softly furnished waiting room. Here youthful servants of the temple, most of them female, all of them provocatively clad, waited to be chosen by customers. From this anteroom corridors branched off, and Kasimir chose one under the icon of a staring eye. Ignoring low-voiced invitations from the employees on the benches, he went that way alone. According to the directions he had received at the last minute from Almagro, his way to the private regions of the temple lay through the Hall of Voyeurs.

The Hall of Voyeurs was almost dark. At regular intervals small, very narrow corridors branched off from it. Closed doors blocked off several of these passages, meaning that they were occupied, each probably by only a single worshipper. Kasimir had never entered a Hall of Voyeurs before, but as he understood the arrangement, the walls of each branching corridor were pierced by numerous peepholes, opening into a selection of lighted rooms. In these rooms servants of the temple, joined sometimes by exhibitionistic customers, were more or less continuously engaged in a variety of sexual performances.

Ignoring the opportunities presented by empty observation posts, Kasimir went straight on to the far end of Voyeurs' Hall. There, in accordance with Almagro's briefing, he discovered a latrine—Kasimir could hear one of the real flush toilets inside working as he approached.

Once inside the dimly lighted and evil-smelling facility, Kasimir fumbled and stalled, feigning intoxication, until other customers moved on and he felt reasonably sure of having a few moments free of observation. Then he hurried to a service door, really only a panel set into a wall, whose lock he had been told was broken.

Actually, as he discovered in a moment, the door or panel was held in place by no lock at all. Typically sloppy Red Temple building maintenance, he thought as he eased the light panel aside, worked his body cautiously through into the dark cavity beyond, and then maneuvered the loose panel as closely as possible back into place.

Now he was standing in a darkness greater than that of the dim latrine, and on an awkward and uneven footing. Kasimir decided to wait, before moving another centimeter, to give his eyes a chance to become adjusted to the gloom.

Soon he was able to discern that he was definitely in an unfinished portion of the building, where he stood surrounded by its darkened skeleton of timbers and stone piers, along with a lot of empty space. There was no real floor anywhere in sight. He was standing on a narrow beam, and even a small step in the wrong direction would earn him a nasty fall. A floor or two below him, the furnished and inhabited rooms were rendered visible in outline by little sparks of light that here and there leaked out through the joints between their walls and ceilings. Also from down there somewhere came loud, drumming music, and wisps of other and more human sounds emanating from the hundreds of occupants.

Looking up, the view was different. A solid roof at about the sixth-floor level blocked out the sky. There was almost no light at all above except for a few more stray gleams of that unearthly looking illumination that had first caught Kasimir's eye when he was still outside the building.

And Robert de Borron—or someone—must indeed be at work up there, three levels above where Kasimir was hiding, for the sounds of the sculptor's studio, an irregular pounding accompanied now and then by voices, came drifting down.

The next thing Kasimir had to do was to get up there.

Some meters distant horizontally from where he stood—it was hard to judge distances in this great darkened cavern where there were only tantalizing hints of light—the light from above was coming down more freely than elsewhere. Traces of the strange illumination shone out through the leaky sides of a large, roughly defined vertical column, that Kasimir presently realized must represent the shaft of the freight elevator used to haul de Borron's heavy blocks of stone up to his studio. That elevator shaft, if he could get into it, certainly ought to offer a way up.

Having got his bearings as well as possible, Kasimir began to work his way in the direction of that vaguely glowing column, two or three meters square and extending its way up from ground level. The task, he discovered almost at once, was even more difficult than it looked. His only means of progress was to edge nervously along a narrow beam, his pathway interrupted at intervals by the thick columns of stone and timber holding up the upper floors. Once he had moved away from the paneled rear wall of the latrine, he had only space on right and left.

He had made only a few meters' progress by this means when his way was blocked more substantially, this time by one of the projecting side corridors of the Hall of Voyeurs, complete with its set of performance rooms. The only way to get past this obstacle was to go over the top, and presently Kasimir found himself creeping across the broad upper surface of a thin ceiling. At one point the surface bent alarmingly beneath his weight; he sprawled out flat, as if he were on thin ice, and centimetered his way forward holding his breath.

From inside the lighted room just beneath him there issued moans and rhythmic cries that suggested torture. Of course in a Red Temple other kinds of sensation were more probably the cause. Still, with every movement Kasimir made, the thin panels—and the plastering, if there was any—of the ceiling beneath him threatened to give way. He expected momentarily to go crashing and plunging down amid the bodies mounded on some bed. When that happened, the men with their eyes at peepholes in the lonely adjoining corridors would see a different show than they had expected.

Kasimir surmounted the barrier of the rooms at last. Now, feeling more and more like a beetle burrowing through the woodwork, he was back on his narrow beam again, working his way closer and closer to the silent, faintly glowing elevator shaft. No hoisting was in progress now, he was sure. If it had been, he would be able to hear men or loadbeasts straining at a windlass somewhere, and the creaking of the network of pulleys and cables he had once glimpsed from above. Anyway the sculptor's work was supposed to be nearly done now, and it seemed likely that all his massive workpieces had already been hauled up.

It occurred to Kasimir to wonder briefly why the workshop had not been situated at ground level, and only the finished statues hoisted. But then he supposed that space on the lower levels of the temple would probably be at a premium, already occupied by the various Houses of worship. And then too, secrecy would probably be easier to maintain at the higher level. Might that have been a consideration with de Borron and his employers from the beginning of the project?

Closer and closer Kasimir drew to the enclosed shaft, until at last he reached it. Putting an eye to a chink in one of the roughly enclosed sides, he could see loops of chain as well as lengths of thick rope hanging inside the shaft, whose interior was bathed in near-daylight brilliance falling from above. Kasimir felt sure now that those must be Old World lights up in the studio, relics of the age of technology whose human masters had ruled the world even before Ardneh lived, before Ardneh's Change had come upon the world to restore the dominance of magic.

Right now, as Kasimir had felt sure would be the case, the ropes and chains hung motionless, the hoisting machinery was idle. Not so the workshop above. A number of people were there, he could tell by the intermittent murmur of voices; and at least a few of them were working, as evidenced by the continued sound of tools.

The next step toward reaching the studio was to get inside the elevator shaft. With his eye to a crevice, Kasimir could see that the inner sides were ribbed with crossbracing that should make an ideal ladder once he got within reach of it.

To get inside that shaft it was necessary to pry one of the ill-fitting side panels loose. That proved to be no great trick once Kasimir had brought his small, sharp-pointed dagger into play. Crude nails loosened quickly. In a few moments the panel was free, and Kasimir was able to slide his body into the shaft, where he clung to the ladderlike sides with a fair degree of security.

Looking up, he could see the big pulleys, wound with chains and ropes, at the top of the shaft. He could see also a part of the overhead of the sculptor's studio, illuminated with that wondrous light, whose source was still invisible.

Before he began to climb the last few meters to his goal, Kasimir, trying to be thorough, moved his loosened panel back as nearly as possible into its proper position. He glanced down once, into darkness—heights had never bothered him particularly—and then started climbing the shaft's ribbed side.

He had about nine or ten meters to ascend, and he moved up as quickly and silently as possible. As he got closer to the top he could see that the head of the elevator shaft was barricaded from the workroom by nothing more than a rude length of rope, stretched as a precaution across the side of the shaft that was open to the room.

As he neared the top of the shaft, he crossed over to the side where the light was dimmest. Even here it was uncomfortably bright for a man who was trying to hide, and he was going to have to be careful to avoid being seen before he had the chance to observe anyone else.

At last, moving very slowly now, Kasimir was able to raise his eyes above the level of the studio floor, and look out into the more distant parts of the big room. Most of it was indeed as bright as day, in the flood of illumination from what Kasimir now saw were indeed two Old World lanterns, each resting on its own small table.

Never before in his life had he seen Old World lights as big as these. But these lamps could hardly be anything else.

And standing between the two lights, almost exactly equidistant from them, with her pale flesh glowing like soft marble in their radiance, her naked back turned toward Kasimir, was Natalia, posing as a model.

CHAPTER 13

A S a secret observation post, the head of the open elevator shaft suffered from at least two major drawbacks: First, any observer who stationed himself there was far too likely to be seen by the folk he was trying to observe. And second, if he was discovered, he had nowhere to retreat to safety.

But a ready solution was at hand. The empty elevator shaft came up at the edge of the huge workroom, and the three sides of the shaft away from the studio were not tightly enclosed. Kasimir needed only a moment to slip out of the shaft onto the rough floor behind the nearest of the draped canvases that had been hung around the high unfinished walls of the studio. He could see more reason for these hangings now, see them as an effort, not entirely effective, to keep the Old World light from being seen at a distance and arousing people's curiosity. The fewer people who knew about de Borron's efforts here, the fewer would be likely to come around and bother him.

Once Kasimir had established himself behind the canvas, he had only to examine the cloth barrier in front of him, using reasonable caution to keep from moving it very much, until he located a small gap between two imperfectly overlapping pieces. When he put his eye to this aperture, he was able to examine most of the room in front of him while remaining virtually invisible himself.

Now he had a good view, from a different angle, of the two Old World lanterns on their separate tables, seven or eight meters apart. Each light source was a white globe approximately the size of a man's head, almost uncomfortably bright if you looked straight at it. Each globe was supported on a stout dark cylinder with a broadened base, that held it above its table by about half the length of a man's arm.

Ordinarily Kasimir would have found such rare Old World artifacts intensely interesting. But not just now. To begin with, there was Natalia, posing nude halfway between the lights. She was standing in front of a white cloth hung as a backdrop, on a low dais or stand that looked as if it could be rotated on demand.

And there was Robert de Borron, standing with his back turned almost fully to Kasimir. The artist was four or five meters from Natalia, and right beside him was the almost-finished statue he was working on. The statue, larger than life like the others in the studio, was of marble, almost pure white, and it rested on its own small foundation of short but heavy timbers. Close along one side of the marble figure rose a scaffolding, a sort of wide ladder, to enable the artist to reach the upper portions of the work.

Natalia had a robe lying beside her on the rough planks of the floor. She was facing toward both the sculptor's and Kasimir's left. Her pose was erect, standing with hips thrust forward, one foot a little in advance of the other, her arms curved wide as if inviting an embrace. In front of her, and slightly more distant from her than the artist was, a pair of Red Temple security guards in soiled and shabby crimson cloaks had frankly abandoned any pretense of paying attention to their duties, and were devoting themselves to staring at her.

She was managing to ignore them completely.

Beyond both sculptor and model as Kasimir looked at them, far across the broad expanse of the shallowy L-shaped studio space, a handful of other workers were toiling at some tasks that Kasimir did not bother to try to identify exactly. Now and then, out of the relative dimness in which those other people labored, a thin cloud of white stone dust drifted, slight air currents carrying it gradually closer to the lights. But some of the people over there seemed to be working on wood; Kasimir looking at them got the impression that they might be simultaneously demolishing one small scaffold and putting another one together. The sounds of their hammering tried with little success to echo in the large but cloth-draped space.

Besides the statue that de Borron was working on, four or five others were still standing about in the studio. All of these appeared to have been finished by now.

The glow provided by the Old World lights was certainly as strong as daylight in the vicinity of the sculptor and his model, but even at its brightest it was subtly different from the light of day. De Borron's face, plainly visible to Kasimir whenever the sculptor turned his head a little, showed clear as a marble carving in that light. But for once the man's expression was not a study in arrogance. Instead there was something strained and pleading in his look, as if the artist were praying to his Muse.

But none of this, not even the sight of Natalia posing unclothed, claimed Kasimir's attention more than momentarily. Within a few seconds after he had made his peephole in the cloth draperies, Kasimir's attention was entirely riveted upon the object in de Borron's hands.

The sculptor was now indeed working with the Sword of Siege.

The hidden observer could be very sure of this, even though very little of Stonecutter's length was actually visible. Almost the entire weapon was out of sight, sandwiched between a pair of thin, flat boards that were held firmly together with clamps. From one end of this sandwich a dull black hilt protruded, and from the other end, that nearest the work, a few centimeters of bright steel.

Attached at right angles to the flat boards making up this improvised sheath were rounded wooden handles. These offered good grips for the artist, who needed only the few exposed centimeters of the blade to work the stone.

But the most ingenious part of the Sword-holder's design, as Kasimir observed it, was the way in which the whole sandwich of Sword and wood was suspended from overhead, on what looked like a fishing-rod of slender steel, with counterweight attached. By this means the sculptor's arms and hands were freed of the continual burden of the weighty Sword, his muscles were liberated to concentrate upon the demands of art and of the client's deadlines.

Obviously the work was going very swiftly now, and doubtless the artist, despite the occasional expression of anguish that passed across his face, was basically satisfied with how it went. The Sword as he used it to cut stone made little thudding noises. These seemed to have little or no connection with the physical work it was accomplishing, being rather a by-product of its magic. Kasimir needed a minute or two to convince himself that such an inappropriate sound was really coming from the Sword, and was not an echo of the coarse pounding by the workers in the background.

But the dull little thudding sound was proceeding from the Sword, all right. Under the sure control of de Borron's strong hands, Stonecutter's irresistible point was peeling and scooping delicate little chips of stone from the white marble shape. Already the work had taken on at least the crude shape of its model in all its parts, and some of those parts looked completely finished. Only the final stages of carving and smoothing remained to be done.

It was obvious that the work had been going on in this swift fashion for some time. For hours, probably, if the drift of tiny, distinctively shaped chips and shavings around the sculptor's feet offered any reliable indication.

The amplified likeness of Natalia, subtly transformed by de Borron's skill, was rapidly emerging from the stone. But despite the evidence of rapid progress, and the fact that de Borron appeared pleased and fascinated with his new tool, it was apparent to Kasimir that the artist had not yet mastered the Sword to his own satisfaction. Fascination was far from contentment. The artist was intent on learning everything that this magical device would let him do.

He was muttering to himself—or perhaps to his Muse—almost continually as he worked. Kasimir was not quite able to make out any of these comments.

The studio was not as busy as it had been during the day, but a few more people were present, all of them Red Temple personnel of one kind or another. Chief among these, the High Priest himself, now came strolling around the corner of the L, heading in the direction of the laboring artist. The priest had his hands clasped behind his back, and his expression was one of impatience held in check by deliberate toleration; it must appear to him now that his precious deadline was going to be met after all. In no more than a few hours, perhaps, the installation of his precious gambling tables in this space could begin.

The official spoke. "So, it appears that you are going to finish on time, de Borron."

The sculptor, without removing his eyes from his model, muttered something in response. Stonecutter continued to make its dull incongruous noise, and thin stone leaves released by the bright blade fluttered almost continuously to the floor.

"What's that you say, sculptor?"

The man with the Sword in his hands looked up. "I said, 'Yes, if I am not bothered too much by fools.'" This time the answer was spoken with fierce clarity.

The man in the red robes flushed. "One day, stonecutter, you will push your arrogance too far."

But with that the exchange of sharp words died out; de Borron had already turned back to his work and Kasimir, watching, thought it doubtful that he had even heard the priest's reply.

Meanwhile some of the other people in red livery were also strolling closer to where the master artist worked. A couple of them, besides the two enthralled with Natalia, were from security. Two more, women, were probably minor officials, Kasimir thought, come up here to see where the gambling tables were going to be when the re-modeling was finished.

The two supposed guards who had abandoned all thoughts of duty in favor of gaping at the model were gaping at her still. Only when one of these moved closer for a better look, actually getting himself into the sculptor's immediate range of vision, did de Borron bark something that sent both men into a hasty-retreat.

The High Priest, who had earlier retreated a few steps, said something in a low voice that Kasimir did not catch.

The sculptor heard him, though, and snapped back: "If you want me to finish quickly, then in the name of all the gods get out of my way and let me work!"

Kasimir was just wondering whether he ought to start back down the elevator shaft—he foresaw that getting out of the temple again would take time—and report to Wen Chang as quickly as possible that the Sword was definitely here, when his thoughts were interrupted by a faint and furtive sound coming from somewhere to his right.

Turning his head sharply in that direction, he saw that

some of the ropes and chains that hung down into the elevator shaft were stirring slightly, as if someone below were pulling on them or at least had touched them.

While Kasimir had been busy making his own unauthorized entrance into these private parts of the temple, it had not even occurred to him to wonder at how easy it all was. You expected security to be lax in a Red Temple. But now he wondered suddenly whether his entrance had not been suspiciously, ominously easy. Whether a path might not have been deliberately left unguarded; not for him, of course. For someone else, and he had happened to find it.

There were more sounds from the elevator shaft, very faint sounds. Sounds that he would not have heard or noticed if he had not been listening intently for them.

Someone else was coming up to the studio, by the same route Kasimir had taken.

If Kasimir stayed where he was, the new arrival or arrivals would be certain to discover him as soon as they reached the top of the shaft. Maybe it was Red Temple security, after all alert enough to do some checking up on loosened panels. Maybe it was someone else.

As quietly as he could, Kasimir scrambled away from the opening of the shaft, moving into the deeper shadows along the wall of canvas draperies.

From beyond that wall came Natalia's voice, speaking suddenly and clearly. "I need to take a break," she said.

Kasimir, satisfied for the moment that he was safe from discovery, fumbled at the cloth in front of him again until he found another tiny hole, which enabled him to once more look out into the studio. He was in time to see Natalia grabbing up her robe from the floor and pulling it around her, while at the same time she shot a swift glance toward the open elevator shaft. It was not a look of puzzlement, or idle curiosity; instead it was full of calculation.

She had heard the sounds there too, and Kasimir got the impression that she had been expecting them.

"Can't you wait?" de Borron barked at her, automatically protesting the interruption of his work.

"No, I can't." Tying the belt of her robe, the tall young woman tossed back her drab hair defiantly. The Old World light did nothing for its color. "We've been at it for hours. I don't know how much longer I'll be able to hold my arms up like that."

"All right, I suppose you're due for a break." The artist's voice was tired. He was rubbing his hands together now, as if to restore circulation in his own tired limbs. He had let go of the apparatus that held the Sword, so that Stonecutter in its odd wooden sheath bobbed lightly in midair, dependent on its fishing-rod support.

Now Kasimir, looking back toward the elevator shaft while holding himself motionless in shadow, could see and hear two people—now three—arriving at the top and climbing out, crouching in the very place where he had been only a few moments ago. Whoever they might be, they were not Red Temple security. These people were clad in close-fitting dark clothing, including masks. Kasimir saw a long dagger in one hand. He had thought for a moment that the new arrivals were all wearing swords, but when he got a momentary glimpse of them in slightly better light he saw that they were actually wearing swordbelts with long empty sheaths.

And, whoever they might be, Natalia was definitely expecting them. The way she had glanced in their direction and then started a diversion was good evidence of that.

Whoever they were, there was no doubt in Kasimir's mind that they were going for the Sword.

From beyond the wall of fabric Kasimir could hear the sculptor's weary voice: "We can put up a prop for you to rest your arms on." Then de Borron's voice grew louder, barking orders at the people who were still banging away at their work on the other side of the big room.

A moment later all the sounds of hammering had ceased. Kasimir, with his eye again to his latest observation hole, saw that the people on the far side of the room had now put down most of their tools and were coming this way.

The Sword of Siege, with no one very near it at the moment, hung gently bobbing in its homemade tool-holder. A few meters from the Sword, de Borron was pacing back and forth, pushing his hands against the small of his back as if to ease the muscles there.

Natalia was stretching herself too, and rubbing her side under her robe where perhaps the cramp was real. Now, as if following a sudden impulse of curiosity, she moved to stand close beside the low table holding one of the radiant Old World light-globes. Then she reached out one hand to touch the dark material of the lamp's base.

"How does this work?" she asked in a clear, innocent voice. "Why is there no heat?"

"Don't fool around with that light, girl. Stop it, I tell you! That's not your—"

But de Borron's shouted orders were ignored. Natalia's fingers had found the control they sought, and suddenly the lamp went dark.

The other lamp, the one nearest the elevator shaft, was still lighted, flooding the big room with plenty of illumination for everyone to see what happened next. In a moment the remaining lamp had been snatched from its table and extinguished by the first of the three dark-clad figures who now burst out of concealment and came running into the room from that direction.

Kasimir had already made up his mind to act, and when he saw the dark figure running for the one remaining light source he knew that the moment for decisive action had come. The barrier of draped cloth in front of him was no impediment at all. Even as the studio went almost entirely dark, he pushed between the folds of hanging canvas, heading for the Sword.

He was certain that a number of other people would be rushing toward the same goal, but he felt sure of having at least a moment's start on most of them. And when the lights went out he was already moving in the right direction.

As his legs drove him forward the few necessary strides, he heard the blackness around him come alive with oaths, cries of surprise and fear, and sounds as if people were colliding with one another. There was even what sounded like a clash of steel blades; perhaps the Red Temple guards were after all not totally incompetent, or perhaps they had only drawn swords out of fear for their own lives.

The bulk of the unfinished likeness of Natalia, and its scaffolding, loomed up just ahead of Kasimir and to his left, backlighted by the faint red glow that came through crevices from the lights along the front of the temple. The same dim light showed Kasimir something else: Despite the speed with which he was rushing for the Sword, he was not going to be the first to reach it. De Borron was there ahead of him, and the sculptor already had Stonecutter out of its wooden sheath before Kasimir could come to grips with him.

The sculptor had Stonecutter's hilt in his right hand, and was ready to use the Sword as a weapon, when Kasimir crashed into him, determined to wrest the blade away. Kasimir's left hand closed in its hardest grip on de Borron's right wrist.

The physician was no trained warrior, but rough games had been a part of his growing up and of his youth, and he possessed considerable stocky strength. De Borron was perhaps just as strong, but when the two men fell together Kasimir was on top, and most of the sculptor's wind was jarred out of him in the impact.

The Sword fell free. For a moment only it lay unattended on the floor of the studio, almost within reach of the struggling men; and then someone snatched it up. Kasimir had only the impression of a lone running figure, unidentifiable in the near-darkness, grabbing the Sword of Siege in passing, and running with it in the direction of the elevator shaft.

A moment later the wrestling match had reached an end, by common consent. Kasimir and de Borron were both back on their feet, trampling and clawing at each other in an effort to gain some advantage in the pursuit of this most recent Sword thief.

Around the running pair, other skirmishes were still proceeding under cover of darkness, with oaths and cries and sounds of impact.

Kasimir, glancing to one side, caught a glimpse of Natalia, distinguishable by her robe and her pale legs running below it, running in the same direction he was. This time he could be sure it was not she who had seized the Sword and was getting away with it.

This time, he vowed grimly, no one was going to do that, unless it was himself.

Someone was giving the trick a great try, though. The person carrying Stonecutter had now disappeared in the general vicinity of the head of the elevator shaft, and Kasimir assumed that he—or she—must be climbing down the rickety interior sides, or sliding down the chains and cables, in near-total darkness. But how would anyone be able to carry a Sword while doing that? Suddenly Kasimir understood why the latest set of intruders had been wearing empty Sword-sheaths at their belts.

Running up to the shaft himself, the physician in his haste came near diving into it headfirst. His entrance was not quite that precipitate. Having climbed the sides of the shaft before, he was better able to handle it in darkness than most of those pursuing would be.

De Borron, reaching the top of the shaft only a step or two behind him, delayed the start of his own descent briefly. He took time out to bellow uselessly for lights, and for more guards to come and save the Sword.

Then, despairing of any effective help, the sculptor swung out boldly on the chains and ropes. On the end of a loose line he started an almost free-fall plunge into the dark depths below, and had to grab at another chain to save himself.

Meanwhile Kasimir kept doggedly to his own more patient method of getting down, and whoever was carrying the Sword ahead of him and below him still maintained a lead in the descending race. Kasimir looking down could barely see a movement, shadow deeper into shadow, and only some faint sounds, clinking together of the long chains, drifted up.

Now a brief outcry in a familiar voice came from above, and Kasimir glanced in that direction. Something had delayed Natalia, but she had reached the shaft at last, and was struggling with de Borron a couple of meters above Kasimir's head.

In a moment the sculptor was somehow pushed free, or lost his grip on chains and ropes, and started to fall down the shaft. At the last possible moment before disaster he saved himself by regaining his hold on one of the cables or chains.

Once more steel weapons clashed in the near-darkness. The members of the intruding group, one above Kasimir's position and one now somewhere below, had drawn blades to defend the Sword-bearer, and indeed he or she must certainly be using the Sword itself, meanwhile trying to hang on with one hand.

Someone climbing in the gloom nearby lashed out at Kasimir. He stuck to his climbing and succeeded in getting away from this attack. If the attack should be renewed he thought he would have to draw his dagger and try to fight with one hand while he hung on with the other.

With a sharp splintering sound, a loose slat in the wall nearby gave way under someone's grasp. There was a scream and a falling body, followed after a sickeningly long interval by a crash in the darkness far below.

But there was no indication that the person carrying the Sword had fallen.

Scarcely had the sound of that first fall died when de Borron, still a meter or two above Kasimir and just to one side of him, fell again. Someone or something had knocked the artist loose from his grip inside the shaft, and he tumbled past Kasimir, screaming a string of imprecations that were cut short suddenly when he hit the invisible bottom.

And, half that distance below Kasimir, at about the level of the highest inhabited rooms, the vague shadow he had tentatively identified as the Sword-bearer left the shaft, to glide almost silently into some kind of opening in its wall.

Kasimir followed.

His pursuit of the latest thief went on relentlessly, crossing narrow beams and leaping gaps over darkness, going more recklessly with each momentary frustration.

Nor were any of the other pursuers giving up on the confused chase. Rather the number of hounds seemed to be growing, with the guards of the Red Temple forming a gradually increasing presence. However tardily and ineptly they were being mobilized for action, they were everywhere in the building, and they greatly outnumbered all the other participants together.

Kasimir now had lost sight of Natalia completely. But not of his primary quarry, the sinister shape who bore the Sword. The figure tried to lose him and the other pursuers, leaping from one narrow beam to another. But Kasimir, his blood now aroused to the full excitement of the hunt, would not be shaken off. His quarry climbed a stony column, dropped down again, and leaped another gap. But Kasimir stuck with the other as if his teeth were already fastened in his prey's flesh.

They were both centimetering their way across the thin ceiling of one of the orgy rooms on the third floor when Kasimir at last caught sight once more of Natalia's unmistakable bare-legged figure. She was starting to creep toward the quarry too, though holding on with one hand to a solid support. Whether she meant to strike at the Swordthief or aid him Kasimir could not—

The ceiling underneath them all was giving way.

This time it was really—

The slow-motion sensation of desperate action took over. Kasimir knew a moment of despair, a moment of resignation; there followed in an instant an almost anticlimactic splashdown. He, along with numerous fragments of ceiling, had landed upon what he first took for a gigantic bursting waterbed. But when he went in up to his waist, he realized that the first impact of his fall had been borne by a flimsy raft afloat upon a shallow perfumed pool. Half a dozen naked bodies, looking clinically exposed and vulnerable, were thrashing in the shallow water now, and from the bottom of the tank unsavory things came swirling up. Wine and food, their fragile containers broken, were churning in the water, scattered into garbage.

Whatever performance had been in progress on the raft was over now. Another body, that of a security guard, fell through the ceiling, drenching Kasimir afresh with a great splash as it landed right beside him. The quondam performers were rolling, swimming, scrambling for shelter outside the pool, intent on getting out of any of the target area before more people fell.

An audience, some fifteen or twenty strong, was looking on.

There were two rows of chairs, the rear row elevated,

making something like a small grandstand. All of the seats were full. The occupants of the chairs, a jaded-looking and weary crew, brightened enough at the violent innovations to offer a small round of applause, even as the Red Temple guards came crowding in through both doorways.

Kasimir, still waist-deep in the noisome artificial pond, looked round him in despair. There were plenty of blades in sight now, drawn and ready in the hands of the Red Guards who came bursting in the room's doors, and dropping through the newly opened ceiling. Swiftly their attention was concentrated upon Kasimir.

And again the Sword was gone.

CHAPTER 14

A BOUT an hour after dawn next morning, an elderly and majestic individual, announcing himself as the personal representative of the Hetman, and accompanied by an armed escort that augmented his already formidable dignity, came calling upon Wen Chang and Kasimir at the Inn of the Refreshed Travelers.

Despite the early hour, Wen Chang was wide awake and ready to receive visitors. Kasimir, on the other hand, had to be awakened, a task that was not accomplished without difficulty. The young physician had been intensely questioned by the Red Temple authorities until well after midnight, and then released only on Captain Almagro's written acceptance of responsibility for any further crimes and outrages that this self-proclaimed investigator might commit.

The early-morning business of the Hetman's representative at the inn was soon stated: The Magistrate Wen Chang, and his chief associate, one Kasimir the physician, were courteously but very firmly invited to attend a meeting that was due to begin as soon as they could reach the palace, and was to be presided over by the Hetman himself. The purpose of this meeting was the discussion of certain strange events known to have taken place recently in the city, and the resolution of the resulting problems.

172

Despite Wen Chang's attempt to question him, the Hetman's representative would be, or could be, no more specific than that.

As the two investigators were concluding their hasty preparations for departure, with the representative of the Hetman waiting in the room just below, Kasimir asked Wen Chang in a low voice: "Shall I tell them everything that happened to me last night?"

The narrowed eyes of the Magistrate widened momentarily. "I presume that you have told *me* everything?"

"Yes, of course."

"Then I see no reason why you should not repeat the same story to the Hetman. Truth is very often an effective weapon; and we mean no harm to anyone in this city except Sword-stealers."

Wen Chang and Kasimir were soon as ready as they could be; they descended to the courtyard and mounted for the ride to the palace. Their escort remained courteous, and the two were not searched, but once in the street they were surrounded continuously by mounted troopers. A light rain was falling again, adding to Kasimir's thoughts of gloom; he took heart from the fact that Wen Chang appeared not at all discouraged.

As their small cavalcade entered the square in front of the Hetman's palace, Kasimir observed that the scaffold that had been erected for tomorrow morning's execution had somehow been severely damaged, and was now undergoing reconstruction. There were signs that fire had destroyed portions of the original wooden structure, while other parts of it had been knocked down and broken. The rebuilding was being carried out under military guard.

Raising his eyes, Kasimir saw that this morning there was a face looking out at one of the small barred windows that here overlooked the square. Looking carefully, he was able to recognize the man he had earlier seen riding in the tumbrel, on the occasion of Kasimir's first visit to this square.

Why should Benjamin of the Steppe, or anyone else, trouble to stand at a window to watch the instrument of his own death take shape? It would seem to indicate a morbid, helpless fascination, certainly. Kasimir gazed up with a kind of sympathy at the face in the small window. But if the prisoner was aware that he had a commiserator, he gave no sign.

Wen Chang, taking in all of this with a glance or two, informed the dignitary in charge of their escort that he intended to pause for a moment. When this was allowed, the Magistrate called over the officer in charge of the military guard, and questioned him.

The officer, of junior rank, plainly enjoyed the chance to be seen talking in public to these important-looking people who were on their way to the palace. He provided what information he could on the situation regarding the scaffold. During the night just past some of those persistent rural protesters had tried to burn the platform down. When rain prevented that, they had mounted the wooden structure with axes and hammers and tried to knock it all apart. The Watch had finally come on the scene and driven them off, but not until the devils had managed to do quite a bit of damage. Never fear, though, the instrument of execution would be ready in time, and this time would be kept under careful guard—there would be a live hanging, drawing, and quartering to begin the Festival tomorrow morning.

Kasimir, who had no intention of attending that kind of a curtain raiser, muttered something about the hopelessness of people who protested by trying to burn a scaffold. Wen Chang was scowling—it was hard to tell just what his reaction was. But as the Magistrate signed that he was ready to ride on again, his eyes twinkled for just a moment.

Their pause in the square had been brief, and only moments later Wen Chang and his associate were being escorted through a rear gate and into a narrow yard behind the palace itself. There all dismounted, leaving their riding-beasts in the care of grooms.

Inside the palace the Hetman was awaiting them in an audience chamber of moderate size, two floors above the ground. A number of other people were also already present, including Captain Almagro, who looked grim and bone-weary.

But most of the small gathering turned actively hostile gazes toward Wen Chang as he entered. The High Priests of both Red and Blue Temples, each accompanied by his own small retinue of advisers, stopped talking and glared at the newcomers on their arrival.

Kasimir was surprised to see that Robert de Borron was also present. Last night Kasimir had reported to Wen Chang that the artist was probably dead following his tumble down the elevator shaft. And indeed, de Borron was in bad shape, with one leg and one arm splinted, and bruises evident on his face.

The silence of the Red Temple's High Priest was only momentary. As soon as that official had recognized Wen Chang and his associate, he immediately accused them in a loud voice of not only taking part in the raid on his establishment the previous night, but of organizing the attack as well.

And of carrying off Stonecutter. "The Sword of Siege is ours by rights, and I demand that you return it to us at once!"

For once the glowering artist gave every evidence of being in complete agreement with what the High Priest said.

That official went on: "I shall make the charges more formal and specific." He grabbed a scroll from an aide and began to read from it. The Magistrate and his associate were accused of conducting a raid last night upon the Temple of Aphrodite and Eros, particularly the House of Flesh, and there conniving in the attempted murder of the sculptor Robert de Borron, and also conspiring with person or persons unknown to steal and sell a treasure of incalculable value.

Wen Chang, who still had not responded, waited calmly until the string of accusations should be finished; this took some time, as the Blue Temple people, unwilling to wait, were trying to get in their own accusations and arguments at the same time.

Meanwhile the Hetman had been sitting silently in his place at the head of the table, evidently willing to let the uproar run its course for a time, in the hope that some facts constituting useful information might emerge. Presently it was evident that nothing of the kind was likely to happen, and he drew his dagger and pounded on the table with the pommel. Almost instantly he was granted the boon of silence.

Kasimir had never heard any personal name for the current ruler of Eylau, and he had gathered that lack was a usage established by tradition as long as the person was in office. The Director of Security at the Blue Temple was operating under a similar rule or tradition.

The present Hetman, whatever his name, was a short, stout man, dressed in an elaborate style that Kasimir considered as bordering on the effeminate. There were rings on almost all his pudgy fingers and his coloring was muddy and unhealthy looking. About forty years of age, he looked as if he might at one time have been very strong physically, but had let himself go to seed. As Kasimir observed him throughout the meeting, the impression he gave was one of fading moral strength as well as physical, of an overriding, undermining insecurity.

Kasimir like all other thinking observers knew that the

position of the city-state governed by this man was insecure as well. Eylau was chronically beset and buffeted by the larger powers surrounding it, and sometimes also by international entities like the great and well-nigh universal temples.

The silence obtained by the Hetman's dagger-pounding was of brief duration. He allowed the silence he had won to stretch on a little too long, and the Blue Temple people took advantage of this leniency to burst into verbal action.

What they wanted, they said, was protection against robbers. This danger, they said, had escalated almost infinitely, now that a tool like Stonecutter was in the city, in unknown criminal hands.

"No one's property anywhere will be safe, as long as that Sword is in the hands of irresponsible people!"

Before the Hetman had decided how to respond to that—or Wen Chang could formulate a reply—the Red Temple had seized the floor again, its leaders protesting that they were the ones who had actually been robbed, and had a real grievance to present.

The Hetman, exasperated at last, gave up all effort at a dramatic pause, all pretense at judicial calm, and shouted hoarsely for order. His voice, or something in the way he used it, was even more effective than his earlier dagger-pounding, and he was granted his wish immediately.

This time the silence lasted somewhat longer. As it endured, Kasimir found it possible to hear, faintly, the continual hammering from out in the square where the reconstruction of the scaffold was still in progress.

"Now," said the ruler of the city, looking around the room. He had a bold, commanding voice when he wanted to make it so; but despite the tone and the determined look Kasimir had the definite impression that the Hetman was uncertain of just what ideas he ought to present to the orderly attention of his audience, now that it had been granted him.

It was with a subtle appearance of relief that the Hetman's gaze at last came to rest upon Wen Chang. The voice of practiced boldness asked: "And you are the famed Magistrate?"

"I am, Excellency," replied the lean man, bowing. There was no pretense of any particular modesty in the answer, and the bow was the movement of an experienced diplomat.

"Good." The direction of the Hetman's attention shifted slightly. "And I suppose you are Kasimir the physician?"

"Yes sir, I am." Kasimir bowed in turn.

The stout man sitting in the elevated chair drew in a deep breath. "As you have just heard, it is charged against you both, among other things, that you have conspired to steal a piece of property belonging to the Red Temple. Very valuable property, too, I might add. What have you to say to this accusation?"

Wen Chang replied smoothly. "Only two things, Excellency. In the first place we have stolen nothing, and we do not have the Sword. And in the second place, the property in question—I assume the Sword of Siege, one of the Twelve Swords of the gods, is meant—does not belong to the Red Temple. It never has." Raising his voice, Wen Chang overrode protests from that direction. "Not only are we innocent of the theft of Stonecutter, but we are engaged on behalf of the rightful owner to recover his property for him. The Red Temple has no more legitimate interest in that Sword than does the Blue, or than the people who have it now."

The protests emanating from the Red Temple delegation only increased in violence and noise.

Wen Chang needed help from the Hetman, in the form of more dagger-pounding on the table, before he could regain the floor.

When a semblance of order had been re-established, and the Magistrate granted silence in which to proceed, he said: "It is true that Doctor Kasimir, acting as my agent, was inside the Red Temple last night. He entered legitimately, as a paying customer. He was not trying to kill or injure anyone, or to steal anything. His only purpose—in which, regrettably, he failed—was to recover the Sword for its rightful owner."

"Ah," said the Hetman. "You keep coming to that point. Who is this rightful owner?"

Wen Chang continued smoothly. "My immediate client, Excellency, is Prince al-Farabi of the Firozpur tribe." That created a stir of surprise in the room. The Magistrate went on: "Not many days ago, the Sword we seek was stolen from the Prince's camp in the desert, some three days' journey from Eylau.

"But the Sword of Siege, as Prince al-Farabi will be first to admit, was only his on loan—a matter, I am told, of Stonecutter's powers being needed to root out some bandits from a particularly inaccessible desert stronghold. The true and rightful owner of the blade is Prince Mark of Tasavalta, with whom I am sure Your Excellency is well acquainted, if only by reputation."

"Of course," said the Hetman after a brief pause. He acknowledged some kind of acquaintance with the well-known Prince almost absently, as if his mind were running on ahead already, assessing what the implications of this claim were likely to be if it was true. Tasavalta was not a next-door neighbor, but rather many kilometers to the north of his domain. Nor was it a particularly large country. But the Tasavaltans were said to be formidable in war; the reputation of their ruler had spread farther across the continent than this.

Now there came an interruption. Robert de Borron, refusing to be kept silent by the Red Temple people with him, struggled out of his chair despite his injuries, and came pushing his way forward, leaning on the central table, demanding to be heard.

The burden of his impassioned plea was that a greater matter than treasure or even human lives was here at stake—and that was Art. Now that he had held the Sword in his hands and had begun to discover how much it could do, what marvels a sculptor like himself would be able to accomplish with such an instrument—well, all this talk about property rights and money value was really beside the point.

The sculptor looked across the table at the Blue Temple people almost as if he really expected them to agree with him. They gazed back. In the face of such heresy their countenances were set like stone beyond the power of any blade to carve.

Meanwhile the Hetman—perhaps from shrewdness, perhaps from chronic indecision—listened to the artist's outburst tolerantly. De Borron grew angry at being tolerated. He had tried to speak respectfully, he said, but perhaps that had been a mistake. Nothing, certainly nothing and no one here in this room, should take second place to Art.

He was silenced at last only by a serious threat from the Hetman to have him removed from the conference chamber and, if even that failed to keep him quiet, locked in a cell.

Next someone in the Blue Temple camp brought up the suggestion that de Borron himself might have arranged to have the Sword stolen and spirited away.

Once more a minor outbreak of noise had to be put down.

"Captain Almagro." The ruler's voice was no louder nor bolder than before, but still the Captain blanched. "You are a senior officer in the city Watch. I want you now to tell me in plain words just what did happen inside the Red Temple last night; include everything that your investigations have discovered since the event."

Almagro, who had perhaps been expecting to hear worse from his master, spoke up confidently enough. To begin with, there was no doubt at all that the Sword had been there in the temple, and that it was now missing. But in the Captain's official opinion, there was also no reason to doubt any of the information that had just been provided by the famous Magistrate.

The Hetman nodded, as if he had known that all along. "My own magicians inform me that it is common knowledge, among those in a position to know, that the Prince of Tasavalta has had Stonecutter in his arsenal for some years."

This time the interruption came from the Red Temple representatives. After a hasty consultation among themselves, they put forward a spokesman who protested that, with all due respect to His Excellency's wizards, it was also common knowledge that the Swords, like other pieces of property, changed hands from time to time.

"We maintain, sir, that we were acting in good faith when we, as we thought, recently acquired certain rights to the Sword of Siege."

Wen Chang broke in sharply. "Exactly what rights were those, and from whom did you think you were obtaining them?"

The Red Temple people were still considering what their answer to this ought to be when the meeting was interrupted from outside by the entrance of one of the Hetman's aides. This was a middle-aged woman, who went straight to the ruler's side and imparted some information to him in a very soft whisper.

The Hetman heard the message with no change of expression. Then he nodded, dismissed the messenger with a few quiet words, and turned back to face the assembly at the table.

"Prince al-Farabi himself is now here in the palace," he

announced, looking sharply round to gauge his audience's reactions. "And he is coming at once to join our meeting."

A stir ran through the gathering, but Kasimir saw nothing he considered helpful in anyone's reaction. Only Wen Chang, as usual, remained imperturbable.

Within two minutes, amid a flourish of formal announcement at the door, al-Farabi indeed entered the audience chamber. The Prince was wearing what looked like the desert riding costume in which Kasimir had seen him last, and Kasimir noted that his clothing was actually still dusty with traces of the desert.

The two rulers, using one of the short forms of ceremony, exchanged the proper formalities of greeting. As Kasimir watched he was thinking that according to strict protocol the Prince would somewhat outrank or would at least take precedence over the Hetman, though both were heads of state. It seemed unlikely, though, that exact rank was going to be of any practical importance.

After his official welcome by the Hetman, the Prince exchanged brief greetings with all the members of the meeting, taking them generally in order of rank as prescribed by protocol. When he came to Wen Chang, who was well down on the list, Kasimir thought that Prince and Magistrate exchanged significant looks, though he could not tell what the expressions were meant to convey.

As soon as the formal salutations had all been completed, al-Farabi resumed at some length his lamentations for his lost Sword.

Eventually mastering his feelings with an evident effort, he faced the Magistrate again. "I understand that Stonecutter was seen here in the city last night, but that it was impossible to recover it then?"

"That is true, sir."

"Ah, woe is me! My burden of sorrow is great indeed!"

Standing informally now with the two investigators as if

they were old friends, the Prince related how, for the past several days, he and several dozen of his tribesmen had been out in the desert, trying in vain to pick up the trail of the villain or villains who had stolen Stonecutter from his camp. But, al-Farabi lamented, he and his trackers had had no success at all—which he supposed was scarcely to be wondered at, considering the nature of the ground and the ferocity of the windstorms that had lashed the area over the past several days.

Wen Chang broke in here to ask if any of the winged messengers dispatched by Lieutenant Komi had managed to reach the Prince.

"Regrettably none of them did." Al-Farabi looked freshly worried. "Is there news I ought to know? On entering the city today I came directly to the palace, feeling that I must consult with my brother the Hetman, and so I have not seen Komi. I have heard nothing."

"There is no news, sir, that is of vital importance for you to learn at this moment—only a few matters relating to the personal affairs of your troops."

With that settled, the Hetman called upon Kasimir to relate his version of events on the night the Sword was stolen from the tent. The ruler listened to the relation with a look of intense concentration. Then he wanted to know Kasimir's version of the events in the Red Temple during the night just passed.

Again Kasimir obliged. From the expression on al-Farabi's face as the Prince listened, Kasimir could tell that he had been expecting to hear nothing like this. As to what he had been expecting to hear, Kasimir could only wonder.

Called upon for comment again when Kasimir had finished, the Magistrate took three or four sentences to say in effect that the situation was indeed most interesting.

The Hetman snorted. "I rejoice to hear that you find it interesting! But is that all that you can find to tell us? We were hoping for something of more substance from the great Wen Chang."

The Magistrate bowed lightly. "I might of course add that the situation is very serious. But I believe it is far from hopeless."

"I am glad to hear that you think so." The ruler looked round at others in the room as if to sample their reactions. "You see, then, some prospect of eventually being able to recover the Sword?"

Before answering, Wen Chang turned to face the people from the Red Temple. He said: "I must return to an earlier question, one that was never answered. You say you thought you had honestly bought certain rights to Stonecutter, or to its use—with whom did you bargain? Whom did you pay?"

The Red Temple spokesman looked at him haughtily. "As it seems now that we were bargaining in error, I don't see how knowing that is going to help."

"It may be of considerable help in recovering the Sword. Come, who was it? Certain disreputable people of the city, was it not?"

"I fail to understand why—"

"Did you not in fact know that you were dealing with a well-organized criminal gang?"

"Well, and if we were? We had hopes of being able to return the Sword, which we assumed might have been stolen somewhere, to a legitimate use in society."

Robert de Borron was unable to keep himself from bursting forth again, once more putting forth his claim that the demands of Art could justify any such dealings.

Someone from the Blue Temple, not wishing to have fewer words to say than anyone else on this occasion, pronounced: "No one's claims to the Sword are going to mean anything unless it is found. I would like to know how the world-famed investigator we have with us plans to go about recovering it."

The Hetman, determined to assert himself, seized this opportunity. "It does seem," he told Wen Chang, "that so far your efforts have contributed nothing to that end."

"It may seem so, sir."

"What evidence can you give us that you are making progress?"

"At present I can give you none."

Eventually, under pressure, the Magistrate pledged to the Hetman that if given a free hand he would be able to provide some information on the Sword's whereabouts, if he had not succeeded in actually recovering the blade itself, within the next twenty-four hours.

This was taken up by many of the people present as a promise that the Sword would be recovered within a day. All were eager for that—if Stonecutter were to remain in the hands of nameless thieves, it was hard to see how any of the legitimate segments of society could hope to profit from it in any way.

So, Wen Chang could more or less have his way for twenty-four hours. In the meantime, according to the Magistrate's recommendations, the Blue Temple would be more heavily guarded than usual, as would all the city's other main depositories of wealth. And all patrolmen of the Watch, wherever they were on duty, would be alerted to watch for Stonecutter.

With that the meeting broke up.

CHAPTER 15

THE Prince was of course invited by the Hetman to partake of the hospitality of the palace. Declining the invitation would have been diplomatically difficult if not impossible, and so al-Farabi was more or less constrained to dine and lodge there, along with the small retinue he had brought into the city with him from the desert.

Though it was plain to Kasimir that the Prince would have preferred to leave the palace at once and have a long talk with Wen Chang, there was no opportunity inside the palace for the two men to converse without a high probability of being overheard. In the brief public exchange of conversation they had before parting, the Magistrate managed to convey to his royal client the idea that things were not really so bad as they might look at present. Wen Chang affirmed earnestly that he still had genuinely high hopes of being able to recover Stonecutter.

Kasimir, listening silently to this reassurance, could only wonder how such hopes might possibly be justified. Reviewing in his mind the situation as it stood, he did not find it promising. The twenty-four hours of Wen Chang's grace period were already passing, and nothing was being accomplished. Of course Wen Chang might have learned something encouraging during the hours he and Kasimir had been separated; the two of them had had no real chance to talk alone since Kasimir had been routed out of bed this morning.

Now, just as Kasimir and Wen Chang were reclaiming their mounts from the palace stables, they were joined by Captain Almagro. The Captain had a meaningful look for each of them, but he delayed saying anything of substance as long as they were still within the palace walls.

The delay, Kasimir discovered, was to be even longer, for as soon as they were outside those walls the Captain left them, with a wink and a wave. Kasimir, not understanding, watched him go.

"He will soon rejoin us, I think," the Magistrate assured him.

"If you say so."

They started for their inn, this time without stopping to watch the rebuilding of the scaffold.

Kasimir had expected the Magistrate himself to have a great deal to say as soon as they were away from the palace. But now, on the contrary, Wen Chang was content to ride along in near silence. Instead of joining Kasimir in trying to plan a last desperate attempt to recover the Sword, he seemed almost to have given up. His precious twenty-four hours were passing minute by minute, and if anything he appeared more relaxed than he had before the meeting at which the deadline had been imposed upon him.

If this was only resignation to the whims of Fate, then in Kasimir's opinion it was carrying that kind of attitude too far. As for himself, he saw no need to carry patience to extremes.

"Well?" he demanded, after they had ridden in silence to a couple of hundred meters' distance from the palace walls. "What are we to do?"

A dark eye gleamed at him from underneath a squinting

brow. "Have patience," his companion advised him succinctly.

Kasimir found this, in the circumstances, a thoroughly unsatisfactory answer. But he had to be content with it until they had reached their inn.

There they found Almagro waiting for them in the courtyard, having evidently completed whatever urgent errand had drawn him away. The Captain was impatient too. "Where can we talk? I've got quite a lot to say."

Wen Chang gestured. "Come up to our suite—it is about as secure as any place can be, outside a wizard's palace."

When the three of them were established in the third-floor suite, with Komi and some of his men on watch in the room below, Almagro began to talk, quietly but forcefully.

His pleas that Wen Chang get busy and find the Sword without delay were considerably more urgent than Kasimir's might have been.

"Magistrate, if you know where the damned thing is, or might be, then let's get it and deliver it without delay." The Captain was now obviously worried for himself. "Whatever might or might not happen to you two if you fail, nothing good is going to happen to me. My neck is on the line. I've stuck it way out for you, and His Mightiness the desert Prince is not going to put himself out to protect me."

Wen Chang responded with every appearance of sympathy. "He might very well offer you protection if I ask it of him. And I shall certainly ask it if I think it necessary."

"If? Look here, Magistrate, tell me straight out—do you know where that Sword is now, or don't you?"

"If you mean, can I walk straight to it and put my hand on it—no. Can I send a message from this room, and have it brought here to me within the hour? Again my answer must be no. Nevertheless I do have some definite ideas on the subject of Stonecutter's location."

"Hah! If you have any useful ideas at all, I wish you'd share them with me!"

"The time is not yet right for that . . . look here, old friend. You have trusted me in the past. Can you not trust me once more?"

The Captain blew out a blast of air that made his mustache quiver. "I've seen you act like this before . . . damn it all, I suppose you know what you're doing."

"Thank you. I appreciate the confidence. Now, have the arrangements that I requested been completed?"

"They have." Almagro looked at the room's windows and the closed door. "If you mean about that fellow Umar. We've picked him up, and brought him into the city, as quietly as we could. One of my own men is now temporarily in command out at the quarry."

"Were you able to determine anything from the records out there, about which prisoner or prisoners might be missing?"

"Nah. My people brought in what records they could find, and I've taken a look at them. Hopeless, I'd say. Kept by a bunch of illiterates."

"I feared as much." Wen Chang rubbed his own neck, as if the long strain were beginning to tell on him. "And where are you holding Umar now?"

"At one of our auxiliary Watch-stations. It's a very quiet little place, hardly used for anything anymore, out near the Paupers' Palace. I doubt very much that anyone besides the men I trust know that he's there. The men who took him there and are watching over him are the most trustworthy I have."

"Good." Now Wen Chang was nodding eagerly. "I want to talk to Umar at once."

Kasimir shook off his own recurrent tiredness as well as he could, and made ready to accompany Wen Chang and Almagro through the streets yet once more.

Leaving the inn, they rode through the streets upon a broadly looping course, the Magistrate doubling back and changing his route unpredictably in an efficient effort to determine whether or not they were being followed. At length he was satisfied, and they set out straight for the Paupers' Palace.

Their trip through the streets was somewhat delayed by these precautions, but otherwise uneventful. Presently a familiar landmark came into Kasimir's sight—the isolated, disconnected, crumbling section of high stone wall, with the winged scavengers rising from its top and settling there again, shrieking in their quarrels over food.

At one side of the stretch of barren ground that centered on the wall of exposure stood a small stone building, seventy or eighty meters from the wall and at least half that distance apart from any other structure. This, Almagro indicated, was the Watch-station. The building, Kasimir estimated, looking at it from a distance, could contain no more than two rooms at most. He supposed its chief claim to usefulness, if you could call it that, was its position that would allow the occupants to keep a close eye on the corpse-disposal operation.

They had ridden within fifty meters or so of the building when Almagro abruptly reined in his mount, then just as suddenly spurred forward. Wen Chang was riding at a gallop right beside him.

Kasimir dug his heels into the flanks of his riding-beast and stayed right behind them. He was actually the first off his mount as the three men reached the station. The stout front door of the little building was standing slightly ajar. In the shaded area just inside the entrance, where it would be invisible until you were almost upon it, lay the body of a man in Watch uniform. The man was sprawled on his back in the middle of a considerable pool of blood.

Kasimir took one look at the wound that had opened the

man's throat, almost from ear to ear, and forbore to look for signs of life. The blood was starting to dry on the stone floor, and the insects were already busy around the corpse.

Almagro, standing over the dead man now with his short sword drawn, said a name, which Kasimir took to be that of the murdered man; then the Captain and the Magistrate, both with weapons ready, moved farther into the building, toward a doorway leading to the rear.

Once more Kasimir was right behind them.

The second room of the small structure was dim and almost windowless. The heat of the sun upon the thin stone walls was turning the chamber ovenlike; and here was more blood, much more blood, this time spreading out in a fanshaped, partially dried puddle that had its source inside the single barred cell with which the building was equipped. There was another dead man in there, lying on the floor of the still-locked cell, and in this victim's distorted face Kasimir could recognize the valuable prisoner Umar.

For a few moments the drone of insects, and the cries of those distant, larger scavengers upon the paupers' wall, made the only sounds in that dim room. Then Wen Chang asked his old friend to unlock the door of the cell.

The Captain fumbled at his belt, where there were several sets of keys. He seemed to be having trouble finding the proper one. "How was he killed, in there?" he asked in a querulous voice. "He can't have done it himself, there's no weapon."

The Magistrate shook his head impatiently. "He was lured to the bars, by whoever killed the sentry. Lured by the promise of being set free, I suppose . . . how should I know the details?" Wen Chang was angry at the loss of his witness, perhaps at his own mistakes as well, and disposed to be uncharacteristically surly.

Once Almagro had found the proper key and opened the cell door, Wen Chang and Kasimir went into the cell, both trying to avoid stepping in the puddled blood. The Magistrate also drew up his trouser legs with a slight fastidious movement.

Soon after Wen Chang had begun his examination of the body, he turned to announce that the man had been attacked from behind, and that his killer was left-handed.

Almagro, his expression at once idle and thoughtful, had been looking into the cell from outside, hanging on to the bars of the door. But he reacted sharply to that.

"Left-handed?" His voice rose, in both pitch and volume, from each syllable to the next. The others turned to look at him.

"Left-handed? That tears it, then! About three years ago, right after I came to work for the Hetman, there was a fellow in the city they called the Juggler. Another name he went by was Valamo of the Left Hand. He was the smoothest assassin I've ever run into anywhere. The deadliest and smartest . . . it was only through a woman that we ever caught him. Even then we knew he'd done a lot of things we couldn't prove. We could prove enough, though. The judge thought that execution was too good for him."

Wen Chang's eyes glittered. "And so he was sent to the quarries?"

"Yes, he was, by all the gods! 'Course I'm not sure it was Kovil's quarry where he ended up. But it might well have been. He was one of the few you don't forget in this business. All this"—and with a savage gesture Almagro indicated the abattoir around them—"this is just the kind of thing he did. He knew, somehow, we had a good witness here, a man who could tell us a lot. And he came to shut him up for good."

"This Valamo, or Juggler, worked alone then, as a rule?"

"In the important things he worked alone as much as possible. Though he could always recruit people in Eylau to

192

work with him, when he thought he needed someone. Had a reputation, that one did. Still has, evidently. I do believe that most of the regular gang leaders were afraid of him . . . so now it looks like the Juggler's back."

"How did he happen to acquire that name?" asked Kasimir.

Almagro's gaze turned toward him. "Nothing very strange about that. It's what he did, they tell me, before he found his real profession. A street performer, doing a little acrobatics, a little sleight of hand, a little juggling. Those people are never very far within the edge of the law anyway."

"True enough," said Wen Chang. "Though there have been times in my own life when I have felt almost completely at home among them . . . but never mind that. What does this Valamo look like?"

Squinting into the air, the Captain took thought carefully. "By now I'd say he must be around forty years old; though by the look of things here he's lost no skill or toughness. Anyone who could survive three years on a quarry gang . . . he's just average height, no taller than the Doctor here. Something of a hooked nose. His hair was dark when he was young, but when I saw him it was going an early gray—so it's likely just about completely white by now. His face would be lined and sunburnt from the quarries, so I'd say he's likely to look a decade or two older than he really is—what's wrong with you, Doctor Kasimir?"

"Tadasu Hazara," said Kasimir, after a pause to swallow. "That was the name he gave when he came to the inn, and talked to me about wanting to buy antique weapons. He must have thought that I was a genuine dealer, and was just making sure. Then he proved to himself that I was a fake." The physician paused and looked at his companions. "How could Kovil have hoped to control such a man?"

"Kovil did not lack in confidence," said Wen Chang

dryly. He stood back from the blood and waved a hand about. "Old friend Almagro, this slaughter must of course be reported."

"And am I to report also that Valamo of the Left Hand did it?"

"Yes, I think so. All the pressure that we can put upon that gentleman will not be too much. As for you, Kasimir—"

"Yes?"

"I want you to go back to the inn and rest," said the Magistrate, surprising his hearer. "Rest, but do not sleep too deeply, for this Juggler may even now decide to pay us a visit there. And soon there will be another job for you to do."

CHAPTER 16

KASIMIR returned to the inn, where Lieutenant Komi was waiting to greet him with eager questions about the most recent developments. Kasimir, not having been told to keep any secrets, brought the officer up to date as best he could.

Komi shook his head gloomily when he had heard the story of the double murder. "It sounds like bad news; I must find out what the Prince wants me to do now."

"It certainly doesn't sound like good news to me either. But be sure to leave a few reliable men here if you go off to the palace seeking orders."

"I will. Don't worry, my men are all reliable."

Climbing the stairs wearily to his third-floor room, Kasimir lay down on his couch to rest. For a time, the cries of peddlers in the street outside kept him awake.

The peddlers moved on eventually to the next street, but by now Kasimir's thoughts were disturbing enough to prevent his sleeping. He kept seeing the murdered men in the small stone building. Somehow the worst horror was the look of peace upon their faces; even the man in the cell, whose expression was unnatural, seemed to have died calmly. It was as if each of the victims in turn had welcomed the figure in whose guise death came upon them.

Neither of them appeared to have taken alarm before the end.

At last Kasimir fell asleep, and with sleep came strange dreams. Someone whose face was hidden in a gray hood was stalking after him with a great steel Sword, trying to coax him to put down his dagger and his cudgel. Then in his dream Kasimir looked down for his right hand, and saw that it was gone, lopped off along with his wooden club.

He awoke sweating and gasping, to find Wen Chang bending over him. For just a moment the horror and strangeness of the dream persisted, and then Kasimir realized that the frightening alteration he perceived in Wen Chang's face was only a result of the Magistrate's just having removed the outer layer of some kind of a disguise.

"What's going on?" Kasimir demanded, almost before he was fully awake. There was something in his mentor's attitude that made him think more action must be imminent.

Wen Chang was standing back now, regarding him calmly. "I have arranged another task for you to perform, my young friend—if you choose. It might help our cause immeasurably, but I must warn you that it is very dangerous."

Kasimir sat up, scratching and rubbing his head. "Now—after we raided that warehouse—after you sent me into the Red Temple—now you think it necessary to warn me that our task is dangerous?"

The Magistrate had seated himself in a nearby chair. "Yes," he said, "I do. There were certainly dangers in those places that you mention. But the risk to be faced now may well be of a different order of magnitude. The fact is that I have been able, through some difficult and indirect negotiation, to arrange a deal with the Watch-station murderer."

Despite himself Kasimir was aware of a chill. "Well, I

won't argue that he doesn't require a special warning. I suppose this deal involves the Sword?"

"Of course."

"What makes you think that the Juggler has it now, instead of Natalia and her group?"

"You misunderstand, Kasimir. The fact is that our friend hopes and expects to obtain the Sword from us, in return for a down payment of cash, along with his pledge of co-operation in other matters."

Kasimir, who had just got to his feet, slowly sat down again. "However did he get the idea that we have it?"

"I fear someone must have provided him with misleading information." The Magistrate's eyes twinkled slightly.

"How?"

There was no answer.

"So he wants Stonecutter from us. What do we hope and expect to get from him?"

"I have told him that we want a thousand gold pieces as a down payment, and a pledge, plus his co-operation in future operations."

"And what do we really want?"

"I want his head," said Wen Chang simply.

There was a little silence. "I see what you mean," said Kasimir at last, "about the danger."

"Yes; about that. Understand, Kasimir, that I would not ask this of you if I thought the part I wanted you to play was truly suicidal. But I will think none the less of you if you—"

"Oh, yes, you would." The physician got to his feet. "That's all right. I, on my part, would think something the less of myself if, having come this far, I were to fail to see this matter through to a conclusion. Tell me what you want me to do."

The Magistrate, smiling and obviously relieved, leaned

forward to exchange a firm handclasp with his younger associate. Then he sat back in his chair.

"Seldom have I made any plan for the express purpose of killing someone. But I think that in this case it is essential. I have already spoken to Almagro on this matter and he sees no objection. I have spoken also to Lieutenant Komi, as Prince al-Farabi's deputy, and he agrees with me. You and I will have help—but so will the Juggler, who has obviously recruited people from the underworld of Eylau."

"I am sure our allies are at least as capable as his. Tell me what you want me to do."

"You will have a special part to play tonight. You will carry to our meeting with Valamo a wrapped bundle of the proper size and shape to persuade him that we are indeed bringing the Sword. He insists on seeing it at our first meeting, before our negotiations are carried any further. There are good reasons why I cannot undertake to play the part of the Sword-carrier myself, but be assured that I shall be nearby."

"I had assumed you would be."

"Almagro and Komi and myself, with additional help, are going to be as close as we can. But we cannot guarantee your safety should our enemy become suspicious."

"Which he can hardly fail to be. But I understand. I tell you I mean to see this business through."

At this point Lieutenant Komi appeared at the head of the stairs. The officer was carrying under one arm a weighty bundle, definitely the wrong shape for a Sword. When this was placed on a table and unwrapped, it proved to be a mail shirt, the steel links as finely wrought as any Kasimir had ever seen.

"This is for you to wear tonight, sir," Komi informed Kasimir, somewhat grimly.

"Indeed. Under the conditions, I think I will not refuse."

In response to Kasimir's questions, the officer informed

him that the garment belonged to Prince al-Farabi himself, but Komi did not think his master would mind its being loaned out in the present circumstances. Komi also stated that the mesh of the shirt, magically reinforced, was so fine and tough that it ought to be able to turn the point of even the sharpest poniard.

While Kasimir was preparing to try the garment on, he asked Wen Chang curiously: "How did you manage to establish communications with Valamo?"

"Only indirectly, and with considerable difficulty." The Magistrate was spreading out a coarsely woven, dull-brown cloth almost the size of a blanket upon the largest table in the apartment. Kasimir's view of this operation was cut off for a moment as Komi helped him pull the mail shirt over his head; then he could see the Magistrate holding up a sword in a plain leather sheath.

"Also borrowed," he said, "from our friend the Prince." The weapon had a brown wooden hilt and an ornate guard; its overall size looked the same as Stonecutter's, but no one able to get a good look could mistake this blade for one of the Twelve forged by a god.

Wen Chang put the sword on the table and began to bundle it up carefully in the brown cloth.

Kasimir asked: "Do we expect the Juggler to accept his treasure without taking a close look at it?"

"We expect, if all goes well, to complete our business with him before he has had a chance to do so." The Magistrate tied his bundle lightly shut and stood back, surveying the effect. Then he hoisted it in one hand, as if testing the weight. "As long as the bundle remains closed the likeness is certainly good enough."

"Where is the meeting scheduled to take place, and when?"

"The time is tonight. The place is the small bazaar at the end of the Street of the Leatherworkers. Rather, that is where you are to carry the Sword, and await further instructions."

"I suppose I am to go alone?"

The Magistrate shot him a glance of amusement, tempered with concern. "You would be willing to do that? No, fortunately our rivals in this matter are too realistic to demand any such foolish behavior on our part. You will have two companions when you arrive at the bazaar, and for some time thereafter. We must expect that at some point an attempt will be made to separate you, the sword-bearer, from your escort."

Kasimir sighed. "Naturally I suppose we must expect treachery from the other side."

No one bothered to answer that. Komi was making certain adjustments in the shirt, which hung with a depressing weight upon Kasimir's shoulders.

"And speaking of treachery," Kasimir insisted, "how do we plan to effect our own?"

"The details of that must wait upon events," said Wen Chang. "Your responsibilities will be, first, to carry this." The brown-cloth bundle was thrust suddenly into Kasimir's grip. "Second, to take direction from me; and third, should that no longer be possible, to use your own wits to the best advantage possible."

Two hours after sunset, flanked by the Magistrate and a sturdy Firozpur sergeant, Kasimir was standing at the south end of the Street of the Leatherworkers, where an intersection with two other busy though narrow thoroughfares had created a square of modest size. One of the city's innumerable open-air markets had grown up in the space thus made available, and was doing a thriving business on this evening, despite the occasional brisk shower and the threat of a real downpour conveyed by heavy background thunder. Again Kasimir found himself in a part of the city no more than a hundred meters, he estimated, from the Tungri and the energetic life that clustered around the river and the docks.

"Why did you decide to give this thing to me to carry?" he asked in a low voice, turning his head slightly toward the Magistrate, who stood at his right hand. "Not that I am unwilling—but I should have thought you'd prefer to have it in hand yourself."

"At the most crucial moments of negotiation," said Wen Chang, "I prefer to have both hands free. Also I chose you because I consider you—after myself—the most quick-witted person available . . . ah. Here, if I am not mistaken, comes our next contact."

An urchin only a little older and bigger than the child who had carried Natalia's message was approaching them steadily through the random traffic of bodies in the bazaar. His eyes were fixed on Kasimir, who held the sword-shaped bundle in his hands. In a moment, as soon as the boy was sure that Kasimir was watching him, he turned sharply and led the way down Leatherworkers' Street.

"Slowly and calmly," said Wen Chang. "After him."

Moving single file with Kasimir in the lead, his bundle held tightly under his left arm, the three men followed.

They were led beneath the flaring oil lamps of Leather-workers' Street, and into another bazaar at the other end of the short, crooked thoroughfare. Kasimir, glancing up just as they reached this second marketplace, saw something that almost made him stumble—a small, dark shadow flitting just above the brightness of the nearest lamp. It had to be one of Komi's—or someone's—winged messengers. The lieutenant must be nearby, and must be somehow trying to use one of the creatures to follow their progress through the maze of streets.

On entering the second bazaar their youthful guide had suddenly turned aside, darted under one of the vendors' carts, and in an instant disappeared from view. It was not to be thought of that men of affairs carrying a Sword would follow him in this maneuver; the trio came to an uncertain halt, watching and waiting for further instructions.

The smells of dough frying, and of meat and peppers roasting on a skewer, enlivened the air here. Somewhere in the background, men clapped hands to the rhythm of a drum, and female dancers whirled in torchlight. A small caravan of laden loadbeasts urged other traffic momentarily out of the way of their slow progress.

Then, unexpectedly, their guide was back, walking out of the kaleidoscopic churn of moving bodies, coming from the direction of the dancers. This time the urchin moved past the three men purposefully, and walked straight on through the outer gateway of a low stone building at the start of the next street. Once inside the gate he paused, looking back just long enough to make sure they were following. Then he walked on into the building's courtyard.

The Firozpur sergeant, hand on his swordhilt, followed. At Wen Chang's gesture Kasimir followed two or three paces behind the sergeant; and he could hear Wen Chang's soft footsteps coming along at an equal distance behind him.

The open passage leading into the courtyard went round a right-angled corner, so that now the busy street was out of sight. The torchlit enclosure in which they found themselves was small, no more than five meters square, closed on three sides by the mortared stone walls of a low building, each wall containing one or two heavily barred windows. There was one door, even more impressively fortified, in one of the walls. Save for themselves, the courtyard was empty. Kasimir caught only the briefest glimpse of their guide, small bare feet vanishing onto the roof at the top of a fragile-looking drainpipe.

"Now," said a sepulchral voice, moderately loud, speaking from within the darkness inside the barred window on Kasimir's right. Nerves triggered by the sound, he spun that way.

"Show us," added a tenor from the window that was now behind him. He turned again, seeing Wen Chang and the Firozpur sergeant at his sides turning more slowly.

"The Sword," concluded a voice that Kasimir had heard once before, in the courtyard of his own inn. This time it came from within the window Kasimir had originally been facing.

Kasimir held up the weighty bundle.

"Unwrap it," ordered the central voice, its owner still invisible behind a protective grille.

"Not so fast," interposed Wen Chang. "We should like to know who we are dealing with. And that our path of retreat out of this courtyard is still secure."

"Stay where you are," said the Juggler's voice. "Show me the real Sword, and you will be able to retreat fast enough."

"First you will identify yourself somehow." The voice of the Magistrate sounded as firm as that of a judge seated on the bench. "Or else this dealing proceeds no further."

There was a pause. Then something, a small, harmless-looking object came flying out of the darkness of the barred window to bounce at the feet of Kasimir. Looking down, he saw it was a juggler's ball. The energy of the small sphere's bounces died away, and it came to a full stop almost touching the toe of his right boot.

Kasimir glanced at Wen Chang, who shrugged and with a confident small gesture seemed to indicate that Kasimir should undo the bundle he was carrying. Kasimir hesitated marginally, then set one end of the wrapped sword on the ground, and pretended to be trying to untie the cord that held the wrappings together. He could only assume that

Wen Chang would manage some interruption at the last second.

The sounds of the bazaar, the music of people blithely indifferent to villainy, drifted into the three-sided enclosure.

"Hurry, get on with it!" the voice of Tadasu Hazara urged, from out of darkness.

"I'm trying," Kasimir protested, endeavoring to sound irritated rather than frightened. "These knots—"

"Cut them!"

From somewhere, almost lost in the noise of the open street behind Kasimir, a low whistle sounded. In the next instant, as if coincidentally, Wen Chang stepped forward to give Kasimir a hand. "Here, let me."

Kasimir let go and stepped back—and recoiled as from the murderous lunge of a madman. Wen Chang had grabbed up the bundle, still tied shut as it was, and lunged with it straight against the white stone wall in front of him.

There was a minor thunderclap of impact. Wen Chang drew back his arms and thrust again with the concealed blade, slashing and sawing with demonic energy. Stones and their fragments burst from the wall, showering and bruising the astonished Kasimir, while the hammerlike sounds of Stonecutter rose into the night.

Inside each of the three dark rooms behind the window bars, pandemonium burst out. Someone fired a crossbow bolt out of the window at the right, a dart that by some sheer good luck missed the Firozpur sergeant, who was near its line of flight. Kasimir was not quite so lucky. The impact, just under his right armpit, felt like that of an oaken club swung in a giant's fist, and for a moment he staggered off balance.

Now there were cries and the clash of weapons in the rear of the central room, from which the Juggler's voice had sounded. Someone was beating down a door back there, and torchlight shone through, even as a section of the front wall went down before Wen Chang's continuing assault with the Sword. The inside of the room was suddenly open to inspection, but Valamo was gone.

Kasimir looked down at the pavement near his feet; the crossbow bolt was lying there, a wicked-looking dart whose needle point was barely tipped with red. His own red blood. The physician put a hand under his outer shirt and felt the fine mesh of the heavy mail beneath; there in one place the perfect pattern of the links was slightly strained and broken. There was a wound in his bruised flesh, but it was superficial.

And now armed men were swarming everywhere. It appeared that most of Valamo's support had evaporated on the spot. An outcry went up; that gentleman himself had just been spotted trying to get away over the rooftops.

Inside the otherwise barren room from which the Juggler had been speaking, there was a ladder and a trapdoor. Kasimir, halfway up, saw Wen Chang, still on the ground, throw the Sword, still wrapped, up on the roof ahead of him, where presumably some trusted figure was waiting to take it in charge and keep it safe.

And now the Magistrate was on the roof himself, leading the pursuit, shouting: "We must not let him escape!"

The pursuit led in the direction of the river.

The buildings in the neighborhood were mostly low, the streets more often than not mere pedestrian alleys, narrow enough for an active man moving at rooftop level to leap them with a bound. Kasimir's wound did not much trouble him, and he forgot about it once he was caught up in the excitement of the chase.

The moon, perversely from the point of view of the fugitive, was now out, near full and very bright. The broken clouds that would have dimmed its light seemed to avoid it wholly. The figure that must be the Juggler was moving on, leaping and running, in the direction of the river, keeping half a roof ahead of the nearest pursuer.

Kasimir was gaining ground slowly. In a moment the man, one of the Watch, who had been closest to the fleeing Valamo tried to jump too broad a gap, and disappeared with a cry of despair.

Now Kasimir himself was closest to the enemy. Glancing off to one side, he was astounded to catch a glimpse of someone else running in the night, moving away from Valamo rather than toward him, and carrying some object. Light, timing, and distance were all against Kasimir, but he thought that he might have just seen Natalia. Or perhaps it was only that he expected to see her now in every scene of action.

He had no time now to try to puzzle the matter out. The river was very near ahead; the quarry was being brought to bay.

Someone's slung stone whizzed past Valamo's head; the shot had been too difficult in moonlight. The white-haired figure turned on a parapet, two stories above the water's edge. Kasimir, running up, knew that he was going to be too late. There were men rowing a small boat in the stream just under the place where the Juggler perched, men who called up to him with urgent voices.

Valamo turned toward Kasimir, and made a graceful gesture of obscenity. The acrobat's body crouched, then lunged out in an expert dive that ought to land it in the water just beside the boat.

Running out of shadows, the figure of Wen Chang appeared beside the leaping man at the last instant. Moonlight glinted on the faint streak of a bright rapier.

The Juggler's body, pierced, contorted in the air. A choked cry sounded in the night. The graceful dive became an awkward, tumbling splash into the river.

Wen Chang, panting with the long chase, his own sword still in his hand, stood watching beside Kasimir. No one saw the submerged man come up.

CHAPTER 17

BEFORE nightfall Wen Chang, Kasimir, and Komi had made their way wearily back to the inn. Kasimir's wound—an ugly bruise, and minor laceration—was throbbing, and at his direction his companions helped him wash it, then took salves from his medical kit and applied them. Wen Chang needed no directions to apply a professional-looking bandage. Kasimir was still functional, doing as well as could be expected.

Meanwhile Komi had retreated below to look after his men, and the Magistrate had ordered food brought to the upper room. While he and Kasimir were eating they conversed.

"I cannot believe that I had Stonecutter in my hand and lost it." Kasimir was loud with growing anger.

Wen Chang did not reply.

"It was you yourself who took it from me. You who passed it on to someone else."

Still no answer.

"Magistrate, I saw you wrap a fake Sword in a bundle. Then you gave the package to me. But later the Sword in the bundle was genuine. I saw it, in your hands, hack to bits a wall of solid stone. I heard the sound of its magic as it did so. The Sword I was carrying was genuine, and I am sure you knew it."

Wen Chang appeared to be meditating.

"I know you are the real Wen Chang, and I cannot believe that the real Wen Chang is a criminal."

At last the narrow gaze turned back to Kasimir. "Thank you." The words sounded sincere, and curiously subdued.

"Then, am I going mad? Or is it not your objective, after all, to get the Sword and return it to its rightful owner?"

"That is my objective," said the Magistrate stiffly, for the first time sounding offended. "I have undertaken it as sincerely as any commitment in my life."

"Then—" Kasimir made a helpless gesture. "Then I am at a loss. If I am to be of any further use to you, I must know what is going on. Was the seeming appearance of the real Sword some result of magic? But no, you do not like to use magic, do you?"

"Magic is not the tool I prefer. Kasimir, if you cannot see what is going on, now is not the time for me to tell you. For your own good, if my efforts should fail."

"Then tell me this at least. Are there magic powers, a curse, arrayed against us? The Sword comes almost into my hands, again and again, and then it flies away—generally into the hands of that woman."

"There is no curse upon us that I know of. We face no overwhelming magic." Wen Chang drank tea from a mug and put it down. "I have heard that the Sword Coinspinner moves itself about freely, refusing to be bound by any merely human attempts at confinement, whether by means of solid walls or of spells. I have not heard that about Stonecutter, or any of the other Swords."

"Then what is the explanation? All I can see clearly is that Stonecutter's gone again," Kasimir declared, in what sounded more like an indictment of Fate than a lament. "You wrapped an imitation in a bundle here; and when I unwrapped the same bundle there, the Sword inside was genuine. I can imagine no nonmagical explanation for that."

Unless, of course, Kasimir's thought went on, *you substituted the real Sword for the imitation by some sleight of hand. You could have done that easily enough. I wasn't really watching. But that means you had the real Sword here, and didn't . . .*

No, Kasimir told himself firmly. That would make no sense at all. The Magistrate himself was trustworthy, if anyone was. He, Kasimir, had committed himself to that.

Unless . . .

"If it was true that we were faced by some overwhelming magic," said Wen Chang, as if he were calmly unaware of all that might be going through Kasimir's mind, "impossible for us to understand or overcome, then there would not be much point in worrying. However that may be, I am going to get some sleep while I have the chance, and I suggest you do the same."

Kasimir was on the verge of pointing out that more than half of the Magistrate's twenty-four-hour grace period had now elapsed, but he decided that would be useless, and took himself back to his couch. The salves were working, and his wound pained him hardly at all. He dozed off hoping that enlightenment might come in dreams.

But this time there were no dreams. It seemed to Kasimir that he had barely closed his eyes, when he was awakened by a remote pounding, as of mailed fists or heavy weapon-hilts upon some lower portal of the inn. Groaning and cursing his way back to full wakefulness, he rubbed his eyes. By the time the sound of boots ascending the stairs became plain, Kasimir was sitting up and groping for his boots.

A few moments after that, Lieutenant Komi, also freshly awakened, was at the door of the upper suite. "A robbery attempt is reported at the Blue Temple," the officer informed Kasimir tersely. "It seems certain that the Sword of Siege was used."

Kasimir groaned. "An attempt, you say? Was it successful?"

"It doesn't sound like it to me. But the messengers didn't really tell me one way or the other." Komi glanced down the narrow stairs. "Naturally, you and the Magistrate are needed at the Blue Temple at once. The Hetman commands it personally."

"Of course. All right, we'll go. Give us one minute. And get your men up and ready for action. We're probably going to need them again, though for what I don't know."

"They'll be ready before you are."

Wen Chang was sleeping as peacefully as an infant when Kasimir intruded upon the inner chamber to bring him the news. But he woke up with a minimum of fuss, and gave no indication of surprise at this latest development.

Everything was soon in readiness. The trip on ridingbeasts through the evening streets was uneventful. This time the Hetman had sent a larger escort, and the level of their courtesy was noticeably less.

When they came in sight of the Blue Temple, Kasimir beheld a swarm of people, many of them bearing torches or lanterns, gathered at one corner of the fortresslike edifice. The High Priest Theodore himself was present, to grab Wen Chang by the sleeve as soon as he had dismounted, and attempt to hustle him forward like a common criminal.

But somehow the hustling was not to be accomplished in that fashion. Wen Chang remained standing where he was, erect and dignified, while the priest stumbled, slightly off balance, as he moved away, and had to recover his own dignity as best he could.

A confused babble of accusing voices rose. Kasimir, now that he could get a good look at the corner of the massive wall, had to admit that it certainly did look as if the Sword had been used on it. Carvings had been made in the stone blocks, deep and narrow cuts that must have required a very sharp, tough tool. And there on the pavement below the cutting were the expected fragments of stone.

Kasimir picked up one of these fragments and held it close to someone's torch. There was no mistaking those smoothly striated markings—yes, the Sword of Siege had really been here, and had been used against this wall.

"It looks," said Kasimir, "as if Natalia's gang isn't going to be easily discouraged."

The Blue Temple priests, as they were not slow in explaining, had an extra reason to be upset. They had been spending time and effort, and presumably even money, in an effort to have their walls rendered proof by opposing magic against the powers of Stonecutter. All this had now proven to have been time and effort—and money—wasted.

Komi said: "The thieves must have been frightened off by a patrol or something, before they could dig in very far."

Wen Chang nodded soberly. "But I wonder how far they fled when they were frightened off?"

"What do you mean?" the Director of Security demanded of him sharply.

"Has it occurred to anyone here that the same band of thieves, armed with the same Sword, might even now be at work beneath our feet? Tunneling out of reach and sight of ordinary patrols, or other defensive measures. Intent upon creating their own entrances to the treasure vaults below?"

This was of course said in full hearing of the High Priest and other Blue Temple officials. They immediately dropped their angry attempt at confrontation with the Magistrate, and began to cast about in search of some way of meeting this new threat. One man immediately went down on all fours to put his ear to the pavement. In a moment almost a dozen people, including the Magistrate himself, were doing the same thing.

Kasimir also gave that tactic a try. But he gave it up in a

matter of moments, unable to convince himself that he was really able to hear anything that way.

Others were having more success. One of the relatively minor temple officials was certain that he could detect the sounds of steady digging. Presently two or three others were in agreement with him.

Wen Chang stood up, shaking his head, and said that he could give no firm opinion. His senses were growing old, he said, and were no longer to be absolutely depended upon.

There was some minor excitement as Prince al-Farabi, accompanied by a couple of mounted retainers, came galloping up. He had come, the Prince said, as soon as he had heard the news of the attempted robbery.

He, at least, continued to address Wen Chang with great respect. "What are we to do, Magistrate?"

The investigator stroked his beard. He said, "If it is possible to pin down the direction of these underground sounds more precisely, starting a countermine might be one useful tactic."

Several people took up the suggestion at once. The numbers of low-ranking workers present had been growing steadily, as first one official and then another took it upon himself to order some further mobilization; and now a call went up for digging implements.

Meanwhile the party of dignitaries, some of them keeping an eye on the two investigators as if afraid they might try to escape, adjourned by more or less common consent to inside the temple. There they descended in a body into one of the deeper treasure vaults, and here again there was much listening, with ears now applied to walls.

More lights were called for, and soon supplied, so that even the darker corners of the many underground rooms could be illuminated. More guards were called for too, though it seemed to Kasimir that the place was inconveniently crowded with armed men already.

By this time someone—Kasimir was certain only that it was neither himself nor Wen Chang—had suggested that the robbers' new plan might not be to dig a tunnel at all, but rather to undermine an entire section of the building, so that walls, roof, and everything would collapse suddenly, in a cloud of dust and a pile of rubble. In this disaster and the ensuing confusion, the suggestion was, there would be little to prevent the brigands' bursting up from underground like so many moles, and looting to their hearts' content.

Theodore was trying simultaneously to counter this and other perceived threats. He had another problem, in that his vaults were crowded with authorities and aides from several organizations and of all ranks, from a head of state on down; and each authority, wanting to make his presence known, had something to say. Already a swarm of laborers armed with picks and shovels were—presumably on someone's orders—descending into the lower vaults to begin the task of opening the floors there and getting the countermining under way. Some other leader, driven into a frenzy by this invasion of the sacred precincts, was trying to organize a force of clerks and junior priests to move some of the musty piles of wealth elsewhere. Still others were trying to delay this tactic, until they could come to an agreement on where the treasure would be safest.

In the midst of all this turmoil, Mistress Hedmark and one of her aides appeared. They had come down from their quarters near the gem room to see what was going on; terrible rumors had reached them up there, and there had been nothing to do but see for themselves.

The suspicion crossed Kasimir's mind that Mistress Hedmark might now actually have the Sword in her possession, and that she and the Blue Temple had worked all this wall-carving, and the rumors of tunnels, as a distraction to keep suspicion from themselves. Somehow the situation had that kind of feeling to it. But Kasimir had not a shred of evidence, and he kept his wild theories to himself for the present.

Meanwhile Wen Chang, as might have been expected, was maintaining his calm amid all this confusion. The flurry of accusation against him and his partners had died down now; but when, as still happened now and then, someone blamed him to his face for being responsible, he answered mildly if at all.

As the hours of the night dragged by, nothing at all seemed certain to Kasimir any longer, except that the robbers had not yet managed to cut their way into the temple. Beyond that he had more or less given up trying to keep track of the theories and fears regarding where the blow was likely to fall, and the various efforts to forestall it. Instead he sought out a quiet corner where a pile of empty treasure sacks offered a reasonably soft couch. Relaxing, his back against a wall, the young physician entered a period of intense thought. Or tried to do so; the effort was made no easier by all the noise and activity around him.

When he saw Wen Chang moving quietly toward an exit, he followed. Outside the temple the air was much cooler and easier to breathe. Others, seeing Wen Chang and Kasimir go out, followed suspiciously.

But the Magistrate gave no sign of trying to get away. He looked at the moon, full and near setting now, and breathed of the damp air, and stretched his arms.

Kasimir sat down again, and before he knew it he was drifting into sleep . . .

Something, perhaps it was revelation, came to Kasimir in a dream. And suddenly he understood much that had been hidden from him. He awoke with a start, having the impression that someone had been shaking him. No one had, unless it were possibly his own Muse.

What a damned fool he had been.

Somewhere beyond the tall buildings of the city, the sun had definitely come up.

And, shortly after dawn on this first day of the Festival, another urgent summons arrived for Wen Chang and his associate. This one came directly from the palace, and the face of the messenger who brought it was ashen in the early light. His master the Hetman must indeed be in a rage.

Benjamin of the Steppe had just managed to escape from his cell in the palace. The delegation going to his cell to bring him out for execution had found the chamber empty. A tunnel originating somewhere outside the building had been cut neatly up through the stone floor. There was not the least doubt that the Sword had been used.

The Magistrate, having been apprised of all these facts, turned and repeated them calmly to those who were standing nearest to him—Kasimir, Almagro, and Lieutenant Komi. To Kasimir, Wen Chang's face now appeared wooden with fatigue. With his new insight, he tried but failed to read something more in it than that.

As for Kasimir himself, he did not trouble to hide his feelings particularly. This struck him as the first piece of good news they had heard in some time. Komi appeared to feel the same way.

Almagro on the other hand was professionally cautious and gloomy.

There was no time now for anything like a private conference. The Hetman had sent a carriage for the people he wanted, and the Magistrate and his three associates piled into it.

As the news brought by the Hetman's messenger spread among the dignitaries gathered in and around the Blue Temple, it had the effect of bringing their weary efforts against robbery to a halt. Indeed, it required only a moment of detached thought to see that little or nothing useful was being accomplished anyway. Priests and clerks and guards looked at each other blankly in the dawn, seeking answers that were not to be found in the faces of others as weary as themselves.

Some of the more important of these people found the energy to decide to follow the carriage to the palace.

The High Priest himself did not go to the palace. He was handed a message which he read, frowning with thought, then tucked inside his garments.

He announced that he had too much to do here in trying to put his own house in order, the house of Croesus and the other gods and goddesses of wealth.

Inside the carriage, jolting along swiftly on its way to the Hetman's house, no one had much of anything to say. There were only the sounds of the swift ride.

When their conveyance turned into the square before the palace, Kasimir observed the gallows standing empty in the dawn, the new wood of the construction still damp from the recent rains. The carriage was forced now to slow down, because the plaza was so crowded with people. Of course, a mob would have gathered to see the hanging. Kasimir wondered if now some other victim would have to be found to take the place of Benjamin. He could not entirely avoid the thought that he himself might, before the morning was over, find himself being escorted up those new wooden stairs.

Such was the crush of would-be spectators near the empty scaffold that the carriage had to come almost to a halt. Putting his head out a window, Kasimir got the impression that the crowd was in a lighthearted mood, not too much downcast by the lack of an execution. He supposed that news of the dramatic escape, and the accompanying official discomfiture, provided compensation. Also there might have been an undercurrent of support for Benjamin that would cause people to view this outcome as an even happier one.

Now some mounted patrolmen of the Watch were starting to disperse the throng, and presently the carriage was able to move on. Kasimir, bringing his head in from the window, caught Wen Chang gazing at the scaffold, and there appeared in the Magistrate's eye something of the same faint twinkle Kasimir had noticed when last they passed through this square. This time Kasimir thought he understood, but he said nothing.

The rear gates of the palace opened promptly for the official carriage, and in a few moments its occupants were disembarking within the walls. Very soon thereafter they were all in the main building, being escorted single file up a flight of narrow and very utilitarian stone stairs. The odor of a prison, reminding Kasimir of animal pens and primitive surgery, began to engulf them.

Presently the stairs brought the ascending party to a heavy door, and beyond the door they entered a dark corridor lined with tiny cells. From some of the barred doors the faces of inmates looked out, their expressions variations on madness, fear, and hope.

The four men who had come in the carriage were ushered into one of the cells, already crowded with official bodies. Some already present, who were of lesser ranks, had to vacate the cell before the four newcomers could get in. Voices on all sides demanded that they confront the evidence of their failure.

Now Kasimir was able to see for himself just how the escape had been accomplished. Several officials were pointing out to him and to Wen Chang, as if they might not be able to see for themselves, the fact of a dark, irregular opening in the stone floor. The hole was only half a meter in diameter or a little more, and people getting in and out through it must have undergone something of a squeeze.

The tunnel, as several officials were now explaining simultaneously and unnecessarily, had been started at some distance from the palace, and dug up unerringly to this point through both bedrock and masonry. Actually its other end had already been discovered; the passage had its beginning in the curving wall of one of the great municipal drains that ran right beneath the plaza, a good many meters outside the palace walls.

And there was more the failed investigators had to be shown; the demonstration of outrage was not yet complete. Perhaps, thought Kasimir, it was only getting started. And so far the Hetman himself had not even put in an appearance.

"Look here! Look here!" someone was barking at him.

Now one of the palace officials had brought out an Old World light, a kind of hand lantern, and was directing a bright white beam down into the dark aperture in the floor. In the unwavering brightness Kasimir was easily able to see the distinctive, inescapably familiar little markings left in the freshly carved-out surface of the tunnel's wall. Here was proof—if any proof was needed beyond the mere existence of the tunnel—that Stonecutter must have been used to make it.

For the moment the young man was able to ignore the personal difficulties this tunnel was likely to create for him. He could only marvel, silently but wholeheartedly, at the daring of the project, and at the amount of intense, hurried work it had required.

By now Kasimir had seen enough of the projects accomplished with the Sword to realize that the actual cutting of stone, so easy with the aid of Stonecutter's magic, had been only the beginning of this job. Here all the work had to be done inside a long, narrow tunnel, and all the debris cleared out through the original tunnel entrance, a task that grew more difficult the longer the passage became. The diggers must have shed liters of sweat in the course of this job, and doubtless some blood as well, handling the sharp rock and crawling through piles of it. Pausing for frequent measurements, someone in the rescue party must have known the shape and the dimensions of the prison very well. And they had been working against a deadline.

When had the digging started? Doubtless very soon after the Sword had changed hands there in the Red Temple. Kasimir thought that he could see the history of it now. Right after Natalia and her people had got away with Stonecutter right under the noses of a score or so of guards and priests. Not to mention one very inept young investigator.

Ignoring the continuous babble of accusation that surrounded them both, Kasimir cast a sharp, probing glance at his mentor. Wen Chang's smoothly composed features gave little indication of either the fatigue or the emotions that must be behind them. Still, Kasimir, who was beginning to know his man, thought that he could detect certain subtle signs of—satisfaction.

A hush fell suddenly within the cell. The Hetman himself had come upon the scene at last, and was now standing in the doorway, an aperture so narrow that, even had there been room for him inside the cell, he might have thought twice before attempting to push his corpulent body through.

"What is your answer to this, O great investigator?"

The ruler's question was delivered with what was obviously intended to be scathing sarcasm.

But Wen Chang imperturbably refused to be scathed. "I am not required to have an answer for this, sir. I was never engaged to prevent the prisoner's escaping, therefore his deliverance is not my responsibility."

"Oh, is it not? Well, in any case he is not going to get away for long." The Hetman wiped sweat from his face with a silken cloth. "He could have had at most a few minutes' start before his absence was discovered. And once the discovery was made, the warden acted with commendable speed, notifying the Watch at all the gates of the city by winged messenger. Every man who leaves Eylau is being identified, and every vehicle that departs the city by land or water is being thoroughly searched."

The Magistrate bowed, slightly but graciously. "In that event it would seem that Your Excellency has no cause for concern."

The Hetman's round countenance darkened. But just as it seemed to Kasimir that his learned associate had finally managed to talk himself into serious trouble, a rescuer appeared. The voice of Prince al-Farabi was heard in the corridor outside the cell.

Naturally the Hetman had to turn away from the cell door to greet his peer. Then a moment later he had to move courteously out of the way of the Prince, who was expressing a desire to see the inside of the cell.

A moment later al-Farabi, now accompanied by a couple of his own men as bodyguards, came into the cell loudly proclaiming his wish to behold with his own eyes the evidence that the missing Sword had indeed been here within these very palace walls, only a few hours ago. Perhaps only a single hour!

But the moment his eye fell upon Wen Chang, the Prince broke off these lamentations. In a quite different voice he demanded: "What hope is there of Stonecutter's return?"

The Magistrate began a reassuring answer. But, as soon as it was apparent that the answer would not be simple and direct, half a dozen other voices, angry and weary, broke in on him, and drowned him out. Above all the others rose the near-shout of the Blue Temple's Director of Security.

"If you, O famed Magistrate, who are credited with the power to see into the secret places of the heart, to sift out the honest from the evil-doer—if you had recovered the Sword before now, in accordance with your pledge, then this would not have happened!"

Wen Chang faced the man coolly. "As I have said before, sir, this prisoner's escape was not my responsibility."

"But you are responsible for what you promise. And you did promise to have the Sword for us by now, or at the very least to give us some definite word as to its whereabouts. Very well, sir, I now hold you to your word. Where is the Sword?"

"Sir, your demand is premature. I was granted twenty-four hours of free action, and that period is not quite over yet. I still have hopes of being able to recover the Sword—not for you but for the rightful owner—before the time expires."

At these words, calmly uttered, a stir ran through the little crowd filling the cell.

Wen Chang now turned to look out into the corridor, addressing the Hetman directly. "Your Excellency must admit that the objective to which you yourself assigned the highest priority, the safeguarding of the Blue Temple and the other centers of great wealth within the city, has been accomplished."

"You claim credit for that, do you?"

"I neither claim credit nor refuse it, sir. I merely call attention to the fact."

The Hetman glanced toward the Prince. He wiped sweat from his face again. "Yes, I must admit that. And you say there is still hope of recovering the Sword?" The first rush of his anger had passed now, and he sounded wistful, wanting to believe.

"Yes sir, certainly there is at least hope. Perhaps there is even a good chance . . . you have said that you already know where the other end of this tunnel is, gentlemen. I intend to go there myself, without further delay."

In a moment Wen Chang had shed his dignity entirely, and was lowering himself feetfirst into the dark and narrow opening in the floor.

"Hah!" was the comment of the Blue Temple's Director

of Security, delivered in a tone of loud derision. But having said that much he did not know what else to add.

Everyone else—except for Kasimir, who was preparing to follow his leader—stood motionless and silent, watching Wen Chang's descent and disappearance. Only a moment after the Magistrate was out of sight, Kasimir was waist-deep in the hole himself, and rapidly working his way lower.

The young man, chin at floor level now, groped below him with his toe for the next foothold—there it was. You really had to go down feetfirst, because climbing down headfirst for any distance would be impossibly awkward. And if the tunnel was this narrow through its whole length, as seemed likely, there wouldn't be any place to turn around.

Now the walls of the tunnel wall had swallowed him completely, the cell he had just left was somewhere overhead. Renewed argument had broken out up there, and now he could hear sounds indicating that someone else was following him down. He trusted that whoever it was would avoid stepping on his head, as he was doing his best to avoid treading on the Magistrate's.

The descent took a long time, and was full of turns and twists, vertical drops alternating with horizontal stretches. That the tunnel was a long one came as no surprise to Kasimir. The diggers would have had to begin operations a fair distance away; they would have needed a secure place, a place where they could drop a lot of displaced rock without hauling it any farther to avoid undue attention.

Now Wen Chang had reached the end. He was calling encouraging words back to his assistant in a soft voice, from somewhere not far ahead. And the darkness in the tunnel around Kasimir was beginning to moderate. In another few moments his feet came out into empty space, and then he had emerged.

He found himself standing on a narrow catwalk, that ran beside a deep drain through a rounded subterranean vault. A steady breeze, cool but decidedly foul-smelling, blew through the larger tunnel. The scene was rendered visible by a wan illumination that washed down through small patches of grillwork set at wide intervals into the stone vaulting overhead. The pattern and spacing of that grillwork was somehow familiar; Kasimir decided that they must be underneath a part of the plaza that surrounded the Hetman's palace.

A rat went scurrying away along the narrow ledge on the far side of the drain. Just at the place where the narrow escape tunnel came out of the wall, the flow in the main drain was partially blocked, so that it ran in a series of miniature waterfalls and rapids. The cause of the blockage was several tons of rock, all in pieces of modest size, an impressive pile of sliced-up and displaced minerals, including building-stone, that had been dumped here by the hurried rescuers.

Wen Chang, standing close beside Kasimir upon the narrow ledge, was squinting thoughtfully up and down the gloomy tunnel of the drain. Now from somewhere in his pockets the Magistrate pulled forth yet another Old World light, this one no bigger than a finger, and began to use it.

"In that direction, of course," he remarked, jiggling his little beam of light downstream, "all of these city drains must empty into the Tungri. And almost directly above us, just over here, must be the palace—yes, I think I am sufficiently well oriented now."

Scraping and grunting noises were issuing from the mouth of the little escape tunnel. In a moment these were followed by a set of legs and feet, garbed in the Hetman's military colors. Soon an officer of the palace guards was standing silently on the ledge, straightening his uniform and looking at Wen Chang and Kasimir with controlled suspicion.

"Ah," said Wen Chang to the newcomer. "You may reassure your master that my associate and I are not trying to escape—far from it. But never mind, here come others to see for themselves."

Another man who had been in the cell above was now grunting his way out through the last meter or two of the constricted tunnel. Scarcely had he found footing on the ledge when another came after him. Soon half a dozen, the most eminent of them Prince al-Farabi himself, were decorously jostling one another for position on the little shelf of masonry, meanwhile watching Wen Chang closely to see what he might be up to now. The group also included the Blue Temple's Director of Security.

"No one was coming down after you, sir?" the Magistrate inquiried of the last arrival, when the tunnel had been silent for a little while. "Good! Then we are ready!" And to Kasimir's surprise Wen Chang relieved the crowding on the ledge by jumping right down into the knee-deep stream. Splashing briskly to the other side in a few quick strides, he went scrambling nimbly up the opposite bank of stone.

Kasimir, after only the most momentary hesitation, followed. He did his best to look as if he knew exactly what his leader was doing. Privately he wondered, not for the first time, whether his leader might have gone quite mad.

Wen Chang had put away his pocket light. On reaching the catwalk on the other side of the drain, he paused just long enough to glance back once at the assembly he had just left. Then with an air of indifference, ignoring the cries for an explanation that came from behind, he started walking along the new ledge toward an intersection of drains not far away. Again Kasimir followed.

One after another, the other men came after them. It

was either that or stand waiting in a sewer for they knew not what, or else make the hard climb through the escape tunnel back to the cell.

Their subterranean progress, lighted by the Magistrate's Old World lamp, continued for some minutes. Then the small party came to an even greater branching of the ways. From here an even larger drain led on in the direction of the river, and a waterfall somewhere in that direction was large enough to sound a note of distant thunder.

Here, on a walkway large enough to accommodate a conference, Wen Chang called a temporary halt.

"From this point forward, gentlemen," he taxed them seriously, "he who accompanies me must remain as quiet as a ghost, say nothing, and follow my orders strictly as regards to noise and movement. He who splashes or mutters, whispers or sneezes—I hereby charge that man with full responsibility for our failure to regain that which we seek.

"Whoever cannot agree to these terms must turn back now."

There was silence as his audience looked at him stubbornly, challenging him to make good on his pledge.

Wen Chang was not perturbed. "Then all of you are with me? Good. Follow where I lead, and be as silent as the grave."

CHAPTER 18

A S soon as he had seen the Hetman's carriage depart hastily for the palace, the High Priest Theodore quickly turned away and issued urgent orders to a few of his most trusted associates.

Then he hurried into his temple, where a few necessary personal preparations had to be made. As soon as these had been completed he descended to the lowest level but one of his establishment, then hurried along a half-buried passageway in the direction of the river, passing numerous tired-looking guards as he progressed.

At a dock covered by its own roof and served by an artificial inlet of the river, the High Priest walked past a large ceremonial barge which was used very rarely, and stopped beside a much smaller launch, whose crew, having been sent word of his intentions, was already making ready to put out. Upon the wharf beside this vessel Theodore paced impatiently until a few more people arrived, men he wanted to bring with him on this venture. These sheltered docks were very handy for certain transactions in which the temple sometimes found itself engaged—deals involving some substantial bulk of cargo requiring to be moved in or out. Such goods could be much more readily and unobtrusively transported by water than by moving them in caravans that had to wind their way through all the streets of Eylau.

The Director of Security was notably absent on this occasion, but the High Priest thought that was probably just as well.

The launch had space for only four rowers on a side, and a half deck under which a few more men might lie concealed. Discussing these matters with the captain, Theodore nodded and gestured, and gave more orders.

A couple of minutes later he was standing near amidships in the launch, gliding across the open surface of the Tungri. River traffic was for the moment comparatively light. The face of the water was spotted with remnants of the morning mist that were rapidly being burned away by the sun. The launch in which he rode was, like the much greater barge, a brightly decorated, somewhat ostentatious craft, and was usually employed only during the Festival and on certain other rare occasions. But it had been the only boat quickly available. The fact that this was the first morning of the Festival might make its presence on the river less surprising to anyone who happened to observe it.

The note that Theodore had received just before the Magistrate's departure was still clutched in his right hand. He stood with eyes shaded under a light gold awning, holding lightly to one of its supports, impatiently scanning the fog-spotted river for any sign that any of the busy vessels in sight had any intention of approaching his launch.

The aide who crouched beside him repeated a doubt, voiced earlier, that the note the High Priest had received was genuine.

On his part the High Priest maintained that he could not afford to ignore any communication like this one. Thieves of some kind were certainly in possession of the Sword of Siege, and what was more logical and natural than that those thieves should seek to sell it at great profit to them-selves?

As for taking out the launch in this furtive way, of course it was essential to keep other people, who might take it into their heads to put in their own inconvenient claims, from knowing about the negotiations should the note prove an authentic offer.

Theodore looked down at the note once more, though by now he certainly had it learned by heart. It specified, in crude, block printing, in just what area of the river he was to cruise. He looked up sharply, making sure that the oarsmen were ordered at the proper moment to put about smartly and coast downstream for a while.

Meanwhile the three heavily armed men he had managed to conceal under the half deck were crouching there in awkward patience, now and then shifting their positions stealthily.

The High Priest had also brought with him on this voy-age a wizard, the best available at a moment's notice, but a man who was more a specialist in guarding treasure than anything else, so that Theodore had doubts of how useful he was going to be upon this mission.

And now, just when Theodore was beginning to suspect that the note might after all have been a hoax, the officer in command of the launch touched him quietly on the arm to get his attention. "My lord, someone on shore is signaling to us."

The officer was sufficiently discreet to refrain from point-ing, but in a moment Theodore, following the man's low-voiced directions, had caught sight of a dark gesturing fig-ure on shore, standing almost out of sight between two low abandoned-looking buildings.

The figure was hooded or masked, and dressed in some loose garment that made even the sex impossible to deter-mine at this distance. He—or she—was standing between two dilapidated buildings, and close above the broken outlet of one of the municipal drains, in such a position as to be practically invisible from anywhere but the narrow strip of water where the launch was cruising.

Farther inland, on the same side of the river, Theodore could see the palace, his own temple, and the tall Red Temple too, somewhat more distant.

Under the officer's direction, the launch was now being rowed toward the dock where the beckoning figure waited. When it had drawn within four or five boatlengths of that goal, the figure on shore suddenly moved a step forward and held up an imperious hand.

"Come no closer!" The voice was deep and throaty, but still, the High Priest thought, it was almost certainly that of a woman. "We must talk first. No closer, I tell you, or you'll not see Stonecutter today!" And the figure held up a Sword-shaped bundle where Theodore could see it.

It took an imperious gesture from the High Priest himself to make the officer and the rowers stop the boat; now the oarsmen were laboring to keep her more or less in the same place in the brisk current. Actually they were doing their job well for men who got so little chance to practice.

Theodore sent his most dominating voice toward the shore. "Is that really a Sword you have there? You must let me see it now, if we are to talk seriously."

Silently the figure holding the bundle shook the wrappings free, and let him see the Sword. Theodore, only a few meters distant, had no doubt that he was seeing the real thing.

But he was not going to admit that right away. "I must see it more closely."

The person who held the bare blade swung it, cutting deeply into the side of a stone bollard. The thudding sound of Vulcan's magic was clearly audible.

The wizard on the launch clutched Theodore by the arm, and spoke into his ear, quietly and unnecessarily affirming the genuineness of the article in question.

Theodore put the man aside impatiently.

"Very well," he called ashore. "I am convinced. Come aboard here and we will talk terms; we cannot treat of a matter so important while shouting back and forth like two street peddlers."

"No, my lord, I think not." Yes, it was definitely a woman's husky voice that issued from behind the mask. "Instead you must come ashore. Bring two men—no more—with you, if their presence will make you feel more comfortable."

"Where ashore?"

"Nowhere, most cautious man, but right here in sight of your boat, though she must retreat and wait for you no closer to the dock than she is now. Come, come, will you do business or not? I am taking a real risk. If you won't accept a tiny one that is no risk at all, I'm sure I can find another buyer who is less timid."

Theodore was frowning, but the offer really seemed fair enough to him. You had to expect that anyone who had the Sword to sell would want to take some precautions. He had to admit that the scoundrels had chosen the place well. Within a few paces of that tantalizing masked figure there could well be a dozen man-sized ratholes, openings in the dock or buildings, into any one of which a thief could easily vanish—or from which other criminals could perhaps come pouring out in case they were intending treachery.

Well, Theodore had some good men with him in the boat, and he would risk it. The sight of Stonecutter, almost within reach, was too much to let him reach any other conclusion.

"I accept your terms," called Theodore. Then, quite openly, he gave some final orders to the men who were to remain aboard the launch, and to the pair, newly emerged from under the half deck, who were going to precede him ashore, telling them to be alert, but to take no action except in case of treachery by the other side. He had already given them their secret orders, by which his own treachery would be implemented if and when he thought the chances of success were good, and the secret signal for which they were to watch.

The boat drew near the dock, and in a moment, the two bodyguards had hopped ashore, their own businesslike weapons drawn and ready. The High Priest followed, and then the launch, according to the agreement, eased out again to her previous position.

Theodore, as was his custom, was carrying with him quite a sizable sum in gold coin, plus a few valuable jewels. Quite likely, he thought, the amount he had with him would be enough to impress a small band of hungry robbers; though of course it was not anywhere near the true value of a treasure like the Blade.

Now he stood on the rough planking of the dock, facing the figure that still held the Sword.

The High Priest was flanked by his two bodyguards, good men both of them. If the slighter figure he confronted had any companions present, they had yet to show themselves.

"Let me hold the weapon myself," said Theodore to his counterpart who faced him. "I must be very sure."

He had expected an argument at least when he made this demand, and indeed the figure opposite seemed to hesitate momentarily. But then the cloth wrapping was cast aside, and the sheathed weapon was proffered hilt first.

Theodore reached for the hilt with both hands, and took the weighty treasure into his possession. He looked at the small white symbol on the hilt, a wedge splitting a block.

And, in that very moment when his full attention was on the Sword, the dark-clad woman who had given it to him turned and darted away, vanishing in an instant into a broken hole in the wooden side of the nearest building.

Theodore's bodyguards started and brandished their weapons—but there was no threat. There was only an empty dock before them, and the High Priest their master left standing with the treasure he had so craved in his hands.

Theodore could not doubt that the weapon he had been given was quite genuine. Then why had it been given him in such a—

There were sounds nearby, a buried stirring, footsteps, careless voices of a different quality than that of the bandit woman who had just left. Someone was about to appear on the scene. No doubt the bandit woman had been first to hear these newcomers approaching, and that explained her sudden disappearance.

Or might she have—

Whatever the reason Theodore now found himself in possession of the Sword, he could not decline the chance to keep it. He had only time to resheathe the blade and muffle Stonecutter under his long blue cape. His right hand was gripping the leather sheath near the middle, so that the pointed end of the blade made a stiff extension of his right arm. It was the best he could do at a moment's notice; no one would be able to see that he had the Sword as long as he could stand still with his long cape furled about him.

Only a heartbeat after Stonecutter had been made to disappear, Wen Chang and his physician-associate, with a surprising escort of notables after them, came popping up out of the opening atop a broken drain nearby. Theodore could only stare without comprehension at the sight of his own Director of Security emerging from the sewers as part of the same group. But the Director was not the highest rank accompanying Wen Chang; Prince al-Farabi himself was in the group as well.

The group appeared on the dock very near the water's edge, so they were actually between Theodore and his waiting boat.

He might call in his launch, but he could not move to get aboard without giving away his secret; so the launch stayed where it was for the moment, the rowers pulling easily to offset the current, some ten or fifteen meters from the dock. The men aboard her could perceive no immediate threat to their master in this arrival of the other eminent folk with whom he had been arguing for the past few days. In response to something—perhaps a guarded look from the High Priest—they did however begin to ease their craft a little closer to the shoreline.

Before they had closed more than half the distance, however, a somewhat smaller and much shabbier boat appeared just upstream, loaded to the gunwales with armed men. Lieutenant Komi stood in the prow, and in response to his crisp orders his crew propelled their vessel right up to the dock in the launch's way.

"What are you all doing here?" demanded Theodore of Wen Chang and those who had just climbed up onto the dock with him. All of the new arrivals looked more or less wet and bedraggled, especially around the legs and feet, as if they had been wading through noisome waters underground.

"Why," replied one of the unhappier officials reluctantly following the Magistrate, "we are seeking the Sword." The bitter sarcasm in the words was of course directed at Wen Chang. "And I suppose this, in our leader's estimation, is the very place where we are going to find it." Then the speaker fell silent, seeing a hard-to-interpret expression pass over the High Priest's face.

Theodore was never the man to adopt a meekly defensive attitude. "By following that man you will never find the Sword," he taunted, putting on his utmost confidence. He sneered openly at Wen Chang.

"I look into your eyes, unhappy Theodore," pronounced the Magistrate in turn, his face contorted in his most theatrical squint, "and I am persuaded that you lie!"

And on the last word Wen Chang pounced forward, with the speed of a striking predatory animal, to seize the High Priest. The victim was so taken by surprise by this direct assault that he made no attempt to dodge until it was too late; and so astounded were his bodyguards that they failed to move to their master's defense in time to prevent his being seized.

A second later the Blue Temple men were galvanized into action. But one of them was met by Prince al-Farabi, and the other tripped up by Lieutenant Komi, who reached ashore to thrust a sheathed sword between the guard's legs and send him sprawling. Meanwhile the Prince, displaying an impressive speed of thought and hand, as well as considerable strength, had knocked down the other bodyguard and stood over him with drawn blade.

Theodore, the High Priest of the Blue Temple, was a strong man too, stronger than he looked. And his training in the arts of personal combat had not been entirely neglected. But neither of those attributes were of any real service to him now. Wen Chang, displaying a master's skill and a wiry strength that few would have suspected from his appearance, needed only a moment in which to overpower the High Priest once they had come to grips.

From under Theodore's long blue cape there fell out the Sword of Siege, still sheathed, to land with a muffled metallic sound upon the worn planks of the dock.

The onlookers gaped at it.

Such was the unexpected suddenness with which the Sword had been made to appear that for a moment even Kasimir could almost believe that Wen Chang had produced it through some trick of sleight of hand. But that was manifestly impossible. There was no conceivable way the Magistrate could have concealed such a weapon on his person before his confrontation with Theodore, and no way he could have pulled it out of the bare planks of the dock. The only place the Sword could possibly have come from was under Theodore's voluminous cape.

An instant after the Sword appeared, the Prince cast aside the more ordinary weapon with which he had been menacing the fallen bodyguard, and pounced upon his treasure. With a great cry of joy he unsheathed Stonecutter, and held up the gleaming blade for all to see.

The High Priest, caught red-handed with another's treasure, refused to blush or even to look uncomfortable. In the space of time needed to draw a full breath he was protesting at the top of his voice the high-handed treatment to which he had been subjected. He announced that all present were witnesses to his perfect innocence in the face of false accusations—though no accusations, true or false, had yet been voiced.

This was not a good audience for anyone to attempt to deceive with the technique of the big lie. All present were looking at Theodore with guarded expressions, and Kasimir was quite sure that not one of his audience believed him.

For the present, at least, no one was ready to indict him either. Prince al-Farabi, having retrieved Prince Mark's treasure and his own honor, attached the Sword's sheath to a belt at his own waist, and made loud vows of gratitude to everyone who had helped in any way toward Stonecutter's recovery.

Meanwhile the boatload of Firozpur warriors had pulled out of the way of the launch, which was now allowed to dock. Theodore promptly climbed aboard. He was still loudly justifying his possession of the Sword as the launch, in response to his gesture, pulled away again.

And now the Prince no longer delayed a more practical expression of his gratitude. The chief beneficiary of this was of course Wen Chang, to whom al-Farabi promptly handed over his promised reward, in the form of a handful of sparkling, high-grade jewels.

Hardly was the Blue Temple launch out of easy hailing distance when in a small thunder of hoofbeats the Hetman himself arrived at the dock, accompanied by a small mounted escort. How the ruler had learned of the confrontation taking place here was not apparent, but his vast relief at the sight of Stonecutter was. His first glance toward Wen Chang and Kasimir was by far the friendliest he had yet sent their way.

"Where did you find it?" the Hetman inquired eagerly.

The expression on the Prince's face lost some of its happiness. "Hidden under the garments of the High Priest of the Blue Temple."

There was no point in the Hetman's trying to dispute this as unbelievable. Not when he saw confirmation of the unbelievable in every face before him.

"A mistake, on his part," the ruler offered. "Some misunderstanding."

"A mistake, certainly," said the Prince. "To think that he could get away with such a theft."

"A misunderstanding, I am sure," the Hetman said. "I trust that Your Highness has no thought of pressing charges?"

"If you agree," conceded the Prince magnanimously to his fellow ruler, "that no charges of any kind will be pressed against anyone else concerned in this matter—then I will consent to press none against Theodore, or his organization."

"Agreed, with all my heart." Then a slight frown dimmed the Hetman's joy. "Except of course for the escaped prisoner Benjamin, who is already under sentence of death."

"Agreed."

And with that the gathering on the dock split up, the Prince and a few retainers going to a round of rejoicing at their host's palace. The Magistrate most eloquently begged to be excused, and the Hetman did not press him to come along.

Once they were out of sight of the higher authorities, Wen Chang gave a choice jewel to Kasimir, and promptly made good on his promise to Almagro by sharing his reward generously.

"I can use it," the Captain said. "I am very seriously considering retirement."

CHAPTER 19

IT was about an hour after dawn on the second day of the Festival, which so far appeared to be making good progress despite the lack of a public execution. Wen Chang, after getting a good night's rest at the inn, had expressed an urge to leave Eylau behind him as quickly as possible. Kasimir, feeling that he could hardly agree with any sentiment more, was going with him. Accordingly the two of them had arisen early, packed up their few belongings at the inn, and paid their bill in full—that was no problem, once a small portion of Wen Chang's reward had been converted into ready cash. Prince al-Farabi had graciously offered, and the Magistrate had accepted, the continued escort of Lieutenant Komi and his small troop as far as the next city.

The Prince himself was not on hand for their departure, having agreed to accept another day or two of the Hetman's grateful hospitality.

Kasimir and the Magistrate, riding their well-rested animals side by side this morning, enjoyed their first real opportunity to talk freely together since the Sword's recovery. Certain hints dropped by Wen Chang had confirmed Kasimir in his opinion that the inn might no longer be a safe place for the frankest sort of conversations; the Blue Temple had been humiliated, if not wounded, and it was notoriously unforgiving of any kind of debt.

"I would like," said Kasimir, after the first few minutes of the morning's ride had passed in silence, "for you to tell me a story."

Wen Chang threw back his head and gave vent to hearty mirth. It was a far more open laughter than any Kasimir had heard from him since their first meeting.

"I fully intend to do so," replied the Magistrate when he had laughed his fill. "I was only wondering how best to begin."

"To begin with, do you believe that the Hetman will ever recapture Benjamin of the Steppe?"

"I hope that he will not," said Wen Chang frankly. "And as a matter of fact I consider the Hetman's chances of success in the matter rather small."

"Oh? I rejoice to hear it. But why is that?"

"Well, in the first place, whoever arranged the prisoner's escape from his cell demonstrated considerable cleverness, and one must expect the same cleverness to be applied to the problem of removing the same prisoner from the city."

"That is true. Well, I have no doubt as to who arranged the escape. And I am still thinking of Natalia. Do you know, in spite of all that has happened, in a way I could wish to see her again."

"You should; were it not for her co-operation in loaning us the Sword for a few hours to trap Valamo, and then returning it honorably when it had served its purpose in the city, you would not have the Prince's jewel in your pocket now. But she is busy, I assume, devoting herself to the survival of her lover. Or perhaps Benjamin is her husband; the rural folk tend to believe strongly in marriage, you know."

"I should have guessed at the connection earlier," Kasimir admitted. "She and Benjamin were even wearing similar clothing when I first saw them. And her hair was styled in the same way as that of those foolish women protesters."

"Perhaps not so foolish. Whether or not they were aware of what part they were playing, they served admirably to distract the authorities from the real rescue effort."

"And their partial destruction of the gallows—"

"Made its rebuilding necessary. And the hammering sounds occasioned by *that* covered the thudding sounds emitted by Stonecutter as the tunnel was dug up to the prisoner's cell. Yes, all in all, a very well-organized escape."

"You implied, earlier, that there was a second reason why the escape might very well succeed?"

"There is. I doubt that the Hetman will push his search for Benjamin as hard as he might, now that the escape is an accomplished fact, and he's had a chance to think matters over."

"And why is that?"

"Of course his pride was touched by the escape. But now that he has at least hints from the Prince that Benjamin's continued survival pleases him, and pleases certain other powerful people as well, it is not an unmixed curse. Perhaps by now al-Farabi has even had time to suggest that allowing poor farmers to vote on matters that concern them greatly might render the task of the radical revolutionary more difficult."

"I can see that this custom of voting might ultimately present a great threat to any ruler."

"Indeed. I am not sure that either of the Princes has thought that far ahead himself . . . in any case, I expect the Hetman is still making a real effort to recapture his victim. He is just not pressing that effort as urgently as he possibly could."

"Well, I repeat that I join you in hoping that he does not succe ."

"We shall see."

"And you are sure that Prince al-Farabi shares our hopes."

"My dear Kasimir, I am very sure of that. Almost from the very beginning I suspected that might be his position. The Prince is a worthy man, though there are times when he displays a lamentable tendency to overact."

"Did you mean to say 'over*react*,' Magistrate?"

"I meant to say just what I said. I only wish that there were many other princes who had no worse faults."

"The implication being, of course, that Prince al-Farabi has been taking a leading role in all this theatrical performance with Stonecutter."

The Magistrate nodded. "Some days ago I became convinced—it was a gradual conviction—that the original theft of the Sword from your caravan's encampment was only a deception, intended to prevent suspicion falling on the two good Princes, Mark and al-Farabi, when it became known that Stonecutter had been used to effect the escape of the prisoner Benjamin."

"My own conviction on that point was much more sudden, but I fear that it took place much later than yours. Tell me, how did yours begin?"

"It began with an oddity. With an event that at first seemed not only inexplicable but meaningless—I refer, of course, to the cutting of the double slit in your tent wall."

"Ah."

"Yes. From the moment you reported that puzzling detail, I suspected that all was not as it seemed regarding the theft of the Sword. Yet the more I talked to you, the more firmly I was convinced that you were telling me the truth as you saw it."

"Indeed I was. I see now that I had been recruited and used without my knowledge; that it was arranged from the start that I should be a witness to the supposed crime."

"And the best kind of witness. Respectable, believable, while at the same time—forgive me, Kasimir—not overly imaginative. Honest and disinterested, a young man who would have no reason to lie about anything he saw or heard. And the plan to use you as a witness of course succeeded—even though the 'thief' had to make more than one slash in the tent wall to wake you up."

"Ah!" said Kasimir, and shook his head, remembering. "But suppose I had wakened at the first whisper of sound inside the tent, and grappled with the intruder?"

"Then there would have ensued noise, shouting, a general alarm. I do not doubt that within moments the tent would have been filled with struggling bodies. Somehow, in the confusion, you would have been pinned down while the thief contrived to make his escape with the Sword. Doubtless his success would have been ascribed to magic."

Kasimir thought about it briefly. "No doubt you are right," he said.

"Yes, I have no doubt of it. If ever we have the chance to talk all this over freely with al-Farabi, he will, I am sure, tell us that the man who took the Sword that night was one of the most trusted members of the caravan, wearing a mask so that you should not recognize him. If you had noticed his absence after the Sword was gone, you would have been told that he was one of the party sent out into the desert to try to track the thief."

"No doubt," said Kasimir again. He let out a faint sigh.

"But as matters actually went, you did not jump up and grapple with the intruder. Instead you watched, still half asleep, as he extracted the Sword from the pile of baggage and made off with it. Moments later the alarm was sounded on schedule. The plan was off to a good start.

"The next step it called for was the freeing of an important prisoner from the road-building gang—I suppose he was someone who knew the layout of the prison cells within the palace, so that a tunnel could be dug out within the narrow compass of the walls. Another person with knowledge just as good must have been found eventually, or the plan could not have succeeded.

"But the prisoner was freed as planned, from Lednik's rather sloppy control. And then things immediately began to go wrong.

"The problem was that the two men who were now carrying the Sword began to improvise. Their next step ought to have been simply to carry Stonecutter into the city and deliver it to Natalia and her people, who were waiting for it. They would have been able to start digging the tunnel at once, with a good margin of spare time before the morning when the execution was scheduled. That would have avoided the need for last-moment heroics, and an escape completed barely minutes before dawn on Festival morning.

"But instead—sudden improvisation. For some reason the two decided to detour to the stone quarry, and release another comrade imprisoned there. There would have been certain advantages in being able to enter the city three strong instead of only two. And perhaps the prisoner at the quarry was a special friend of one or the other of those who were carrying the Sword.

"But those two had not reckoned with Foreman Kovil. That red-haired man was of a very different stamp from the easygoing boss of the road gang. Kovil was not only greedy and ruthless, but treacherous, bold, and resolute as well. When the Sword was shown to him he saw in it a chance to trade the life of a petty prison tyrant for that of a wealthy and successful adventurer; and to seize that chance he did not scruple to commit a double murder.

"He had no real chance, of course, of being able to keep his crime a secret from the other men at the quarry, guards and prisoners alike. But those who knew the secret had no reason to reveal it, and every reason to cooperate with the man who still held their lives in his hands. Mere silence was not enough; Kovil needed a couple of more active accomplices, both in the killing and afterward, when he took the Sword into the city to convert it into more useful wealth.

"He thought his second-in-command, Umar, would do to mind the quarry until the sale of the Sword should have been somehow completed. But he needed and wanted one more man. Someone to stand with him and protect his back while he negotiated the secret sale of a tremendous stolen treasure. And then Kovil made his own fatal mistake. Though probably from the start there was no doubt in his mind as to which man he would choose for a job like that."

"The Juggler," said Kasimir, and shuddered faintly.

"Indeed. Kovil went into the city with Stonecutter in hand, and the Juggler at his back, and tried to sell the Sword. Whatever might have been the details of that first bloody skirmish on the waterfront, when it was over only one man was left alive—the Juggler, with the Sword of Siege now in his own hands. In one way or another Kovil had fallen victim to the same treachery he had dealt out to others."

"Meanwhile," Kasimir put in, "Natalia and her people had been expecting the Sword to be brought to them. And when it failed to arrive—"

"They became alarmed. Then they heard about the killings on the waterfront, probably from someone who had actually seen the Sword in the Juggler's hands. And they knew that he had it and would almost certainly be trying to sell it quickly."

"And when did you come to an understanding of all this, Magistrate?"

"Alas, with painful slowness! At the start of course I came into the situation by accident, and through your efforts to be helpful. Al-Farabi could scarcely refuse my help, but he sent his most trusted subordinate into the city with us to keep an eye on us.

"As soon as I learned that the prisoner freed from the road gang was political, and that a connection was implied between him and Benjamin of the Steppe, I thought I understood the beginning of the story. After seeing al-Farabi at that conference in the palace, where he seemed more genuinely worried than before, I was sure of it. Since I sympathised with Benjamin, and with Princes Mark and al-Farabi, my task then became not simply to find the Sword, but to cause it to be used according to the original scenario, before being returned to its rightful owner."

"The original plan being of course to free Benjamin."

"Of course."

"And when did you tell the Prince that you had discovered his deception?"

"That came a little later. In beggar's guise I also managed to establish contact with Natalia and her group. I persuaded her to loan me the Sword for a few hours to get rid of Valamo, who had learned of the tunnel into the prison and was threatening to reveal it to the authorities—unless he was paid off very handsomely.

"I dared not try to trick him unless I could have the real Sword in hand to do so—but I could not explain its presence to you ahead of time. Hence my sleight of hand substitution."

"You might have taken me into your confidence completely."

"It is natural that you should be bitter. But I could not be sure of your reaction . . . at any rate, my task became much easier, once we had got Valamo out of the way.

There was nothing to do with such a man in such a situation, except to kill him.''

Wen Chang looked grim for a long moment, then his features relaxed. "Once the Juggler had been removed from the game board, and the Sword was back in the tunnel-diggers' hands, it was not hard to distract everyone for a few necessary hours with fears of a Blue Temple robbery. In return for my help, Natalia agreed to finally return the Sword to me in the rather impressively dramatic manner that you all witnessed.''

"She is a remarkable young woman."

"She is indeed.''

And now both men fell silent. The little cavalcade they led was now closely approaching one of the great land gates of the city. It was in fact the same gate by which they had entered Eylau only a few days ago. Just ahead, troopers of the Watch were probing with lances and swords into a wagonload of refuse that was being hauled out of the city.

Kasimir whispered a question. "I wonder—will he manage to get out?"

Wen Chang made no reply. The refuse wagon was moving on, and now it was their turn to ride up to the gate. The Watch officer who was in charge saluted the imposing figure of the Magistrate, held brief conversation with him, and then reached into the guard post at the center of the gateway to get a copy of the roster of recent travelers.

He consulted the list, then once more faced Wen Chang respectfully. "Yes sir, here you are—the merchant Ching Hao and party, fourteen men in all.'' Swiftly but accurately the officer counted. "Pass on.''

Kasimir rode on out through the gate without turning in his saddle to glance behind him. He rode on without looking back, though he could remember perfectly well that when the little column left the inn there had been only ten uniformed troopers riding behind Lieutenant Komi. One man, the lieutenant had said, had fallen ill while visiting his relatives in the Desert Quarter, and would be rejoining his unit later.

So, counting the officer, Wen Chang, and Kasimir himself, that ought to make a company of thirteen men in all. And now there were fourteen. But Kasimir was not going to turn around and look. Not for nothing had he spent the last few days in the company of Wen Chang.

THE BEST IN FANTASY

PIERS ANTHONY

ANDRE NORTON

☐ 54738-1 ☐ 54739-X	THE CRYSTAL GRYPHON	$2.95 Canada $3.50
☐ 54721-7 ☐ 54722-5	FLIGHT IN YIKTOR	$2.95 Canada $3.95
☐ 54717-9 ☐ 54718-7	FORERUNNER	$2.95 Canada $3.95
☐ 54747-0 ☐ 54748-9	FORERUNNER: THE SECOND VENTURE	$2.95 Canada $3.50
☐ 54736-5 ☐ 54737-3	GRYPHON'S EYRIE (with A.C. Crispin)	$2.95 Canada $3.50
☐ 54732-2 ☐ 54733-0	HERE ABIDE MONSTERS	$2.95 Canada $3.50
☐ 54743-8 ☐ 54744-6	HOUSE OF SHADOWS (with Phyllis Miller)	$2.95 Canada $3.50
☐ 54740-3 ☐ 54741-1	MAGIC IN ITHKAR (Edited by Andre Norton and Robert Adams)	Trade $6.95 Canada $7.95
☐ 54745-4 ☐ 54746-2	MAGIC IN ITI IKAR 2 (edited by Norton and Adams)	Trade $6.95 Canada $7.95
☐ 54734-9 ☐ 54735-7	MAGIC IN ITHKAR 3 (edited by Norton and Adams)	Trade $6.95 Canada $8.95
☐ 54719-5 ☐ 54720-9	MAGIC IN ITHKAR 4 (edited by Norton and Adams)	$3.50 Canada $4.50
☐ 54727-6 ☐ 54728-4	MOON CALLED	$2.95 Canada $3.50
☐ 54725-X ☐ 54726-8	WHEEL OF STARS	$2.95 Canada $3.50

Buy them at your local bookstore or use this handy coupon:
Clip and mail this page with your order.

Publishers Book and Audio Mailing Service
P.O. Box 120159, Staten Island, NY 10312-0004

Please send me the book(s) I have checked above. I am enclosing $_____
(please add $1.25 for the first book, and $.25 for each additional book to
cover postage and handling. Send check or money order only — no CODs.)

Name _____

Address _____

City _____ State/Zip _____

Please allow six weeks for delivery. Prices subject to change without notice.

BESTSELLING BOOKS FROM TOR